RECKLESS KISS

GRACE HARPER

GRACE HARPER

RECKLESS KISS

By

Grace Harper

The Turners of Copper Island
Book #1

ONE

Archer

"They're going to do what?" Daisy Turner asked, with her teeth gritted together.

The wind gusted inside the canteen of the oil rig when one of their co-workers came through the side. Archer Turner's sister stood with her hands fisting at her sides on the other side of the Formica table. The four siblings had crowded around while Archer explained the situation. A storm raged outside. Experiencing a storm on an oil rig was no fun, but it was calm compared to Daisy's anger. She was the one he worried about the most.

"The oil rig is shutting down. All personnel are to leave within one week," Archer said.

Archer sat next to his brother, Jason. Opposite him his other brother, Luke. Daisy still stood. She searched his eyes, he guessed, to see if he was lying.

"Sit down, Daisy, please?" Luke said, tugging on her fisted hand.

Archer looked at all his siblings. He felt lost with the

news he'd been given a few hours ago. As a senior manager on the oil rig, Archer asked if he could break the news to tell his brothers and sister personally as he knew how this would affect them.

They'd all worked on the same oil rig since they'd qualified in their field of expertise. Archer had worked on the rig the longest for thirteen years while his siblings had joined the company every two years. Their dad had worked on the same oil rig, too. So Archer understood why Daisy was upset. They all wore visible signs of disappointment. It was their last connection to their father, who had passed away seven years earlier. Daisy had only been on the rig a week when their father had died.

"Fantastic. What the hell are we going to do now?" Luke asked, folding his arms roughly, chin up, like the world owed him a favour.

"We'll have to find new rigs to work on," Jason said.

"That means we'll get split up. I don't want to work on a rig if you're not all on it," Daisy said.

That's how Archer felt, too—having his family close meant everything.

"We could head home to Copper Island?" Archer suggested.

He'd been thinking about the prospect of returning to Copper Island for the last hour. Their home, where they were raised, brought back memories, and not all of them were pleasant.

"Go back to the island. What would we do there?" Luke asked.

"Claim some of our inheritance early," Archer stated.

"Aunt Cynthia would never in a million years hand it over. I swear she's doing everything she can to live to a hundred and twenty, so we'll be too old to get it," Luke said.

Archer didn't doubt his reasoning. Bitterness ran through his aunt's veins like a lifeline.

"It's great to hear you so positive, Luke," Jason said, glaring at him.

"I'm being realistic. Aunt Cynthia is an ogre and a dragon rolled into one. She hated dad for dumping us on her. She hated mum even more for walking out on us," Luke said.

"She is a dragon. As soon as we were old enough, we were on the first flight out to the rig once we'd passed all our qualifications," Daisy said. "Going back to Copper Island seems a step back somehow."

"It wouldn't be so bad, would it? If we were all together," Archer said.

His three siblings gave him wary looks, furrowed brows, and matching incredulous expressions.

"She'll never give it to you," Jason declared. "But if you can swing it, I'll come to Copper Island to help you run whatever you're thinking of doing."

"To be clear, I'm not going begging unless you're all in. I want to ask for the hotel business that is run out of Edward Hall. I also want the wedding business and the cottages they let out for long rentals," Archer said.

"The hotel? What do we know about running a hotel?" Luke asked.

"Daisy could finish her accountancy qualifications and do the books. Jason can continue as a chef. I would be a handyman of sorts, as I'm an electrician."

"And what use would I be as a medic? First aider in case a bride breaks her fingernail?" Luke asked.

Ignoring Luke and his pessimism, Archer looked at Daisy, who was visibly crestfallen that she would return so soon after escaping seven years ago. She nodded her acceptance, adding a perfect baleful look. He nudged Luke with his foot, raising his eyebrows for an answer.

"Fine, I'm in too, but I get to choose what I do," Luke said.

"You only know how to do one thing," Jason said.

"Annoy the hell out of me," Daisy muttered.

The four siblings laughed. Archer stretched out an arm and put his hand flat on the metal table screwed to the floor. Jason added his hand, and then Luke and Daisy. Finally, Archer lifted his hand, and they all raised their hands together.

"Let's go home," Archer said.

TWO

It took longer to fly off the oil rig than expected. Long enough for Archer to secure a meeting with his aunt, who ran her life as if she lived in the early 1900s. They made appointments, tea was served, and he had to be in his best suit.

Archer did not own a suit.

Rectifying the situation, he then trekked the entire length of the UK. Their oil rig was in the North Sea, and his childhood home of Copper Island was fifty miles off the south coast of England. A unique island with white sands, palm trees, and clear waters. The tropical feel aided by the gulf stream made it exclusive and expensive to live on. His ancestors were the first to inhabit the small island—mining copper, in the late 1700s and early 1800s. He glossed over his ancestors, who won the island in a duel.

The Turners of Copper Island had money, land, and a grand old house called Turner Hall. Except the hereditary rulebook said, only one Turner could own the island and

5

everything on it at any time. Cynthia Turner was the current sole owner. Their aunt.

Archer hated the place with the ghosts of his ancestor's past. But if it meant they could stay together, he would suck it up. Alongside Turner Hall was Edward Hall. The smaller of the two Palladian buildings used to be for guests visiting the family. For a guest house, it was vast, with twenty bedrooms. Two hundred years ago, decadence ruled the Turners, and minor royalty and dignitaries would often come to stay. A hundred years ago, luxury led the Turners where singers and actors would come. Fifty years ago, superiority ruled the Turners. You had to know someone to be invited to Edward Hall. Except fifty years ago, one Turner did not conform to expectations. The repercussions of one of the Turners saying no turned everything on its head, and not a single person was happy about the outcome.

Thirty years ago, something went very wrong, and their mother high-tailed it off the Island. And since their father died seven years ago, no one visited the Turners of Copper Island unless they were paying guests.

Archer returning was for the good of his siblings and nothing more. Some would tell him he was noble, but Archer couldn't see any other route that would enable them to stay together. He couldn't stand the thought of them splitting up. On the rigs, they worked three weeks on and three weeks off. Thanks to their dad, they were on the same shift cycle. During their three weeks off, their dad went back to Copper Island, but they explored a new country each time.

Except this time, when the four of them had made landfall after their final shift on the oil rig, they parted ways.

Jason, Luke, and Daisy went in different directions for

the first time. Archer told them he'd call when he had an answer from their aunt.

He had to get her to say yes. Left to their own devices, he didn't know if they'd all stay on the straight and narrow. They were all there the day their mother walked out on them, except they weren't aware of what was happening twenty-nine years ago. Daisy was six months, Luke was two, Jason was four, and Archer was nearly seven.

They were all there the day their dad died. Two profound events that bonded them forever. It didn't stop their bickering, but they were a tight group that no one could infiltrate.

Archer took the ferry to Copper Island, getting flashbacks to the numerous times he'd travelled back and forth to the mainland when studying for his electrician qualifications. As soon as the ferry docked in the small port, he was one of the first off, shoving his duffle bag further up his shoulder. It was a hike up to the old house. He wasn't looking forward to it in a suit on a warm Spring day.

Archer took the stone path along the quayside. There were inlets with rock pools and sandy patches of beach on that side of the island. He used to pick periwinkles as a kid in the rock pools and kiss girls on the sandy dunes. The pathway up to his ancestral home was private and only for Turner use.

A yapping sound attracted his attention. Archer looked over to the rock pools near the sea edge and saw a dog barking and running himself ragged in circles. Instinctively Archer knew the dog was in trouble, and the tide was coming in. Kicking off his shoes and socks, Archer picked his way across the rocks to the dog. It looked like a puppy, large brown eyes with a chocolate brown coat wet through. Archer didn't know anything about dog breeds, but he knew this one would grow big when it was an adult. A brown sack was nearby with a rope tied around the dog's back leg.

"Son of a bitch," Archer muttered. "It's okay, buddy. I'll get you to safety."

The other end of the rope had snagged between two rocks, and the dog was trapped. Water lapped at Archer's feet as he untied the rope on the dog's leg and lifted him into his arms. The dog rewarded him by licking his face.

"All right, no need to get too excited. I've no idea who you belong to, but we need to get out of here before the sea sweeps us away, and I don't get too wet."

Hopping back across the rocks with the puppy, Archer put his socks and shoes back on, then wrung out the bottoms of his trousers as best he could. His aunt would have to accept he was less than perfect.

THREE

Archer

Once Archer reached the gates to his ancestral home, he put the dog down on the ground. The puppy whined and sniffed his leg, looking up with doe eyes.

"Listen, you don't belong to me. Go find your owner," Archer said to the dog.

A sharp bark told him the dog was saying no. In his heart, Archer knew the puppy owner had abandoned the dog.

"Fine, but if I walk in to see my aunt with a dog in my arms, it will not go in my favour."

Archer pushed open the side gate and trudged along the pathway to the main house. The dog trotted next to him, sniffing at anything that took his interest. The Georgian Palladian building and the rest of the properties stood on flat land at the top of the cliff. The Turners had lived there for four hundred years. Not that he or his siblings saw a penny of the wealth. With the tradition of the head of the family holding the purse strings, everyone else needed to earn a living to survive.

His aunt was currently the matriarch living up to the premise. You were warm and fed if you stayed under a Turner roof, but no money was handed out. When Aunt Cynthia passed away, the purse would be handed to Archer. Something he didn't want until recently.

He took a deep breath as he approached the shallow, broad steps leading up to the stone pillars in front of the entrance. The dog was in his arms, burrowed deep against his chest like he knew to brace for battle.

In true fashion, the door opened before knocking.

"Mr Archer, it is good to see you back, Sir," Bailey said, greeting him warmly.

"Thanks, Bailey. Do you think you can give this puppy water and something to eat? I have no idea what puppies eat."

"You had a puppy on an oil rig, Sir?"

"No. I found him trying to run from the sea. Somebody had dumped him in a sack."

"That's awful. I'll take care of him," Bailey said, taking the bundle of puppy from Archer. "Does he have a name?"

"No collar, Bailey. I'll come down once I've seen the matriarch."

"Very good, Sir. Miss Turner is in the morning room."

Archer nodded to the footman and left his duffel bag with Bailey and the dog. He strode away through the grand foyer with its ornate marble and sweeping staircase and into the morning room. It still had the same red carpet and aged chairs and sofas. He was sure they were well over a hundred years old. Not that anyone was allowed to sit on them for very long.

He spotted his aunt sitting near the fireplace, wringing

her hands as she leaned into the warmth. She wore a bottle-green jumper with a roll collar. Her hair was up in a low bun, her once all-black hair streaked with white. He couldn't see what else she wore with the thick blanket over her knees. If she wanted to portray a frail little old lady, she had.

"Hello, Aunt," Archer said once he was a few feet away.

"You're late," she answered in her clipped upper-class accent. It was cold, harsh, like a verbal whipping.

"I had to rescue a dog who was drowning."

"Is that why you're traipsing your sodden shoes through the house?"

"I didn't think you'd appreciate bare feet on the ancient carpet."

She gave him a critical glance from head to toe, taking in his suit. It fit him perfectly—dark blue with a matching tie and crisp white shirt.

"Shall I call down for tea?" Archer asked after a too-long stretch of silence.

"Will you be here that long?"

Sighing heavily, he unbuttoned his suit jacket and sat on the sofa opposite his aunt. She'd aged significantly since he'd last seen her at his grandfather's funeral. His aunt hadn't shed a tear at her father's funeral and left the gravesite when the coffin was lowered. She refused to put on a wake afterwards.

"So you know why I'm here?"

"Not a clue. Your letter said you wanted to talk to me, but it lacked details."

"I want us to have a piece of our inheritance early," Archer said.

"Us?"

"Me, Jason, Luke, and Daisy. If dad were alive, he would hand it over."

"Well, he's not alive. I am."

"I can't imagine you enjoying running an exclusive hotel and cottages at seventy-nine."

"I don't run anything. That's what managers are for. And I'll thank you, not to mention my age again."

"Are you telling me no?"

Silence emanated from his aunt. He could almost hear the cogs whirring in her head. That was enough pause for him to know she didn't care much about overseeing the family business.

Edward Hall was a smaller version of the house they were sitting in was half a mile away. It was a mini palace that entertained the minor royalty, celebrities, and the very rich who wanted an exclusive wedding. The hotel was a place to stay for the exclusive guest who could relax without having the press turn up. Five cottages, half a mile away from Edward Hall, the other side from Turner Hall, were let out long term for those who wanted to hide away from some crisis. It was his grandfather who had turned the second house into a business. He was fed up with his friends turning up and spending weeks eating his food and drinking his whisky. His grandfather called the second house Edward Hall after his father.

"I'll give you my answer in the morning. You may go," his aunt said and then rang the tiny bell next to her.

He took one look at her pinched lips and stood up.

"What time should I call tomorrow?" Archer asked, buttoning his suit jacket.

"Not a minute before ten-thirty," she answered.

Archer nodded and gazed at the painting of his grandfather, Archibald Turner before he strode from the room. His aunt adored her father right up to the day she didn't. No one would talk about why they fell out, and now Aunt Cynthia was the only person alive who could reveal the secrets. Jennifer, her dress maid, could, Archer thought, but she was loyal to her mistress.

FOUR

Archer

Landing back in the foyer, he met Bailey carrying a stack of letters.

"Maggie has made you a meal. She's named the damn dog, and all your clothes are being laundered."

"I love and have missed Maggie. She saved my backside more times than I can remember when I was a kid."

"I remember," Bailey answered with a knowing smirk. "I better get these to Miss Turner," he said, nodding to the silver tray and the pile of letters.

Archer turned, slipped through the servant's door, and hurried down the stone steps to the kitchen. It struck him that the old-fashioned ways his aunt still maintained comforted him. It was so outdated, but took him straight back to his upbringing, which was a happy one until it wasn't.

"Maggie," Archer called out as soon as the expansive open kitchen came into view. The round-faced cook bustled towards him even though she wore a white shirt, black trousers, and an apron.

"Come here, my boy, and give an old lady a cuddle," she said with a broad grin.

Maggie Jones was a foot shorter than him, but packed a mean hug when she wrapped her arms around his waist and squeezed him.

"You're not old. It's good to see you, Maggie. How have you been?"

"Keeping well," she said, pulling away and patting his cheek. "I'm feeling my sixty years, I can tell you."

"Is my aunt treating you okay?" Archer looked at her, concerned that the old battle-axe was making her life hard.

"No more than usual. Have a seat at the table. I've made your favourite. As soon as I heard you were coming today, I knew exactly what to make you."

"Beef and ale pie with so much mash I can't eat it all?"

"You got it. Apple pie too," she said and winked. "You've got plenty of time to eat. Your clothes won't be ready for a few hours."

"Is there a bed I can sleep in tonight?" Archer asked when a steaming plate of food that made his eyes water was placed in front of him.

"None of the cottages are rented out this week. If you don't want to sleep under Turner Hall's roof, you can take one of those. They're made up, ready for guests."

"No bookings this week?" Archer asked.

"It's full next week," Maggie said and busied herself at the stove, swapping pans over on the rings.

"Should I get a key from Bailey?"

"Yes. He can take you across when Miss Turner takes her afternoon nap. That's when we all have a rest."

"I'm sure I can find the cottages I used to play in as a kid. Just tell me the name and give me the key."

"Bailey won't hear of it. Let him take you. It'll give him something else to do than wait for people to visit."

"Does she get many visitors?"

"None. Miss Turner scares them all away. You kids are the only family she has left. Where are Jason, Luke, and Daisy anyway?"

"The far corners of the globe. I've come begging on my own."

Maggie let out a long sigh and nodded her understanding, even though he hadn't shared his plans with anyone.

"Hopefully, they'll rock up soon."

"It would be so lovely to hear voices in this house again. It's so quiet with me, Bailey and Jennifer."

"Jennifer is still here?"

"She sure is. Same age as the Mistress herself, but Miss Turner won't let her leave."

"Poor woman," Archer muttered.

"No pity needed for Jennifer. She treats her job like a lady-in-waiting for the Queen. She'll be by Miss Turner's side until her dying breath."

"Where is Jennifer now?"

"Getting Miss turner changed for her nap, no doubt."

"Is she in good health?"

"Perfect health. She'll outlive us all. She prefers to cat nap as she can't sleep for more than four hours at night."

Archer laughed at the sentiment because she wasn't wrong. His aunt was strict, formidable, and stubborn as hell. He realized his aunt always knew he had sneaked back after being out until the early hours. She would've seen him sneak back in if she was up early.

"Is that how we got busted for being out all night? She saw us?"

"Yeah. I know you've never been into her rooms, but a leaded glass door is in the far corner. It leads to a small flat area where only one table and chair will fit. When you were teenagers, she would make herself a pot of tea and sit at the table. The seat had a full view of the lawns, and she would see when any of you used to sneak across the grass as the sun was coming up."

"How do you know?"

"Jennifer used to tell us," Maggie said, then laughed. "There are no secrets in this house. Someone always knows something. But they rarely tell."

Archer shook his head, grinning at the memories of his teenage years. He finished eating his early lunch. Having a full dinner at ten-thirty in the morning didn't phase him. Working on the oil rigs sometimes meant you ate your food when you could, especially if there was a storm.

He said farewell to Maggie and walked back up to the foyer to find Bailey.

"I'll give you the cottage nearest the house, less walking for me," Bailey said.

"You are fitter than me, Bailey. How are your family?"

"They're all very well. Thank you for asking."

They walked in amiable silence along the pathway to the cottages, past Edward Hall and the walled-in garden. His aunt could always be found in the walled garden when they were kids, reading a book and spying on what they were getting up to. All generations living under one roof, the whole family, meant there was zero privacy to get up to no good. He and his siblings had to be stealthy in their adventures, but somehow his aunt always knew what they'd done and who. And now he knew how.

As they approached the first cottage, memories of sneaking into the empty houses came flooding back. Smoking, making out, and for him, losing his virginity to Susie Cooper when he was fifteen.

The smaller path leading up to the front door had grass and small shrubs on either side. It was a typical Georgian cottage.

"Here is the key. You should find everything you need inside. Maggie will bring over your laundry later," Bailey said, giving him a key with an enormous metal disc as a keyring.

"No danger of losing this heavy thing," Archer commented.

"No, Sir, or putting it in your pocket either. Ridiculous things. The guests hate them."

Without waiting for a reply, Bailey turned and left Archer in front of the closed door and strode down the path towards Turner Hall.

A shiver ran down Archer's spine. It was like time had stood still on Copper Island. Could he handle living back at Turner Hall? He had to, for the sake of his siblings.

Archer looked at the windows on either side of the front door and noticed the curtains were closed. Stepping further back, the three upstairs windows also had closed curtains. He unlocked the door and stepped inside, getting used to the darkness in the ground-floor rooms. Each of the cottages was named after his female ancestors. The house he stood in was Emma Lodge, after his great-grandmother. The entranceway still had the same flagstone flooring and white-washed walls. In the room to the left was the living room, vastly updated since he was last home with modern furnishings. He pulled open the curtains where dust particles flooded the room, highlighted by the sunlight. It made him sneeze multiple times. He mused that there had been no residents for some time if the dust levels were anything to go by. As he checked the sitting room across the hall, every room was immaculately appointed. The country-style kitchen and dining room were the same. He opened the curtains in all the ground-floor rooms before jogging up the stairs and into the four bedrooms upstairs. There were five when he was a teenager. Empty back then, but now they had colour-coordinated furnishing with an ensuite for the primary bedroom at the end of the hallway. Opening the windows to let fresh air in, he glanced at the small back garden with wooden furniture under coverings. There wasn't much room before the vast lawns reached the pathway down the cliff to the private beach.

"Something is definitely not right here," he said aloud.

Archer needed a shower and a change of clothes. He could smell salt water from his adventures in the sea rescuing the poor dog.

Pressing the switch for the shower, there was a loud bang, and the lights went out.

"Great, just what I need," he said.

FIVE

Erica

"Why won't you give him a divorce?" the young woman asked Erica.

The two women were standing in the bathroom at the Oscars. If Erica was drunk, she'd think this was a movie set. But nope. A heavily pregnant woman stood before her and wanted to know why she wouldn't divorce her husband.

The man who she divorced a month ago.

Without saying a word, stunned by the question, Erica unbuckled her clutch bag and lifted out her phone. Then, she dialled her ex-husband in without taking her eyes off the woman.

"Hey, babe," he said cheerily.

As far as Erica was concerned, they'd had an amicable divorce and had remained friendly. Erica didn't answer for a moment, dropping her hand with the phone to her side.

"What's your name, sweetie?" she said, barely holding back the anger she felt.

"It's Monica," the woman replied.

Lifting the phone back up to her ear, she kept narrowed eyes at her ex-husband's mistress.

"Babe, babe, are you there? I'm watching the Oscars on TV. Your category is on next."

"How long have you been fucking Monica?" Erica asked.

Smooth as silk, Erica was calm as a millpond on the outside, but a raging inferno was inside her rib cage.

Yanny, her manager, had told her that her husband was cheating a year ago, and she said that was preposterous. They divorced because he said he was lonely and barely saw her between movie shooting, promo, and everything else she did as a top Hollywood actress. It seemed she was the idiot.

"Hurry up and answer. I've got an Oscar to collect," Erica said.

"You don't know you've won," her husband replied, all joy gone from his voice.

"Well, at least you've admitted infidelity. It should make divorce proceedings easy."

Erica kept her side of the conversation as if they were still married. She wanted to make Gregg, her ex-husband, squirm, but she wouldn't do his dirty work for him. She didn't know or care why he hadn't told the mother of his child he wasn't married anymore.

"We're divorced," he said. "What the hell is going on?"

"Let's find out, shall we?"

Erica put the call on speaker and placed the phone on the vanity unit between her and the woman in front of her.

"How long?" she asked into the phone

"I don't know what you're talking about?" Gregg replied.

"Come on, Greggybaby," Monica said. "Tell her it's over

so we can get married. I want to get it done before I give birth."

A little bit of bile rose up at the sound of Monica cooing to Gregg. Her American accent grated on Erica's nerves. A stark contrast to Gregg's clipped British accent.

"Monica?" Gregg said in surprise. "What are you doing at the Oscars?"

That was enough for Erica to have confirmation. Then, she switched the speaker function off and again brought the phone to her ear.

"How long? By the look of her bump, it's at least seven months," Erica asked.

Why did Erica want to know? She was divorced from the man. That's right, and the paparazzi would have a field day if it got out.

"Well, you didn't want to have kids, and I wanted a family. You were always travelling, and I was lonely."

"So, you thought you'd have a whore on the side while lazing about like a househusband while I worked to keep you in that lifestyle?"

"I am not his whore," Monica replied.

"You are, sweetheart. You fucked my husband and are having his child while he was married to me."

"Erica, baby, please, can we talk about this?" Gregg said, whining his way through his words.

"Not a chance in hell. We'll never speak again. My lawyers will contact you," Erica said and ended the call.

No lawyers would contact him, but Erica kept up the ruse. Gregg could get himself out of his mess. She wasn't going to help him. He'd never worked a day in his life. He lived off his parent's money, and then when they married, he let Erica pay all the bills and his social butterfly lifestyle.

"You've got what you wanted. I hope you'll be happy

with Gregg. Good luck," Erica said and dropped her phone into her clutch.

Gregg had no money and didn't get any money from her as he signed a prenup.

Bending to look in the mirror, Erica dabbed her fingers on her lips to check her lipstick and strode past Monica, who was picking her jaw up off the floor.

"Where the hell have you been?" Yanny, Erica's manager, hissed when she sat down.

"And the Oscar for Best Actress in a Leading Role goes to," the world-famous actor on stage said.

"I got delayed," she whispered.

"Smile for the camera, Erica. You might win," Yanny said through gritted teeth next to her.

Erica wasn't in any mood to smile. A few minutes ago, she'd been confronted by a twenty-year-old demanding she give her husband a divorce so they could get married. A few minutes ago, Erica discovered her husband had been cheating on their marriage. With a woman, ten years her junior, showing off a spectacular baby bump.

The divorce was finalised a month ago. What made Erica angry was her ex-husband had said there wasn't another woman when he asked for a divorce. Yet the young woman looked ready to give birth.

Everything about the scene was a cliché. Erica was cornered in the bathroom. Mirrors were everywhere to capture the hurt and betrayal dripping off her face as she applied her lipstick, staring at the other woman.

The silence deafened her in the rows behind, waiting for the name to be called. All the best actress nominees were in the front row. Everyone looked fabulous. Erica's money was on Meryl Streep, winning the Academy Award.

"Erica Taylor," the actor announced.

Rapturous applause echoed around the hall. Everyone surrounding her was on their feet. Some hugged her. In a daze, she looked at Yanny, slowly blinking to make sure it was her name called out. He nodded, giving a peck on her cheek.

"Go up there and give your speech," Yanny said.

"I can't. You were right," Erica said.

"Right about what?"

"I want to leave right now."

"You can leave as soon as you give your speech. I'll have everything ready. Now, get your arse up there right now."

He pinched the skin above her elbow for good measure to get her to focus.

Erica had known Yanny since high school, and pinching was what he always did to get her to focus. She lifted the hem of her dress and walked up the half a dozen steps to the stage. Only a few more paces and she was being hugged and kissed by the actor while someone else put the statue in her hand.

Erica looked to the side and back out to the auditorium, pasting on her showcase smile. She grinned wide as she looked down at the statue in her hand. It meant nothing, nothing at all. There were no feelings of pride.

"I just hugged Jack Nicholson," she said as laughter bubbled out of her throat.

Laughter rippled through the audience. Erica had lost her breath, unable to find her words. She'd written a speech, but she couldn't remember a word for the life of her. Silence fell on the room, expectancy thick in the air at her words.

Jack Nicholson stepped to her side, turned his back to the audience, dipped his chin, and gave her a squinted gaze. He placed his hand on her shoulder. It centred her enough for her to collect her thoughts. Once he was sure she was okay, he stepped away to the side.

"I think we're besties now," she told the audience. "I am so thankful to the Academy for this award. I am speechless because I was sure Meryl would get it."

That was the last thing she remembered about her speech. Her private jet was on standby to get her home. Erica didn't remember flying home, falling asleep in her jewellery, dress, and full makeup.

SIX

Erica

She rolled off the bed the next afternoon and crawled on hands and knees into her bathroom. Her house in Kensington was soundproofed enough that she couldn't hear anything from outside. Making lie-ins possible is a noisy city.

Erica had won her first Academy Award for best actress the previous evening, but it was like she knew nothing. Including how to stand. Shuffling inside her walk-in shower, Erica shifted her body to lean against the tiled wall. Then, lifting her hand, she turned the dial and let the water flow over her. Tasting the salt on her lips, she realised her silent tears had started streaming down her face.

Minutes passed as she sobbed in the torrential downpour of water. Clawing at her dress, she tore and ripped the material. The constricting underwear underneath her Oscar-winning dress had clips and ties, but after a few tugs, her breasts were bared, her legs were free of her stockings, and all that was left was a tiny pair of panties. Ripping the material at her hip, she pulled them free and tossed them on the pile of clothing in the far corner of the wet floor.

The reaction to finding out her husband had cheated on her was heartbreaking. Gregg had wanted a family straight away, but Erica wanted to wait. He said he was okay with waiting. They'd only been married five years when the divorce was finalised. She didn't fight him because she felt guilty for leaving him alone for weeks on end to pursue her acting career. Gregg was highly educated but had no business acumen or desire to work. He was lonely, so she let him go.

He wasn't lonely at all. He had a twenty-year-old to keep him company. Erica didn't consider herself old at thirty-two, but Gregg was hooking up with a woman fifteen years younger than him, and it hit her in the stomach. Children would've come in the next couple of years. He didn't have to wait too much longer.

On high alert, Erica wondered if she'd bolted the door so he couldn't get in the house. Turning up to talk things through would be Gregg's style. The thought of seeing him again brought acid water into her throat. It was enough to motivate her to her feet. Snatching a silk robe off the hook in the bathroom, she hurried down two flights of stairs to her front door. She hurriedly checked all the locks, thanking her absent memory for locking up before crawling into bed.

Her phone was face down on the hallway carpet. She lifted it to see the screen cracked so severely that she wondered if it had hit a wall before landing on the floor. Her phone was dead, battered, and would unlikely never work again. There wasn't anyone she wanted to talk to, anyway.

Dashing back up the stairs, she entered her shower and turned off the water. Collecting her clothes, Erica dumped them in the bin and then turned the water back on again. She needed to wash off the night before and figure out what she would do.

Back downstairs half an hour later, she'd plugged her phone in and was surprised it was working. Making a call to her assistant to get a new phone delivered, she avoided all social media and news and then called her manager.

"I remember nothing between the second line of my speech and about an hour ago. Tell me I didn't humiliate myself."

"It's good to hear your voice, love. No is the answer. You asked me to take you to the airport, but then you were going to do that anyway, but you also asked me to get you a sleeping pill for the flight. So I came with you, helped you inside your home, and left you alone at your request. But, of course, I didn't leave you alone. I stayed for a few hours to ensure you slept soundly and returned to my place."

"I'm sorry I acted like a diva," she said.

The phone was on speaker on her kitchen counter, and Erica had her head in her hands as she spoke.

"Are you going to tell me what happened?" Yanny asked.

"My shithead ex-husband's whore cornered me in the bathrooms before my category was announced. She-Monica, demanded I give my husband the divorce he apparently keeps asking for a while she stroked her swollen belly."

"Fuck," Yanny said. "I'm on my way. Get the kettle on, lovely."

"Thanks, Yanny," Erica said, trying and failing to hide her sob.

"I won't be long. Hold tight," Yanny said and ended the call.

Erica put the phone face down as messages flooded her screen. She hated her reaction to Gregg and Monica. What did it matter now? She was divorced. Deep down, she knew why it hurt so much.

She'd always believed marriage was for life.

SEVEN

Erica

True to his word, Yanny arrived at her front door within twenty minutes.

"Yanny, thank you for coming," Erica said, her shoulders sagging as soon as she closed her front door.

"So far, no one knows that your ex-husband has been a dickhead, but there is gossip on why you were like a rabbit caught in the headlights. The narrative is more about you and Jack Nicholson than anything else."

"Thank goodness for that. I can cope with speculation about being linked with a man twice my age. But it will get out that my ex-husband, who the world thinks I'm still married to, has knocked up a teenager. She looks so young."

"Have you got any milk?"

"Probably. The housekeeper takes care of that."

"I need coffee, let's go into your kitchen, and we can go through your schedule."

Erica had never been so pleased she had Yanny as a manager. Nothing fazed him. He took everything in his stride and never lost his temper or his cool. She made them a French press coffee, and they sat at her kitchen table. They were facing each other across one end of the table like playing battleships with the laptop lids back-to-back.

"I had a complete meltdown when I woke up. The beautiful dress I wore to the ceremony is ruined. I tore it off me. Gregg made a mockery of our marriage. I'm not saying I'm blameless, but to keep her a secret? He would've known she was pregnant when he asked for a divorce. I can't imagine it was a one-night stand."

"I've been single since I was born. I don't have any advice. Now, your next movie doesn't need you for another two months. What will you do with your time, apart from learning your lines and morphing into a synchronised swimmer?"

"I think that's enough to handle. I can swim, but I'm not used to holding my breath underwater or staying in the water for long periods."

"It's possible that is something you should've considered before you accepted the role to play Esther Williams in her biopic?"

"Possibly."

"Should I arrange a season pass for the local swimming pool?" he said and laughed.

"That's not going to work. I need to find a private pool."

Yanny was silent as he tapped at the keyboard. Then, her intercom buzzed, making her jump.

"Don't answer that," Yanny said.

"Why?"

"Do you want to know that your husband was in LA and not in London when you collected your award?"

"Seriously?"

"Yeah, there's another thing too," Yanny said, frowning at his laptop screen.

"That's not a good expression. What's going on?"

Yanny turned the laptop screen to show her a video on a popular online gutter press magazine. Her ex-husband and Monica were kissing like teenagers on the Hollywood Walk of Fame. Erica didn't have to check that they were standing on her star.

On the third cycle of viewing the video, the doorbell rang with urgency. Erica knew the press was brazen and stepping onto her property.

"I'll just check it's not the postman, lovely," Yanny said quietly while Erica stared dumbfounded at her ex-husband's audacity. She wanted her private life kept away from the public, and he displayed it in full view. Worse still, everyone would think he was cheating on her.

Another thing occurred to her. Gregory Potter, her husband of five years, had never kissed her as passionately as he kissed Monica. Not even in the heady first few weeks of dating. Sadness gripped her for a few moments until Yanny returned to the kitchen.

"It was the postman. I've left it all in the hallway."

"Thanks, Yanny. Where's a good place to run away to?"

EIGHT

Archer

Bailey greeted Archer an hour before he was due to meet Aunt Cynthia. He ushered him into the kitchen, where Maggie sat him down and fed him breakfast. The puppy he'd rescued was sleeping on a dog bed in front of the small, lit fireplace like he'd lived there his whole life.

"What did you call him, Maggie?" Archer asked.

He sipped on his coffee while watching the clock. Even if he was a minute late, he knew his aunt would say no to his plea, just for his tardiness. She'd evict him from her land in the next breath.

"Teddy," she said.

Teddy raised his head and looked at Maggie and then at Archer. He let out a woof and got up to pad across to him. Archer dropped his hand for the dog to sniff and lick. Once Teddy had approved of his rescuer, he flopped down at Archer's feet and went back to sleep.

"How is the lady of the house today?" Archer asked.

"A pain in my goddam arse," Jennifer said as she

stomped into the room. "Do I have you to thank for her foul mood?" Jennifer asked, picking up the tea towel and pretended to flick Archer's arm.

"I haven't seen her today, so you can't blame me," Archer said with a broad grin, standing to bring the aged woman into a hug.

"It's good to see you, Archer. Are you staying long?"

"That depends on the Mistress of the house. If she says no, then I'll be on the next ferry off the Island."

"For all our sakes, I hope she says yes. Your brothers and sister coming back to live here would be the greatest news we could hope for."

It was an extreme statement. Archer hadn't spoken to any of the staff since his grandfather had died. Coming back to Copper Island hurt in too many ways.

"Sir, it's time to head upstairs if you don't want to upset Miss Turner," Bailey said, coming into the kitchen.

"Okay, Teddy, the moment of truth," Archer said to the dog, who got up while Archer stood. Teddy let out a yap and nudged Archer's leg.

Archer looked to Bailey and stood for inspection. Bailey assessed his suit, shirt, and tie with a grey eyebrow raised.

"I feel the need to retie your tie, Sir," Bailey said.

"I'd be honoured. For old time's sake. Even as a kid, I never could get it to sit straight."

"I suspect that's why you chose a job on the oil rigs than working in the City, Sir."

"There may be some truth in that."

Everyone laughed at the comment as Bailey and Archer left the kitchen and ascended the stone stairs up to the main foyer. Every piece of furniture was pristine, perfectly placed. There wasn't a spec of dust anywhere. Memories came back from sliding down the banister and being caught by his grandfather, who tanned his backside so he couldn't sit without wincing for a week.

"I'll take you into the morning room. Miss Turner is finishing breakfast."

"Thanks, Bailey."

Archer stood in the middle of the morning room. One side had waist-to-ceiling windows lined with a criss-cross of lead. His grandfather's writing desk stood in the far corner. Archer wandered over and tugged on a drawer on the left. He smiled wide when he saw a fat cigar. His grandfather had let him smoke one when he was eleven, and Archer had never choked so much in his life.

"Rifling through the drawers already. I'm not dead yet," the clipped voice of his aunt said from behind him.

Archer thought she was a ninja the way she'd crept in and stood directly behind him without him hearing. Not having perfect hearing was a downside to working in the rigs and the machine noises. It hampered nothing in everyday life, but people creeping up on him would always take him by surprise.

"Just taking a walk down memory lane, Aunt Cynthia," Archer said.

He plastered a genial smile on his face before he faced her.

"Let's talk," she said, walking away to the red velvet sofas by the fire. It was too early in the day for the fire to be lit. However, the sun streaming in the window kept the room warm for most of the day.

He mirrored her position on the sofas precisely as he'd done the previous day. Archer dared not say anything until she was ready. At the moment, his aunt was brushing off invisible dust from her plaid skirt. This was a trait his old headteacher used to do to intimidate him. But his headmaster wasn't a patch on his aunt for intimidation. The uncomfortable wait was excruciating, but he had to keep perfectly still.

"I've thought about your proposal," Aunt Cynthia said.

"That's great news," Archer replied, smiling wide.

"Wait until I have finished before you assume you'll get everything you came here for."

He felt the whiplash of her words but didn't physically react.

"I'm listening," he answered.

"I'll hand over the business for Edward Hall and the cottages," Aunt Cynthia said.

"Fantastic," Archer said and stood.

"Sit back down, Archer Turner," she said, giving him an icy glare.

Archer returned to the sofa and felt his smile wither away with her continued stare and pinched lips.

"I'll sign over the paperwork, but there are conditions," she said, raising her palm when a smile played on his lips again.

"Okay," he said hesitantly.

"You only get the business itself. You don't have any hold over Turner Hall or Copper Island land."

"That sounds fair," Archer said.

"I haven't finished."

Archer kept quiet, keeping eye contact but barely breathing.

"You are to get married before I sign the papers."

"What?"

"And you have three months, or the deal is off."

Aunt Cynthia dropped her chin to stare at her lap. She cleared her throat and smoothed her hands down her a-line plaid skirt. Archer dropped his eyes to her shoes, positioned neatly together and to the side.

"A wife?"

"A wife, Archer," she answered. "I don't mean an engagement—a wedding where I am attending. You can get married in the family chapel. A single man living under my roof at your age brings all kinds of trouble. Next, I'll hear that you've got half the town's single women pregnant."

"Seriously? What kind of man do you take me for?"

His aunt gave him a hard stare. "You look exactly like your father."

That comment got a reaction from him. He stood, buttoned his jacket, and stepped away from the sofa. His aunt had agreed to look after them while his dad was on the rigs, but she still harboured so much distaste for him.

"Thank you for seeing me, Aunt Cynthia. Will you permit me to sleep on this and come to you tomorrow?"

"Of course," she answered and then rang her bell.

Bailey entered the room a few seconds later, but Archer was already striding past him and out of the morning-room. Bailey followed him through the servant's door and down the steps. Archer's strides were longer. He took the steps two at a time as he descended. When he reached the bottom and stood on the flagstones, he put his hands on his head, waiting for Bailey to catch up.

"Do you have something stronger than tea, Bailey?"

"Right away, Sir. Take a seat in the kitchen, and I'll bring it through."

"Thanks, Bailey," Archer said.

Teddy came bounding down the hallway, tripping over his enthusiasm to reach Archer's feet. As soon as he landed with a plop on his shiny shoes, he let out a yap. Archer reached down and picked him up.

"Do you want to live here, Teddy?"

A double bark came out of Teddy's mouth. Archer had no clue if two barks meant yes or no. It didn't make the news any easier to digest.

How the hell would he find a wife in three months?

NINE

Archer

Teddy wouldn't let Archer leave the kitchen without him. He jumped and ran around his legs as Archer tried to inch out the kitchen laden with two plates of food for lunch and dinner. Maggie knew him well enough that he would stay in his cottage until he'd decided his future. His siblings' future. It was as if Teddy knew Archer needed him.

"I guess I have a dog now," Archer said, bending down and scratching behind his ears. "Do you know what breed he is, Maggie?"

"He's a Dobermann, a big dog when he's an adult and lots of exercise. So think carefully before you accept him," Maggie said.

"Okay, understood. I'll take him overnight while I work out what I'm going to do," Archer said.

"Take him for a couple of hours, keep him outside, then bring him back. You're in a guest cottage. We don't want dog hair over all the carpets and furniture."

"I'd better leave him here if you're okay with that? I've

already got to fix the electrics in the cottage, probably not the place for a dog, anyway."

"What happened?"

"I turned on the shower and blew a fuse. I flipped the fuse, but there has to be a reason it happened."

"Good job, we have an electrician here, isn't it?" Maggie said as she gave him a grin.

"Are you sure you're okay with Teddy?"

"Positive."

Maggie whistled for Teddy to come to her, and he did. Archer left the kitchen by the back door and walked back to Emma Lodge. The grounds were simple but expansive. To his surprise, the outdoor pool was still there and looked like it was fully functioning. Wandering across the lawn, Archer expected his aunt to yell at him to get off her grass through the window. In the opposite direction, a man walked towards him carrying a rake. They met by the side of the pool.

"Hi, I'm Archer," he said, holding out his hand.

The man looked to be in his forties. With a head of thick wavy fair hair and a tanned face, the man pulled off his gardening glove and shook Archer's hand. "I'm Ralph, the gardener. Good to meet you. Bailey talks about you and your brothers and sister a lot."

"I bet he's shared some stories," Archer said good-naturedly.

"A few. Are you coming back to live here?"

"It's a possibility. Is the pool fit for swimming?"

"Sure. Miss Turner arranged for the pool to be over-hauled a couple of weeks ago. Bailey says she's never stepped a toe in the pool, so we're not sure why she wanted it ready."

Archer suspected why, two weeks ago was when they'd

got notice to leave the island, and he'd organised a meeting with his aunt. He'd spent most of his youth in the pool, and so had Jason, Luke, and Daisy. His dad had lectured them they needed to be able to swim if they lived on an Island. He hammered home the point that they needed to be able to swim better than anyone because they never knew when someone might need help.

His dad had always worked on the oil rigs. Archer had never known him to do anything else. As children, they'd grown used to seeing him for three weeks and not seeing him for another three. He'd learned to swim in the swimming pool. They all had.

Their dad wouldn't let them swim in the sea until he was satisfied they could handle the ocean, currents, and riptides. He'd taught them to recognise the dangers of the sea. Demystified it, but at the same time respectful of mother nature.

"Good to know it can be used. I might take a dip later," Archer said.

"Of course, Mr Turner. I live in the town, so if you want to go for a beer, let me know, and I'll bring you up to date with what's happening."

Archer took in the man, he looked familiar in his green overalls.

"Thanks, Ralph. Please call me Archer. Have you worked here long?"

"A few years. My father and grandfather worked here as gardeners. My grandfather is long passed, but my father is still alive and cantankerous. He's retired but can still tell me what I should be doing on the grounds."

That was why he looked familiar. Archer remembered his father and grandfather.

"My advice? Write it all down. Record him, absorb

everything you need to know. You never know when you'll need to know something, and he won't be there to ask."

Ralph dropped his chin, and Archer silently begged him not to say it. "Yes, I will. I'll bear that in mind. I never met your father, but I hear he was a fantastic man."

And there it was. It was the kindness that brought a lump to Archer's throat.

"Thank you, he was amazing. I'm sorry to hear about your grandfather. He was fabulous with all us kids running over his lawns. I'll see you around."

Archer nodded and walked away, instantly regretting pointing out that life wasn't forever. Just because his dad had died early, he didn't need to remind everyone else. Sending a group message to his siblings, he arranged to have a family call in an hour. Hopefully, the time differences wouldn't be too hard on them. As far as he knew, Jason, Luke, and Daisy were all in Europe.

Archer couldn't find an obvious problem with the electrics in the cottage. The shower didn't trip the second time he switched it on. He changed into his board shorts to take a dip in the pool, hoping his aunt would permit it. She would never directly come out into the grounds to tell him off, but she would send someone to advise him. At least now, she had the excuse of age and the extensive grounds, but back when they were kids, there wasn't any reason she couldn't come and tell them off personally.

Archer checked in with Bailey and Maggie to be on the safe side to ensure it was okay. He swam laps until he was worn out thinking about his aunt's condition. The far end of the pool neared the edge of the grounds overlooking the cliffs and out into the Atlantic Ocean. Swimming up to the edge and hauling himself up, he looked out to sea. Working on the rigs seemed so long ago, even though it was only a week. He knew in his heart he would agree to his aunt's deal, but he still needed to hear what his siblings had to say.

Climbing out of the water and snatching up a towel, he dried his skin and walked back to his cottage.

Setting up his tablet on the table in the rear of the cottage, he sank into the outdoor armchair and logged into their online meeting room.

Luke was already online.

"Hey, where are you?" Archer asked.

"Barcelona. How's Copper Island?"

"Interesting. I haven't been into town yet, but the house hasn't changed at all since I was last here."

"Doesn't surprise me. Is she going to give us the business to run?"

"That's what I want to talk to you about. Where are the other two?"

"Physically, Daisy is in Rome and Jason," Luke said.

"Is here. Keep your pants on," Jason said as his voice came through before his live feed flashed up.

"You look like hell, Jason," Luke said.

"Let's just say it was a good night. But, cut short this morning by this meeting. A bit formal, isn't it? Turner Hall rules already rubbing off on you?" Jason said.

Daisy came into view, and the screen split into four squares. "Hey, guys, how are you all?" she said.

She grinned wide when Jason gave her an eye roll. "It's been a week Daisy."

"I know, but it's the longest I've been away from you since University," she replied with a pout.

"True," Archer said. "Look, we can catch up later. But, first, I need to let you know what the deal is here."

"Is she going to let us run the business?" Jason asked.

"She will," Archer said, and cheers went up in all three windows. "But," Archer added and raised a finger.

Like a set of dominos, they all slumped one after the other. "What are the conditions?" Daisy asked.

"She isn't going to give us control of any land on Copper Island."

"That's okay. We don't want the land until we inherit it," Luke said. "Is that it?"

"Not exactly," Archer said. "We're not allowed to have anything to do with the running of Turner Hall."

"So long as Maggie can cook for me, I don't care about that," Jason said.

"Maggie is excited you might be coming back. I'm sure she won't have any trouble feeding you. Strangely she's permitted use of the swimming pool, recently had it overhauled," Archer said.

"Aww, she still has a soft spot for us," Daisy replied.

"I don't think she's capable of such things," Luke said.

"Still. Turner Hall is off-limits apart from sleeping. Edward Hall is still the hotel and venue for the business, plus the five cottages are with the deal."

"They're for the wedding parties, aren't they?"

"As far as I can tell, they're rented long term, rather than for the weekend. So I'm not too sure what's going on there. The one I'm staying in is clean enough, but it hasn't been used for a while. Plus, I nearly electrocuted myself on the shower electrics."

"Good job you're an electrician then," Jason offered.

"That's what Maggie said," Archer replied.

"Amazing. What about Bailey?" Daisy asked.

"He's still there, too, as well as Jennifer."

"Christ," Jason replied. "She must be eighty by now."

"There is one more proviso to have the business," Archer said.

Jason, Luke, and Daisy waited expectantly, staring at him and then looking at each other on the screen. Archer scrubbed his face with his hands and blinked away the blurring he'd caused.

"She thinks I am my father's son and says we can only take over the business if I get married."

Luke burst out laughing.

"Fuck," Jason replied.

"No way," Daisy said.

Archer let the news sink in for a few minutes as they talked over each other, arguing whether Archer should take the deal.

"You're a catch. I'm sure you'll find a wife," Daisy said, bringing her phone into view.

"What are you doing, Daisy," Luke asked.

"Setting up a profile for Archer on a dating app," she said.

Luke laughed and sat back with a smug smile.

"Put the phone down, Daisy. I need you all to be serious for a moment. She wants me to get married in the family chapel. Not just engaged, married. That's serious stuff, just because she thinks I'm going to whore my ass around the town and get half the single women pregnant," Archer said.

"Shit. She said that?" Luke asked.

"Yep."

"But dad loved mum. It's not like it was a one-night stand. They got married as soon as they found out she was pregnant with you, Archer."

"In the family chapel," Jason added.

"I know that, and you all know that, but I think when

mum walked out, Aunt Cynthia assumed he was forced into it because she didn't hang around."

"Can we not talk about our mother?" Jason asked.

"Sure. Let's go back to the deal. Did Aunt Cynthia mention any clause about not getting divorced?" Luke asked.

"No, she didn't mention it at all, in fact," Archer replied.

"So, find a wife, get married, and get divorced if it doesn't work out. Get her to sign a pre-nuptial agreement first," Luke said.

"It sounds so cold," Archer muttered.

"Look, brother, you don't have to do this. We'll inherit eventually. We can return to the rigs overseas and chance our luck in getting the same place for all of us. We're young enough to wait it out," Daisy said.

"Get a fake wife," Jason said.

"Luke," Archer said, "what about you?"

"I don't know, man, it's a lot for her to ask you to give up. You've always been someone who wanted to marry once and forever. Marrying for a transaction seems beneath you," Luke said.

"Right, you're all saying I have to make my own decision?"

All three of them nodded. "Yes," they said.

"Is it a profitable business?" Daisy asked.

He smiled for the first time in fifteen minutes. Daisy had gained her accountancy degree while on the rigs but had yet to do the final exams to qualify. Her main job on the oil rig they worked on was as a forklift driver.

"I have no fucking idea, Daisy," Archer said and laughed. "Does it matter?"

"It may swing your decision," she warned.

"Okay. I'll let you know in the morning what I'll do. In the meantime, do not send me pictures of your fabulous locations. I don't want to see them," Archer said, sounding grumpier than he was.

"If you want to talk later, Archer, call me," Daisy said.

"Don't call me," Jason and Luke said simultaneously.

Somehow, they were able to bump fists on screen. It lightened the mood how little they wanted to be involved but would ultimately do whatever Archer asked them to do.

"If I agree to her terms, you'll all come home?" Archer asked.

"I'll be on the next flight," Luke said.

"Absolutely," Daisy said.

Jason did his one-shoulder shrug. "Sure," he answered.

"I'm going to take you at your word. Love you all," Archer said.

He ended the call and sat back in the chair, slouching as he pondered if he could marry for money and not love.

TEN

Archer

He woke early the following day. He had a fitful night trying to work through what he should do. There was some merit in finding a wife, being totally upfront that it was for appearance's sake, and then she was free to get a divorce. Were there women out there that would agree to it? He was sure he would have to pay them. Archer had a fair amount of money in savings, but he'd doubted he had enough money to pay a woman to marry him.

He'd taken an early dip in the pool to clear his head. By the time he'd exhausted himself swimming laps, Archer knew what he had needed to do for the sake of his family. Sending a text to his brothers and sister, he told them he would take the deal.

Message after message streamed through, but Archer didn't read any of them. He didn't want to be put off. He'd made the decision and now needed to see it through. Daisy tried to call him, but he didn't take the call. He knew it wasn't an emergency, just moral support when she'd only called once. Dressing more casually this time, Archer took the path up to the main house and went to the kitchen early. He talked Maggie and Bailey through what he planned to do. They both let out a long breath but noted the thinking behind the decision.

"I'm not going lie," Bailey said. "It's going to be great to have you home again. You never know, you might find a wife you actually love.

"Have you got a candidate in mind, Bailey?" Archer said through a laugh.

"Not at all, Sir. That's for you to discover. But I would suggest a night in the town with Ralph. He can tell you who all the singles ladies are."

"Good advice. Take me up, will you?" he asked Bailey.

"Of course, Sir."

Archer trudged behind Bailey up the stone stairs and into the grand foyer of Turner Hall. This was once his home, but he felt like he'd never entered the building before in his life. Foreboding inched into his heart. He had no idea if he was doing the right thing. But if he didn't try, he would always wonder if he could have done more to provide his brothers and sisters with a job and a salary.

His Aunt Cynthia was sitting at his grandfather's writing desk with a fountain pen and a blank sheet of paper in her hand. She gave the impression he was interrupting her morning.

"I'm surprised you came," she said.

"We agreed I would come and give you my answer this morning," Archer replied.

"I'm still surprised. I take it you've decided to take me up on my offer."

"I have. It seems horrendous that you think so little of

me. That I would be so careless with a woman and have an unplanned child."

"Your father was exactly like that."

"It doesn't mean I would be. My dad loved my mother, so getting her pregnant wasn't unwanted."

"The apple doesn't fall far from the tree, Archer."

"Why are you so bitter?"

"Are you going to take the deal or not?"

"I am. I'll be married within three months, and then you will jointly sign the business to me, my sister, and brothers."

"Can you find a woman to love you in that time?"

"I'll have to if I want to get my siblings back all in one place."

"I'll sign the papers to you only on your wedding day, directly after the ceremony."

"Fine."

"I'm sure the day will be perfect," she said and turned her back on him.

Bailey cleared his throat behind Archer signalling the meeting was over.

"Maggie is making you breakfast. Let's go back down to the kitchen," Bailey said.

"I might need a Brandy too."

"Of course, Sir."

ELEVEN

Erica

Erica had flown in a helicopter many times in her career, but this one seemed a little bit special. It felt like she was running away. Petra, her assistant, had booked her a private helicopter. Her luggage had been put on board for her two-month stay on the remote island. Two things surprised her when she got to the small airport in Penzance. The first part was that she needed to be weighed and the second part absolutely nobody recognised her. It was one of those things that she tried to tackle in her mind. She didn't want to be identified but was disappointed when she wasn't, but then that was her ego thinking. The news of her husband having an affair with a young woman and that he was soon to be a father have mortified her. Speculation was going into over-drive that it was a publicity stunt to get the sympathy. That wasn't something she understood because she had just won an Oscar. Why would she want sympathy?

The large helicopter could seat eight, but she was alone.

If she had more of a circle of friends outside Yanny, Erica could've filled the aircraft for her time away. Erica settled herself at the back and stared out the window when they took off. Flying across the water, deep blue seas eventually turned into light blue and then clear water with golden sands.

She had no idea that the small oasis was only fifty miles off the coast of England. The type of waters and sand she'd only seen in the Caribbean. The main island she'd landed on was Copper Island which was bustling with tourists. Erica desperately didn't want to be recognised and pulled the cap further down over her brow with dark sunglasses. She didn't look out of place on the gorgeous sunny day. A couple of men loaded her luggage onto the small boat, and in no time at all, she was speeding across the water to the other side of the small island. Erica had researched Copper Island and found that it was a privately owned island going back four hundred years. There was something about the island's history that intrigued her. She wanted to stay somewhere within flying distance should she need to get back to the mainland. She heavily tipped the two boatmen when she stepped off the sloping concrete quay. They smiled and nodded their heads and climbed back into their boat. Another man appeared in green overalls with what looked like a golf cart with a trailer behind it.

"Are you Erica Taylor?" he asked.

She'd heard that sentence hundreds and hundreds of times in the last decade, but the tone he used wasn't curiosity. As if she wasn't an Oscar-winning actress, but more he was sent to pick her up, and he was just checking a name.

"Yes, that's me."

"I'm Ralph. I'll get your bags into the trailer, and then we can get you to your cottage."

Erica helped him put all the bags into the back of the trailer, feeling slightly guilty that she had brought a dozen suitcases with her for a two-month stay. While she felt like she was running away, Erica also felt like she was temporarily moving house and wanted to have everything around her.

The buggy was surprisingly fast as they drove along the concrete paths between palm trees and thick grass. Semi-circles of houses, shops, and cafes had surrounded the main port, but when she got to the deserted quay, Erica could hear waves crashing against rocks and birds squawking and nothing else.

"You'll have a great time here, Miss Taylor. We'll take care of all of your needs."

"Thank you. Do you work at the house?"

"I'm the gardener, but I double up as a driver if people need a lift up from the quay."

"Thanks for coming to get me. I'm sorry I pulled you away from your day job."

"It's not a problem. That's what I'm paid to do."

They rounded the corner on a tight bend, and she grabbed the metal pole in the open buggy. Then they came to a grinding halt.

"Here we are. I know you've got all five cottages for privacy, but this is the one we thought you would like the most. It's called Emma Lodge. I'll help you with your bags.

"Thanks, Ralph," Eric said.

She gave him a hand again with the bags making it quick. She offered a tip as she had with the boatman, but he refused to take her money.

"All part of the service, Miss Taylor."

She nodded and respected his answer, saying goodbye. As soon as the door was closed behind him, she felt her shoulders drop. Complete isolation for two months if she could get away with it. Erica wouldn't even turn on her internet access.

When Yanny said she would stay in a cottage, she imagined dark corners and low ceilings. A one-storey building. But this cottage was huge. It was like a small house, and the rooms were light and airy. Standing in the middle of the living room with the big plump sofas and armchairs, she thought she could quickly get used to living there.

She took her luggage up the stairs and chose the first room to dump all her baggage. The room had a full set of wardrobes as well as a bed. She would use this as her dressing room. She kicked off her shoes and walked down the corridor to inspect the other rooms. Finding the main bedroom at the end of the hall, she entered and then flopped down on the bed. She'd been travelling for twelve hours with an overnight train journey down to Penzance. What she needed was a shower.

Stripping off her clothes and dropping them on the bathroom floor, she reached into the shower room and pressed the button for the shower.

A bolt of electricity hit her finger and travelled up her arm.

Erica cursed a long streak of expletives while ambling backwards. She steadied herself on the vanity table without falling over completely. She gave the shower a deathly glare and had a quick wash out of the sink.

She returned to her makeshift dressing room and found a pair of shorts and a t-shirt. Then, running down the stairs, she left the cottage. She didn't come to Copper Island to die on her first morning.

Walking with purpose along the path to the next cottage, she reached the front door. It looked like somebody was living in it. She knocked on the door, but there was no answer. Erica could see a grander house in the distance through the tall trees. When she got to that building, it was utterly deserted. Erika could see an even more prominent place, more like a stately home in the far distance. It took ten minutes to get there. The imposing building screamed go away, but she needed to speak to somebody.

Hearing somebody was mowing a lawn, she turned in that direction. Walking around the perimeter of the vast mansion, she spotted Ralph, the man who had picked her up from the quay. Standing with her fists to her head, she waited for him to turn the mower to face her. When she got this attention, she waved. Ralph turned the machine off and jumped down, wiping his hands on a rag he pulled from his pocket.

"Is everything all right, Miss Turner?"

"No, Ralph, I'm afraid it's not. I just stepped into the shower and got electrocuted."

"Oh my God, are you all right?"

"I'm fine, but it's obviously a death trap. Can I move cottages?"

"Why don't I send the maintenance guy around first to see if you can see what the problem is?"

"That would be great. Do you know how long that will be?"

"I'll go and fetch him right now. Do you want a lift back to your cottage?"

"No, that's unnecessary."

Ralph didn't know how to end the conversation, so he turned his back and strode towards the main house. Erica looked up at the building, wondering what kind of family lived inside the four walls. She hoped it was a happy home.

She spied the swimming pool on the other side of the

grounds and noted its location. She would need to use that very soon.

TWELVE

Erica

An hour later, no one had come to fix her shower, and she was desperate to wash away the travel from her skin. She picked up a towel from the stack in her bathroom and her wash bag. Erica assumed all the cottages she'd hired were for her use and should be ready to accept guests. Walking to the nearest cottage, the one she passed up to the main house, she used the keys she was given. The place looked exactly like hers. Same décor, same layout. It made it easier for her to find the bathroom attached to the main bedroom. She stripped off for the second time. Nothing would stop her from getting under the warm water, not even the vague idea that the front door had just slammed shut.

She stepped towards the switch on the wall and reached out to press it when a man appeared in the open doorway.

"Don't press it," he yelled.

But it was too late. Her finger had already started its trajectory and had pressed the button. The man yelled *fuck* and ran towards her. The shock of electricity shot up her arm. Erica let out a scream and stumbled back, and then she fell. The man caught her as she sank to the floor, falling to the floor with her. They landed in a heap on the tiled floor. Erica was sitting on his lap, and he had his hands on her.

A rough palm of his hand cupped her breast while his other hand was on her hip.

"Shit, I'm sorry," he said, whipping his hand away like her skin burned him.

He reached across, snatched a towel off the vanity unit, and draped it over her.

"Thank you, I think," she said.

"How did you know the shower is trying to kill me?"

"The same thing happened to me in Emma Lodge. I fixed that one, but I hadn't had the chance to check in here. They told me you wouldn't be living in this cottage," he said.

"The switch in Emma Lodge attacked me too. Are they all like this?"

"I didn't think so, but I'll get them all checked out straight away."

"Now that you've grabbed my breast, maybe you could tell me your name?" Erica said, making no effort to move away from her position on his muscular thighs.

"I'm Archer," he said, holding out his hand in the awkward position. She took it but didn't shake it. Instead, she held his hand and leaned against his torso.

"I'm Erica, and I feel a bit light-headed," she said.

"I'll pick you up and take you to the bedroom," he said, already rising from his seated position.

"I hope you're a gentleman," she said and laughed.

Talking brazenly had never been her style, but this man was strong, seemingly capable-and he gave a shit that she was about to electrocute herself.

"Always the gentleman. The lady should always come first. Shit. I mean, go first. Fuck. Be first."

She let out a nervous laugh as he stumbled over his words. Then, momentarily startled that Archer was affected by her, she regained her composure.

He carefully placed her on the king-sized bed and ensured the towel completely covered her. Then, taking a large step back, he glanced into the bathroom and then back to Erica. She tried and failed at her perusal of the man who caught her when she fell.

"How are you feeling?" Archer asked her.

"I feel okay now. Thanks for coming in when you did."

Erica sat up with her hand on her towel over her breasts and swung her legs over the side of the bed. Archer's eyes darted to her thigh that was on show.

"I'd gone to your cottage first. Ralph said your shower had tripped out the electrics. When you weren't there, I walked back and saw the light on upstairs here."

"I'd pay a lot of money to get a shower right now."

"I'm really sorry. I'd told the main house and suggested they put your main cottage as one of the others."

"You're not the maintenance man?"

"I'm not sure what I am, to be honest, but I am a quali-fied electrician. There is only one shower I know is working and safe for sure. But there's a catch."

"It's the sea?" she deadpanned.

"Not quite, but it is outdoors," he said with a broad grin.

"Can you turn your back for a second?"

Archer turned around. "I'm sorry my hand landed on your breast, truly."

"Don't give it another thought. It's fine," Erica said.

She would be thinking about it for some time. His rough skin, the short squeeze that he probably didn't remember doing. Did he notice her nipple hardened? She hoped not. He didn't appear to have recognised her, so at least there wouldn't be headlines in the gutter press online within the hour.

Maintenance man grabs Hollywood actress tit

Wrapping the towel around her body and tucking in the edge of the towel securely, she walked to where Archer was standing.

"I need to grab my wash bag, and then we can get going. Is it far?"

"A few minutes walk. You'll need shoes if we take the shortcut."

"Okay," she said, pulling on her deck shoes without socks.

Archer smiled at her, "come on, follow me."

They walked out the back of the cottage and through a gap in the hedge. This brought them level with the end of the tall trees. He took her across the lawn at the back of the cottage she first arrived at, and then they walked between the trees. On the other side, they were almost at the back of the smaller of the large mansions she passed earlier. They walked in silence to Turner Hall, where the swimming pool was located. Archer stopped next to a wooden shack.

"In there is a shower. It's for people who are going to use the pool. There's warm water and a shelf on which you can put your wash bag. On the back of the door is a hook for your towel. However," he said, thinning his lips. "There's no lock. So I'll stand guard until you're finished."

With a wary look, she stepped into the wooden slatted hut with no roof and closed the door. It had a magnetic clasp.

"I can see through the wooden planks," she said, closing one eye and checking out his thighs.

"Do you know you're not completely invisible in there? I can see the direction of your eyes."

Erica jumped back like she'd been caught spying. She heard his chuckle as she turned on the shower using the large silver dial. The water shot out of the shower head and down her back. The cold water soaked her.

"I thought you said it was warm water," she shouted over the shower noise.

"It'll warm up. Stop being a diva."

It wasn't the first time she'd been called a diva, but the water was icy cold and surprised her. His back was turned to the cubicle when she glanced over her shoulder. His arms folded and his feet apart, standing guard. Erica washed her hair and body quickly, so she didn't impose on his time any longer than necessary, and turned the water off. Once her towel was securely fastened, she pushed the door open and stepped out onto the flagstones. The sunshine shimmering off the pool was inviting.

"I can't wait to take a dip in the pool. I'm so glad the booking allowed me to access it."

"Was that a condition of your booking?"

"Yes. I can't believe the luck I had with a late booking."

"How long ago did you book?"

"Two weeks ago. To have all the cottages and the use of a swimming pool to myself is perfect for what I need."

"Do you compete?"

"Swimming? No. I need to increase my synchronised swimming skills. I need to be as perfect as I can be in two months."

"Did you ask for the exclusivity of the pool?" he asked, looking crestfallen.

"I assumed as I had all the rooms booked. Are there others that use it?"

"Just me, but I can swim in the sea if you need access whenever you need it."

"We can share, Archer. I'll need to swim to increase my stamina and lungs, but it's big enough for both of us."

She asked it as a question. Erica was now desperate to see Archer in his swimming trunks, soaking wet from the water. Archer tipped his head to the side.

"What are you concentrating on?"

Erica snapped her head up and looked him straight in the eye. "Nothing, nothing at all. Look, I need to get back and put some clothes on. When do you think you can look at the shower in my cottage?"

"I can come now if you like."

"Great," she said, taking in a large breath and letting it out with a slump of her shoulders.

Having Archer in her house was going to be a distraction. She'd always liked a man who could fix things. Handsy. But she wasn't here to hook up with the maintenance guy or whoever he might be. She was here to lick her wounds and learn her lines. Her afternoon's task was to watch as many Esther Williams films as possible.

They walked to her place, and he looked at her shower once she was dressed. Archer came into the open living room shaking his head in the universal way that told her it would cost her a fortune to fix. Thankfully, it wasn't her financial problem.

"It looks like the same problem as next door. I will check the other three cottages to see if they are okay. If they are, we can move you into one of those."

"And if they're not?"

"I guess I'm on escort duty for a poolside shower."

"Are you a full-service escort?"

Archer gave her a wide-eyed stare with a gaping mouth. She burst out laughing at his shock.

"Relax," she said, waving away his reaction. "I'm kidding. I love movie quotes."

"That's lost on me. I've never seen a movie in my life. Can't stand the things."

"You're kidding?"

"Nope. I lasted ten minutes once, never again. Who wants to sit still for two hours looking at a screen."

"I think they call it escapism."

"There are other ways to escape," Archer said, taking a quick glance at her mouth. "Anyway, I'd better go look at the other cottages. I'll be back in ten minutes."

Erica nodded her understanding and watched him walk out of her house. Her relationship with Gregg had been over for months, and she hadn't lusted after anyone until this guy. A man who hated films. At least she wouldn't have a problem with him knowing who she was while she hid away.

THIRTEEN

Archer

All three cottages were precisely the same as the one he stayed in and hers. He stopped on the path, realising he knew the feel of Erica's breast in his hand. Soft, supple, perfectly sized, with a large nipple.

He wanted to kiss her so badly. The pull he felt when she sat on his lap, curling in against his body while she found her grounding. The electric shock wouldn't have hurt, but it would have surprised her. He was used to being shocked, but if Erica had never experienced it before, she would've been startled.

Carrying her to the bed was over the top, but she was game. It took all of Archer's willpower to stop pulling the towel off her body and burying his face between her trim thighs.

Archer knocked on her front door and pushed the door open, walking in. He called out *hello,* and she shouted she was out in the back garden. I watched her through the window for a few moments while she was talking and waving her hands in the air. Her earbuds were firmly in her ears, with the cord trailing down into the back pocket of her jeans. Then his focus was solely on her backside.

"Eyes up here, sunshine," she said.

Fuck.

Her smile lit up her whole face. Archer wanted that smile just for him, ban her from smiling that way to anyone else.

Ignoring what his dick wanted after seeing her bottom and killer smile, he cleared his throat and went outside to see her.

"The other cottages are the same, but it's an easy fix. I'll get them repaired in the next few hours. I need to go into the town to pick up some supplies. Someone has wired up the switches incorrectly."

"Sounds like someone hasn't done their job properly. However, I have faith you'll sort it out. Are you new to the estate?"

"Kind of. Why?"

"Is the town busy with people?"

"Define busy?"

"Crowded, people looking you in the eye, that kind of thing. Stopping to have a chat. Or is it strangers passing on the street getting on with their lives?"

"The former, definitely. The townfolk can smell new blood instantly. Then they'll charm you into revealing everything about yourself. If you resist, they'll engage other means."

"Christ. I'll stay here."

"You don't like people?"

"Not at the moment. I'm a private person and clam up when asked personal stuff."

"Best you stay here then. Is there something you need? I can pick it up for you."

"Nothing in particular. I thought I could wander around the town and browse in the shop windows. But if I'm likely to be stopped, I'll stay here. Two months is a long time to be cooped up. I want to get some exercise."

"If it's exercise you need," he said with a smirk he couldn't stop. "Then you can walk around the open land up here on the cliffs. It's all Turner land. If you walk to the end of the garden, past the gap I took you through before, there's a well-worn path connecting all five cottages and leading you down the beach below. It's a private beach for Turner use. The townspeople know they're not allowed on the beach. Plus, you can only get to it by that path or by boat."

"Turner use?"

"It's a broad term, but back in the day, both Turner Hall and Edward Hall were filled with family, staff, and a constant flow of friends coming to stay. Whoever was staying in either hall could use the beach."

"And no one sneaks up in the dead of night to go down to the beach?"

"No, for two reasons. One, they wouldn't risk the wrath of my aunt, and two, everyone living on an island knows not to mess about near the sea when it's dark."

"Sounds like you talk from experience."

"Yes, I do, on both counts," he said, chuckling. "I'll be back in an hour or so."

Archer walked away from Erica, thinking about the parts he needed to fix the wiring issues in the cottages. He'd thoroughly checked over the rest of the cottage he stayed in and found no other issues. He hoped that was the same for all five of them. Vowing to check over Erica's house again, he marched faster to the back of Turner Hall to find Ralph. He found him in his shed, sorting through spanners.

"Hey, Ralph, can I borrow the buggy to go into town?"

"Sure. Did you sort the problem at Erica Taylor's cottage?"

"You know her name?"

"I think we all know her name," Ralph replied.

Shrugging, he assumed they ran a tight ship renting out the cottages and running the hotel wedding venue at Edward Hall.

"Someone has wired up the on-off shower switch incorrectly. Do you know how long ago it was done?"

"A few months ago, I think. Your aunt got someone from the mainland to update the bathrooms in all the cottages. She'd got it into her head that bathrooms are the selling point of any holiday cottage."

Archer followed the logic. There was nothing better than a hot shower with a powerful shower head.

"Have they been paid? We need to get a refund on shoddy work if they have."

"I don't know about any of that side of things. I meet them at the quay, take them to wherever they need to go, and then get on with the never-ending job of mowing these lawns."

"But you have a tractor mower. What more could you want?" Archer said in good humour.

"There are small mercies, not that I thought the Mistress would ever agree to such an extravagance. It turns out her hatred for spending money comes below her hatred for unkempt grounds."

"Lucky you," Archer said. "I'll be about an hour."

"No problem. If I'm not here, just hang the keys back

up on that hook." He said and pointed to where Archer needed to get the keys for the buggy.

Snatching them up off the hook, he jumped into the buggy and drove into town. Parking at the dockside, he spied Nathaniel at the far end, coming out of the small warehouse. He started the ignition and moved towards where he was rolling a tyre.

"Hey, Nate," Archer called out.

"Archer?" Nate called back. "Is that you? I heard you were back in town."

"Sure am. Can I leave the buggy here while I go and get some supplies?"

"Sure. What do you need?"

"Wiring and a few tools to fix a botch job. Is McKenzie's still open?"

"Yeah. Old man McKenzie is still at the helm. Selling screws individually."

"I used to love that shop as a kid. He sold everything you could need."

"Still does, mate. Come into town one night. We can have a drink and catch up."

"Will do."

Archer strode away, aiming for the ironmongers. He nodded to people he didn't know and then pushed open the door. It was dark but inviting. High shelving units with every possible nut, bolt, or anything you could need for a household. He passed the plastic door numbers on hooks, still swinging where someone had turned the moveable stand. Everything was in the same place as when he was last in the shop. Heading to the back left, Archer stood in front of the trellis-style wall with metal hangers and dozens of different wire types.

"Can I help you find something?" Old man McKenzie said behind Archer.

"Hello, Mr McKenzie. How are you?"

"Archer Turner? I heard you were back up at the estate. What brings you into town?"

"I need to repair some bad wiring. Can you help with this list?"

Archer handed the list to Mr McKenzie. It would be faster than searching through the shelves. Mr McKenzie smiled wide. The wrinkles and well-worn skin brightened at the task.

"Give me five minutes, and I'll have everything at the till. How's Miss Turner these days? We don't see her in town anymore."

"She is no different from the last time I saw her," Archer replied.

"I can't believe it's seven years since your dad left this earth."

Mr McKenzie was the same age as his father and went to school with him. They were best friends even when his father went to work on the oil rigs.

"It's a hard reality. The Hall is completely different without him there. I still think he will walk around the corner wearing a big grin."

"I miss him too, but it's good to see you back on the island. Are Jason, Luke, and Daisy coming back too?"

"We'll see. Not sure at the moment if I'm staying. I've given myself three months. If everything isn't sorted by then, I'll leave, and the others will find jobs overseas."

"I will send prayers it works out. The island needs you all back."

"Thanks, Mr McKenzie."

The man gave him a nod and set about getting the list of

items Archer needed. He was soon walking back to the quayside and into the buggy. Ten minutes later, he was back at Erica's cottage. She'd left the front door ajar, but he still rapped the door loudly and called out her name.

"I'm in here," she said.

Archer followed her voice into the living room to find her crouched over her laptop.

"The Wi-Fi here is shocking," she said, stretching back in the dining room chair she'd brought through. She'd made a table from a stool and a stack of books to put her laptop on.

"Interesting use of the furniture," he said, pointing to her homemade desk.

"It's the only spot that picks up the Wi-Fi in the house. The dining room table was too heavy to drag in here. If I sit in an armchair, I fall asleep within ten minutes, and I have work to do. I promised myself I wouldn't turn on my internet access, but I'm addicted and not ready to go off-grid."

"How's your mobile signal?" he asked.

"Amazing, but I can't do the work I need on the phone."

"But you could tether your laptop to your phone signal."

She pointed her pen in his direction. "I could, fantastic idea," she said.

"I'll leave you to it while I work upstairs. I need to turn off the electricity, so your work shouldn't be interrupted if you switch to your phone.

He got to work as soon as Erica confirmed she'd switched over and fixed the wiring. He'd found the incorrect wires had been taped together at several points. Archer stripped it out and replaced the damaged section. When he returned downstairs, Erica had moved outside to the rattan chairs. She was on the phone again, so he didn't interrupt her, leaving her a note that it was safe to have a shower.

He needed to repeat the work in all the cottages. He should've done the work when he first tripped out the shower switch a week ago, but he'd got distracted with the other tasks at Turner Hall. He didn't imagine so much work would need to be done in the cottages. Surely the other guests would've used the shower and reported the problem?

FOURTEEN

Erica

"Is it horrific?" Erica asked Yanny.

Yanny hummed for over thirty seconds and said, "not horrific, no."

"You're such a liar. Keeping my private life away from magazines has its downsides. Sometimes I think the celebrities who tell the world every breath they take has it right. Is anyone reporting that we're divorced?"

"No. You made everyone involved sign confidentiality agreements. You have excellent lawyers, so it still looks like he had an affair and got a woman pregnant behind your back."

"I'm going to look like a victim here."

"Technically, he did have an affair, Erica. Just because you got divorced, you were still married when he got her pregnant. He hadn't asked you for a divorce when she conceived."

"But we were not madly in love."

The public doesn't know that. So this is good for him, sadly. He's coming across as a stud."

"I'm a weak, stupid woman who couldn't keep a man happy enough to stop him straying. Men are arseholes."

"Some men are arseholes."

"Sorry, Yanny, I didn't mean you were an arsehole."

"As a man, sweetie, I feel tarred by your sweeping brush."

"Don't be ridiculous. You're the best man I've ever met."

"Aw, thanks, love. I'll keep an eye on the media and tell you if any rumours are being aired."

"Thanks, Yanny."

"How are things on Copper Island? Did I pick a good place for you?"

Erica looked up to see Archer coming through the French doors and walking past where she was sitting. He made the motion of writing a note in mid-air and gave her a wave.

"Erica?"

"Um, yeah. Things are good here. You chose well."

"Who caught your attention? Was he hot?"

"The maintenance guy had come to fix the wiring in the bathroom. He was just leaving."

"Sounds like he was hot if you couldn't multitask talking to me and looking at him."

"He is very nice to look at and seems like a decent guy."

"You sound like you like him?"

"I do. He's someone I could get to know better. The public thinks I'm heartbroken over my arsehole husband, but I've been leading a single life for a while in reality."

"Do I need to give you the rebound guy speech?"

"No," Erica answered, hopefully giving her manager a clear objective to change the subject.

"Fine. I'm sending over a couple of scripts for you to look at. How's the swimming going?"

"I've been here a day."

"You're Erica Taylor."

"True. I'm going for a dip later. I needed to get the house sorted first."

"Okay. Don't be a stranger."

Erica tossed her phone onto the chair beside her and looked across the lawns. How had she gotten to the age of thirty-two and divorced? She had no home she stayed in for very long, spending much of her time on location or holed up in her London home to prepare for her next role. It was no wonder her ex-husband looked for comfort elsewhere. She was never at home.

"Snap out of this," she said to thin air.

Closing her laptop, Erica took her electronics inside and left them on the dining room table. It was time she started her endurance training. Once she was changed into her swimsuit and had donned her Kaftan, she locked up and took the same route Archer had shown her earlier. The sun was still high in the sky and warm in the early evening. The nearer she got to the pool, Erica could hear and then see there was a man swimming laps, front crawl. His muscled arms came out of the water as he sliced through at speed. Archer reached the far end and lifted his body as high as possible, using his hands flat on the side of the pool. Erica thought he would get out of the pool. Instead, Archer stayed in the same position looking out to sea. He seemed deep in thought, gazing out at the ocean.

Not keen to disturb Archer, she dropped her kaftan on the chair near the shallow end and walked into the pool. As soon as she was out of her depth, she began to tread water like she'd been taught. Positioned halfway down the length of the pool, she turned her back to Archer and straightened her legs but kept moving her arms so that she could pivot in the water. When she returned to look at Archer, he was inches away from her.

"Am I interrupting your session?" he whispered, looking at her mouth.

She wanted to kiss him, and his focus on her lips wasn't helping. She sank under the water and stayed there for as long as her lungs let her break the tension. Erica came back up with Archer's hands under her arms. He yanked her out of the water to the surface. He kept his hands under her arms, his wrists pressing against the sides of her breasts.

"What are you trying to achieve apart from giving me a heart attack?" he said.

"I wanted to kiss you, so to stop me from doing that, I sank under the water to practice holding my breath."

"What?"

Erica laughed at his confusion, and delight rolled into one.

"You want to kiss me. Kiss, me?"

"Why not? You're hot as hell. But we don't know each other, so kissing you would seem inappropriate."

"This is like a god damn role reversal. Isn't it supposed to be the man who lusts after the woman making all the moves?"

"Welcome to equality Archer. Do you feel liberated?"

She laughed again at his furrowed brows, the thinning of his lips, and the way he held her more firmly. He seemed to be considering his next move. Erica licked her bottom lip and smiled at him. She was back underwater as he removed his hands from her torso a second later. Erica came to the surface quickly and looked for Archer while smoothing back her hair. Turning in circles, using her arms, she found him back at the other end of the pool, staring at her.

He climbed out of the pool using a move she envied. He hauled his body out with his arms, hooked his foot on the flat, and stood up. She was right about seeing him soaking wet. He was perfect. Erica glanced down his chest, his stomach, admiring his muscles bunched as he breathed deeply, and then she saw his erection, plain as day. Her eyes shot back up to his face. Erica was startled at the pain she saw etched on his face.

"What are you doing all the way over there? Come back into the water."

"I can't," he said, choking out the words. "Believe me, I really want to, but it wouldn't be a good idea."

"Are you married?"

Archer barked out a humourless laugh.

"No, I am not married."

"Girlfriend?"

"No. Just leave it, Erica."

"Boyfriend?"

"I'm straight and, as you can see, attracted to you, but I can't get back in the pool. I'll see you around the estate," Archer said, snatching up his towel, and jogged out of sight through the dense trees at the side of the pool.

"Maybe he doesn't like his women talking directly," she muttered to the water.

Brushing off the rejection, Erica practised treading water, speed swimming, and then her basic synchronised moves, which she'd been taught back in London. Her coach was a gold medallist in the Olympics and a stern taskmaster. Erica knew what she needed to do every day to prepare for her role, but something about Archer's pained expression made her give up on the day and head back to her cottage.

She didn't even know his second name, and already she was feeling hurt by his apparent dislike of being attracted to her.

FIFTEEN

Archer

He'd avoided Erica for a week, trying not to get sight of her. Or smell her perfume. Whatever scent she wore had seeped into the cushions on the chairs next to the pool. He had to wait until she had finished in the pool each day before he took a swim. Some days she spent hours in the pool. He felt like a peeping Tom standing by the tall bushes waiting for her to finish.

Until he found a wife, Archer had little else to do with his time. His Aunt Cynthia had forbidden him to do more repairs on the cottages without her express consent.

Bailey suggested Archer train his new dog Teddy as he would need plenty of exercise daily. Archer spent hours on the internet studying the best food, training, and lifestyle for a Doberman. He hoped like hell he would be able to provide a good home for the dog. He'd gone into the town a few nights and met up with Ralph and Nate. They'd introduced him to pretty much anyone who had entered the bar. A few women had gravitated towards them, but Archer wasn't interested. His mind kept wandering back to Erica up at the estate.

Archer had to find a wife and was already a week into his three months. Once he had a woman who would agree to the ruse, they had to have their banns read in church at least a month before their wedding date—two months, preferably, according to his aunt. She'd told him the vicar preferred to have more time. Archer wouldn't put it past his aunt to time the three months to the second. To his calculations, he needed to find a wife in three weeks.

Frustrated with the deal he'd struck, he called Daisy. She'd know what to do.

"What's up, brother? Found me a sister-in-law yet? I'd love to have a girl on board. All the testosterone has been a bit much over the years," she said when the line connected.

"No. that's why I'm calling."

"Oh, you like someone," she said in her conspiratorial tone.

"Is it that obvious? How do you know?"

"Only to me, big brother. You look like you're in pain. Where are you?"

"My old bedroom," Archer replied, sitting down on the ancient bed. "Aunt Cynthia had me move in when I agreed to the deal. She clearly doesn't trust me."

"Is that the same bed you had as a kid?"

"Yep. I'm going to need a chiropractor by the time this is over. One way or another."

"You've found a girl you can put your proposal to. Except you like her, and she's a decent person, so you're worried she'll tell you to take a hike, thus losing out on the deal you made with the dragon and a shot at a chance of love."

"Christ, how do you do that?"

"It was an educated guess. Otherwise, you would be calling me to tell me to book a ticket home."

"Where are you?"

"Kenya," she replied.

"Did I wake you?"

"Nah, it's only an hour's time difference. So what's she like?"

"I don't know very much about her. I met her a week ago, and we connected. Then she wanted to kiss me, and I said no and ran away. I've known her for a day, but it's like I've missed her this past week. I catch glimpses of her around the estate but have avoided her."

"Why?"

"I told you, she said she wanted to kiss me."

"Then why didn't you kiss her?"

"Because I didn't want her to think I only kissed her to get her to marry me."

"I see your point. Why don't you cook her dinner and get to know her? You're a good judge of character. You'll be able to tell if she's game by the end of the meal."

"Jason's the chef, not me. I can fix her dodgy electrics in her bathroom but not dinner."

"The cottages had faulty wiring?"

"Yeah. The electrician who installed the new bathrooms messed up the shower power switch."

"That doesn't sound good if Aunt Cynthia is using cheap labour. I'm sure Mr McKenzie would've done a better job."

"Probably. Anyway. So you think I should go and see her?"

"Yes. If nothing else, if she says no, you can search for someone else or put an advert in the newspaper."

"I'd get all the weirdos coming out of the woodwork if that happened."

"Then your mission is to charm this girl and sort out a job for me."

"All right, sis, I'll see what I can do."

Archer ended the call and stood up from the bed. Even sitting on the mattress gave him back ache. He went to Maggie in the kitchen and asked if she had any bottles of beer in the fridge. He was taken aback at the choice when she showed him the entire stock. His aunt wasn't a fan of any alcohol, but there were at least a dozen different kinds. He took a six-pack of light beer and hoped Erica liked beer.

He walked across the grounds as the sun was setting behind the trees. It was eight o'clock, and he assumed she'd already eaten. Since Archer had moved into the main house, dinner was promptly served at six o'clock. His aunt had insisted they eat together every night. She made it clear that they would all eat together when he found a wife until they were married and afterwards. He wondered why his aunt assumed he would find a wife on the island and that she wouldn't have a job that conflicted with eating at six o'clock. He imagined she didn't care and would probably find she would add it to the deal if he didn't.

SIXTEEN

Archer

Archer approached Erica's cottage by the hidden gap in the hedgerow. He was taking a chance entering her space uninvited. When Archer walked through, the clink of the beer bottles startled a bird out of the bushes. When he looked over at the patio furniture, Erica stared back at him. She flipped the pages of what she was reading so the white pages sat neatly on her lap and tucked a hand under her chin. Archer's steps faltered when she smiled, sending a jolt to his heart.

His feet kept going, but his heart gave off warning signals like there was a significant engine failure on a helicopter. The sirens blared in his head, screaming that his soul might never be the same again if he went through with this.

Stepping up to the patio area wall, he put the six-pack of beer down on the wall. "Hello, Erica, sorry for coming by unannounced."

"That's okay. I wasn't doing much. What's that you've brought?" Erica asked.

"Beer," he answered, holding them up by the handle. "I wanted to explain something."

Erica nodded to the sofa opposite hers, and he sat down. Then, twisting off the caps of two bottles, he handed her one. She raised her bottle, and they clinked necks.

"Cheers," she said and took a long sip. Her exposed throat moved slowly as she swallowed the liquid. His mind instantly turned filthy at her movements. Taking a long gaze at her body, he was happy to see she was wearing a baggy green dress.

"Cheers," Archer muttered and closed his eyes as he drank half the bottle.

"Have you eaten?" she asked, looking to the open window through the kitchen. "I have cheeses and bread if you're peckish."

He needed to find the words to tell her about his situation, so he grabbed the time delay with two hands. "That would be great, thanks."

"Be right back," she said and placed the stack of papers attached at the corner with a gold clip face down on the table between them.

Her long flowing bottle-green kaftan moved as she gracefully walked into her kitchen. Archer looked into the darkened garden, searching for support from the nocturnal animals. He practised how he would start the explanation but the words stuck in his head.

When Erica returned to view with a tray laden with food, Archer jumped up to take the tray from her. He placed it on the table between the two sofas and sat back, admiring the graceful way Erica walked and sat. It seemed rehearsed, practised a thousand times until it became natural.

Archer reached over the cheeses and bread and took a selection on a cloth napkin. He placed it on the seat next to him—no more stalling.

"What did you want to explain?" Erica asked, then broke off a chunk of cheddar and dropped it into her mouth.

Her eyes sparkled with mischief like she knew what he was about to say. A smile played on her lips as she chewed her food. Never in all his life had he thought a human being as sexy when they ate.

"I wanted to explain why I couldn't kiss you," Archer said, then stuffed his mouth with too much bread.

"Couldn't or wouldn't?" she asked.

"Shouldn't more like."

Archer let out a long sigh and sat back on the sofa, brushing the crumbs off his lap. He stared at Erica, getting the measure of her, seeking answers in her expression to let him know if he could trust her.

Deciding he was willing to gamble, he said, "I'll inherit this one day." Archer looked up at the cottage.

As he looked at the house she had been renting, Erica followed his gaze.

"You're going to inherit the house?" she asked.

"Copper Island," he said and snapped his gaze back to Erica.

She jolted back on the sofa and took a deep breath, holding her palm to her chest.

"You're not the maintenance guy?" she asked with her eyebrows raised. There was still humour in her eyes while she waited for the answer.

"At the moment, who knows?"

"Copper Island belongs to your father, and you'll inherit all this beauty one day?" Erica guessed.

"It's more complicated than that. My father passed away seven years ago."

"I'm sorry, Archer, truly."

"Thanks," he said and paused. "I adored my father, my mother too. They should still be here, running Turner Hall."

"You must be lonely."

Erica said it as a statement. Archer didn't consider himself lonely, not with three siblings he thought the world of and would do anything for them.

"Copper Island has been in my family since the early 1700s when copper was mined here. There is some antiquated rule that only one Turner can own the island at any time. When my father passed away, my grandfather was still alive. My father never got to own or run an inch of this piece of Earth. Everything went to my aunt. I'd hoped to learn from my father how to run everything when I was a kid. But he didn't have any interest in the old ways. He wasn't the eldest Turner either. My aunt is. Something happened that no one talks about back when my dad and aunt were younger. But fate had its way, and she is the matriarch."

"And you didn't get anything?"

"We won't get anything until she passes away. It's how the will was written."

"We?"

"I have two brothers and a sister. So when I inherit as the eldest, I will split it four ways between us immediately."

"What about your mother?"

"I haven't seen her in a very long time. Close to thirty years. She could be dead for all I know."

"Archer," she said.

He couldn't work out if she told him off or pitied him. Erica slumped back on the sofa and stretched out to look up. Most of the back of the cottage was under coverings. The couches were at the edge of a low wall overlooking the lawns.

They fell into silence, not looking at each other. Instead, Archer fixed his gaze on the stars.

"I don't understand the connection between inheriting this island and kissing me? Do you think I'll run off with your inheritance?"

Smiling, Archer looked her way, resting his forearms on his thighs.

"No. Nothing like that. Until recently, my brothers, sister, and I worked on the same oil rig. They closed down the operation, and now we need to find a new workplace. We can split up and work at different oil rigs around the world, but none of us wants to work solo. We've been together all our lives. Well, apart from education. It was either this island or the oil rig."

"Wow. I can't imagine liking my family well enough to spend that amount of time together."

"We're tight, inseparable, you might say."

"Are you going to get to the kissing part?" she asked, licking her bottom lip.

Did she do that on purpose? Archer thought.

"My aunt owns every inch of this island. I thought she would let us run the hotel, wedding business, and cottage rentals."

"That sounds like a good idea. You'll all be working together side by side. Presumably, your skills are transferable."

"Mostly," he said. "Luke will have to adapt the most."

He wasn't sure how much forklift trucking Daisy would be able to achieve, but he had a hunch she wanted to pursue her accountancy qualifications.

"Kissing," she said and did a double lift of her eyebrows.

Archer was feeling the pressure of confessing what he'd agreed to. He had to say it out loud to someone other than his siblings. It sounded crazy.

"I went to my aunt, who, by the way, is nearly eighty, and proposed the idea."

"And what did she say?"

"She had a counter-proposal or a condition. A big one."

Sitting up, Erica took a swig of her beer and gave him a stern look. "This is like drawing blood from a stone, Archer. I'm on tenterhooks."

"She'll hand over the hotel, wedding business, and cottages on one condition."

"You find a wife," Erica blurted out, then clapped her hand over her mouth.

"How the fuck did you know that?"

Archer looked around to see if there were hidden cameras or one of his brothers hiding around the corner, setting him up.

"I saw it in a movie once," she said, her eyebrows almost reaching her hairline.

She wouldn't look him in the eye. The grape on her plate was far more interesting.

"Really?"

"Yeah. Something about him getting his inheritance and proving that he could find his wife to his father. It was only supposed to be for a year, but they fell in love."

"Wow."

"It's a bit far-fetched, but some people are more old-fashioned than their age."

"That's my grandmother to a T."

"So, kissing is off limits while you find a wife? I'm guessing you will find a wife because you care about your siblings. This place reeks of old money and tradition. If you turn down the deal, you could be looking at twenty years waiting for her to die. That's morbid and depressing and no way to live."

"I want to marry for life, ya know? My aunt has very traditional views on marriage. It wouldn't occur to her to have a love match. For her, marriage is about convenience and making sure the Turner line keeps going."

"Good job your mum could have four kids. Less pressure on having children if you were an only child."

"Are you an only child?"

"Yep."

"Do your parents pressure you to have children?"

"They've never mentioned it, which tells me they do."

"There were so many reasons why I shouldn't kiss you. I didn't want to kiss you and then tell you I needed to find a wife. Then I didn't want to kiss you if you thought I had ulterior motives. I didn't want to kiss you, feel your lips on mine, and then stop because I'd have to start dating another woman. My sister has set up a dating profile for me."

"You think way too much. You know that Archer?"

Erica put her plate down on the coffee table, tossed the napkin on top, and stood. Then, she came around to his side of the table and sat next to him on the sofa.

"I'd still like that kiss, Archer," she said and placed her hand over his on his thigh.

"Knowing what you know?"

"Yeah, knowing what I know."

Archer turned to face Erica, who wore her sexy, playful

smile. He pulled her onto his lap with one hand reaching for her neck and the other inching towards her waist. She wrapped her arms around his neck and leaned in. When he closed the gap, pressing his lips to hers, he yanked her tighter to his body.

"This is reckless, Erica," he said over her lips.

"Nothing better than a reckless kiss, Archer."

When he kissed her a second time, he didn't let her go to chat. He twisted his tongue around hers, toying and teasing while she pressed her breasts against his chest. Archer trained his brain to keep his hands where they were in her hair and around her waist. He would risk a kiss with this woman, but he needed to find a wife, and taking this passionate kiss to the next stage was stepping way over the line.

Erica broke away from him, pressing her lips together, trying to hide her grin.

"I'm glad you came to explain why you couldn't kiss me," she said.

"Shouldn't," he corrected.

"With a kiss like that, I could definitely pretend to be your wife."

He cupped her cheek and rubbed his thumb along her skin. "There wouldn't be any pretending, honey. I must find a wife and marry her in the family chapel behind Turner Hall."

"There's a chapel? Is it as under-described as these cottages are? Because these are not cottages, Archer, they're houses."

"I think fifty people would fit in the pews, so it is definitely a chapel."

"Actually get married? Wow, your aunt is not messing about. Where will you find a woman to marry you in such a short time? Three months is not long when you have to announce a marriage a month before the date."

"Two months in my case. Apparently, the vicar wants more time between announcing the marriage and saying *I now pronounce you husband and wife.*"

"Do you know the vicar?"

"Reverend Chivers has been here all my life. He comes to the chapel to do all the services. Christenings, weddings, and funerals. I bet he earns a fortune with all the weddings the business must do."

"It sounds like your aunt knows what she's doing. So a month to find a wife."

"Three weeks. I struck the deal a week ago. Christ, I don't know why I agreed to it."

Erica cupped his cheeks and pressed her forehead to his. "Because you want to help your brothers and sister. It's a noble reason, Archer."

"My aunt doesn't think I'm marriage material. I think that's why she gave the deal. She doesn't have a high opinion of my father and thinks I am a replica of him. As soon as I agreed, she insisted I move into Turner Hall so she could keep an eye on me. No girls back to my room. I feel like a teenager again."

"I guess that's her upbringing. Very traditional. It doesn't mean you can't have sex in the sand dunes or sneak to her place."

"Sex in the sand dunes is painful," Archer said.

"Is it now?" Erica said with an eyebrow raised.

He realised she was still sitting on his lap, happily chatting about his crazy task ahead. She felt good sitting in his arms. He never wanted to let her go.

"There was a third reason I shouldn't have kissed you."

"And what's that?"

"I'll want more, and you'll ruin me for every other woman."

"Then I'll marry you," she said as if she offered to buy a pint of milk.

"You can't stay shit like that."

"Why not? I could play the role of doting wife. Don't you think I'm up to the challenge?"

"You have a life, presumably a lucrative one if you can afford to rent all five cottages. So why would you want to marry me?"

"I've been married before. Divorced now, so the giddiness and the romance of getting married have gone sour. I thought I was marrying for life. It turns out he didn't think the same. He proved that marriage is not for forever, so if you need a wife, I can do that."

"What would you get out of it?"

"Seeing you and your siblings get what you deserve. This island and hell, these houses are big enough that if we start to hate each other, we would never have to see each other. If the Royal Family can do it, then so can we."

Archer gave her a questioning look. "You're crazy," Archer said.

"Maybe so, but you kiss like a dream, so I shall remember your lips forever if nothing else works out."

SEVENTEEN

Erica

"What the hell did I agree to?" she whispered when she woke up the following morning.

She pulled the duvet up to her chin so only her face was visible. If Erica was hoping for a reply, none came. The sun was streaming through the crack in the curtain, telling her she was late for her swimming session.

But what if she bumped into Archer?

Did she really agree to be his wife?

Staying as much under the covers as she could, Erica stretched her arm out to snatch her phone from the night-stand. She'd call Yanny and thrash it out with him.

"What's happened?" Yanny said as soon as he picked up the phone.

"Why do you think something has happened?"

"You never call me. I always have to call you."

"That's not true," Erica replied, thinking of half a dozen times she'd called him in the last month.

"Okay, but it's unusual to get a call from you when you're hiding out."

"I think I've agreed to get married."

Silence drifted down the line.

"Are you still there?" Erica asked, bringing the phone away from her ear to check they were still connected.

"The thing is," Yanny said, hiding his hysterical laughter poorly. "You've recently got divorced, and you said, many, many times, you would never get married again. I saw you two weeks ago. How the holy hell can you be engaged already?"

"Well, the maintenance guy isn't the maintenance guy. He's the heir apparent for the entire island. The problem is, for him and his siblings to run the hotel and wedding business, he needs to find a wife, or his old-fashioned aunt won't sign over the business."

"Does he know who you are?"

"I don't think so. Archer says he hates movies and has seen the first ten minutes of one film in his life."

"Is he hot?"

"Smoking hot."

"Are you being overwhelmed by his six-pack? Deprivation making you desperate? Are you agreeing to marry him to feel good about yourself, so you know you're still desirable when your ex-husband hooked up with a woman a decade younger than you?"

"Ouch and no."

"Then why has he presented you with the same scenario as the movie you've just won an Oscar for?"

"It's not exactly the same. I don't think the aunt will slowly poison him and me while we dine at her table."

"What does he think you're going to get out of it?"

"My desire to see his siblings settled."

"He will not buy that. Why not tell him the truth of why you're hiding out?"

"Because he'll think I'm only marrying him to shove it in Gregg and Monica's face."

"And you're not doing that?"

Silence again, this time Erica.

"I don't think that's my motive. I can get divorced as soon as Archer gets the business."

"How long will that be?"

"Three months. Then I could walk away."

"You're only booked in there for two months. Do you want me to extend your stay?"

"Let me talk to Archer. We didn't discuss any details."

"Did you kiss him?"

"Um," Erica said.

"Erica." Yanny said her name with a sigh.

"I'm totally in control. If we're to pretend to be madly in love, then it's only natural there will be PDA."

"How much did you practice?"

"Yanny." It was Erica's turn to use a name as a warning.

"Erica," he snapped.

"All right, it was a couple of kisses, and that's it. After our agreement, he left me to my lines and disappeared into the darkness of the gardens."

"I'm not sure you'll come out of this deal unscathed lovely," Yanny said gently.

"I'll be fine. It's not like I'm announcing the engagement or the marriage. As with old-fashioned people, it will be sedate and low-key. Archer will get what he wants, and I'll get what I want."

"I'm invited to the wedding, right?" Yanny asked.

EIGHTEEN

Archer

Archer picked up his beer bottle and walked through the empty kitchens at Edward Hall. He waited for his sister, Daisy, to answer her phone. As soon as her face appeared on the screen, he blurted, "I think I've found a wife."

Daisy scrubbed her face with her hand, waking herself up while she processed her brother's statement.

"Go back to sleep. I'll be back in a bit," Daisy said to someone behind her.

"I'm sorry, Daisy," Archer said. "I should've sent a text first."

"It's fine. I'm going to put you face down a second."

Archer heard feet padding around on a tiled floor, and then the phone was back, showing her face while she moved through the bedroom. When Daisy was settled with a glass of water, her knees tucked under her, she put her phone on a cushion.

"I'm all yours. Tell me everything," Daisy said.

"Who is he?" Archer asked, referring to the man she had in her bed.

"I'll send you his LinkedIn profile later."

"Are you safe?"

"You taught me how to be safe. Have faith your skills are being put to good use."

Archer took his overprotective nature for his baby sister to the extreme. Their relationship was tight, just like his brothers, but he ensured Daisy was more okay than the other two brothers. This was the first time the four of them were separated for more than a couple of days and the further apart they had ever been. It didn't sit well that he wasn't there. What if something terrible happened?

"You'll tell me if you're in trouble, won't you?"

"Honestly, Archer, you'd be the first person I'd call. You've got to know that. You're my big brother."

Mollified by her words, he nodded.

"Tell me about her," Daisy prompted.

"She's agreed to be my wife. She even offered when I told her why I couldn't kiss her."

"Did you get your kiss?"

"Yeah. That's the problem. I like her and don't think I can fake the relationship. For me, this is going to be a real relationship."

"What's the issue?"

"For her, it's a short-term thing."

"She said that?"

"Not explicitly, but she understands the deal is only until I get the business. I've abundantly made clear that this doesn't have to be long term."

"You know she could actually like you and want to see where this goes."

"I'm not so sure. She's been married before, and comes

across as jaded about marriage. I don't think she values the institution. For her, it's a piece of paper to help us out."

"From what you've said, you both like each other, as in like like, so it won't be a hardship. What is the agreement? How long? What happens when you get the business? Where will you live?"

Archer winced at her questions. They hadn't discussed any of that. They were too busy kissing.

"I'll probably have to iron those issues out. We didn't talk about many details. I'm going all-in on this, and I think my all-in won't be her all-in."

"How long is she staying?"

"Her booking is for two months, but I need her to stay for at least three to make this ruse work."

"What does she do for a living?"

"I think she's a writer."

Archer had no idea what Erica did. He didn't think to ask. She'd hired five cottages for two months, so he didn't much care what she did for a living.

"You think?"

"Erica's reading a thick printed-out manuscript, so I figure she's here to work through her novel. She wants to be an expert at synchronised swimming. It must be for her book."

"You need to talk to her before she meets Aunt Cynthia. The dragon will go through her like a dose of salts if you don't get to know Erica thoroughly."

"How the hell am I going to sell this to Aunt Cynthia. She'll never believe I've fallen in love inside a week."

"Maybe date her for a month, then introduce her to our aunt. Cynthia misses nothing, so be visible with her around the grounds. Then, when you introduce her, our aunt will already know you've been dating her."

"Sounds good. It will take a month to organise a wedding date, and I've already wasted a week since the deal I made."

"Make sure you tell us the date. We all need to be there to throw rose petals at the happy couple."

Daisy grinned at her words. Archer had never met another person so bright and optimistic as his sister. She could see the good in everyone, including their mother, who she didn't remember. It was the only sticking point between the two of them. He remembered his mother and still couldn't understand why she'd walked out on her family.

"I promise to tell you when we've set a date. Thanks for listening to me. Go back to whomever you're dating, and I'll see you soon."

"I love you, Archer. Take care of yourself. It'll all work out."

Daisy waved her goodbyes and ended the call.

"It has to work out," Archer said aloud to the empty room.

NINETEEN

Archer

Teddy was growing bigger by the day. Maggie doted on him when Archer stopped by for his breakfast and dinner. Then the pair of them would wander the grounds together side by side. Archer put off looking for its owner, fearing he would want to punch a person who left a dog to fight for survival. No one ever came to the estate unless invited, so Teddy was safe unless someone approached him in town.

"Archer, there's been a request made," Bailey said, entering the kitchen with a stack of post in his hand.

"I don't think I've ever heard you use an upbeat tone, but it's sombre than ever," Maggie replied.

Bailey looked to the cook and didn't even smirk. Archer had never seen him smile. The man took his job very seriously.

"Miss Turner had requested you be at home from ten o'clock every night."

"For how long?" Archer asked.

"Permanently, sir."

Archer looked to Maggie, who did not attempt to hide her giggle. He gave her narrowed eyes and then turned to Bailey.

"Did she give a reason?"

"She wants to keep an eye on you. Is there anything you want to tell us?"

"No, no, I don't think so."

Archer heard his voice get higher as each word came out of his mouth. These two people were more like family than his aunt and mother ever were. How could his aunt know about Archer and Erica? He'd only kissed her once.

"I'm sure he'll tell us when he's good and ready," Maggie said, wiping his hands in her apron as she approached the kitchen table.

They both knew he was lying and didn't demand the truth. He'd forgotten that about them.

"It's a bit complicated. How she will keep tabs on me in a big house is beyond me."

"The Mistress will cope," Bailey said.

"I'll have to return to my other home in Scotland to pack up the rest of my belongings."

"Your old bedroom in the east wing," Maggie said. "You can't get any further from Miss Turner's room if you tried. I wonder what she's up to?" Maggie said.

Bailey had sorted the post as he spoke, shuffling them into an order only he knew was correct. One day Bailey and Maggie would retire, and new staff would replace them. Archer put those thoughts out of his head. He needed to focus on the here and now.

Bailey left to deliver the letters to Aunt Cynthia, and Maggie returned to the stove to stir the large pot.

"Maggie, is there still a tide timetable in the study?"

RECKLESS KISS

Archer asked, getting up from the seat. Teddy jumped up from his bed by the large stove and came to Archer's side.

"Yes, it's tacked to the notice board behind your grand-father's desk. Do you want me to fetch it for you?"

"No need, I'll go. I haven't been across to Stuart Island since I've been back and don't want to get caught by the incoming tide."

"Do you want a picnic?"

"Not today, but I'll let you know if I need one."

"Fancy a walk?" Archer spoke down to Teddy. He was rewarded with a yap. Archer hadn't gotten around to a lead for the dog and hoped he could train the dog without having to put him on a leash. "Come on then. Let's go and find you a mummy."

Archer glanced to Maggie, who had her back to him, wishing he hadn't said the words aloud. Hoping she hadn't heard, he left the kitchen and went up the stairs to the main foyer. He strode across the floor to the study and turned the round door handle.

It was locked.

"What's the point of putting a tide timetable in a locked room?" Archer said to the solid wooden door.

Archer turned to the sound of a bunch of keys jingling. Bailey was striding towards him, searching the dozens of keys on a large keyring.

"It had become a habit to keep this room locked since your grandfather passed away. No one comes to the house anymore, but it was his sanctuary when he was home and his father's private room. Let me open the door, and I'll get you a key."

"Thanks, Bailey," Archer said, stepping aside for the man to open the door.

"Take this key, and I'll pick up the extra downstairs. Was there anything you were looking for in particular?"

"The tide times. Maggie said a copy was in here on the notice board."

"It is. You must think me old-fashioned to keep these habits alive for people who have long passed."

"The opposite, in fact, Bailey. I find comfort in the old ways. It's how we all grew up. Good reminders of our childhood. We all spent so much time in here when dad was home and with grandad when dad wasn't home."

Archer saw Bailey get misty-eyed. "I'll leave you to it, Sir," Bailey said, turning on his heel and striding away.

Archer pocketed the key and looked down at Teddy, giving him a stern look. "Best behaviour, okay?"

Teddy yapped.

As soon as Archer walked into the room, Teddy scampered in. The puppy jumped up and kept missing the edge of the battered leather sofa. Teddy gave big eyes to Archer with a soft whine and then back to the couch.

"How about the chair?" Archer asked the dog.

Archer pulled down the old brown blanket thrown over the back to the large armchair in matching battered leather and arranged it on the seat. He then picked up Teddy and placed him on the blanket. After a few twirls, the puppy sat down with his head on his paws, watching Archer move about the room.

"We're not staying long," Archer told Teddy over his shoulder, "so don't get comfy."

Going straight for the bookcase, Archer picked out one of his childhood story books. The yellowed pages of Roald Dahl's novel smelled familiar as if he was still sitting on his mother's lap in the armchair Teddy was lounging. Archer flashed back for a few seconds, feeling his brother moving about in his mum's belly while she read him a story. It was a couple of days later that Luke came into the world. Snapping the book shut, he placed it back in its place on the shelf and strolled the shelves noting that nothing much had changed in the room since he was last in there six years ago. Then, clearing his throat to rid him of the sadness of attending his grandfather's funeral less than a year after his father's funeral, Archer untacked the tide timetable.

An idea formed, and he smiled.

"Come on, Teddy, let's go," Archer said.

The puppy jumped down and did a forward roll, unsteady from the drop-down from the armchair. He scampered to Archer's side and then followed him out of the room. Archer locked up the study and headed back to the kitchen.

"Maggie, can you make a picnic for tomorrow, about eleven?"

"Of course, anything in particular?"

"I'll leave that up to you. It's for two people," Archer added.

Maggie smiled, raised both her eyebrows, and scrubbed a pot in the deep sink under the window.

"I'll have it ready, Archer. Bailey can get some blankets for you too. Leave it to me," she said.

Archer strode over and kissed her cheek before walking to the back door. "Thank you, Maggie."

She waved him away over her shoulder with wet hands.

TWENTY

Archer

Archer and Teddy strolled across Turner Hall's lawns, then around Edward Hall's rear gardens. Then, approaching the side opening that led into the cottages' gardens, nerves hit Archer square in the belly.

What if Erica had changed her mind?

He couldn't delay. If Erica didn't want to marry him anymore, he needed to know and search for a new fake wife.

From his viewpoint, he saw Erica in the back area under the canopy of the patio area. She seemed to gravitate there like she was always meant to live in the cottage. Her over-sized sunglasses sat on top of her head as she read whatever was on her lap. As he walked a couple of seconds later, Erica held her hand in the air and mouthed words. She could've spoken them aloud, but he was too far away to hear. She alternated from looking down and then repeating the action.

When she did it a third time, her head looked at him

approaching, and a broad smile lit up her face. His heart soared in response to her cheerful non-verbal welcome.

She still liked him, but did she still want to marry him?

By the time he reached her chair, Erica was on her feet, the pile of papers face down on the table with her glasses resting on top.

"Hi," she said.

Her smile was still warm and welcoming, but her eyes told him she was nervous. Just the sight of her caused Archer to grow hard. He thought she was lovely in another kaftan, reds, and pinks in a riot of colour, giving her tanned skin a healthy glow.

"Hi," he said, cupping her face in both his hands.

Archer couldn't help himself and kissed her lightly on the lips, brushing against her mouth in a soft touch. Her hands and arms came around his waist and held him. Erica tilted her head and kissed him back. He wanted to deepen the caress, but knowing she was still on board was more important. This would be the last time he would check. The next time he greeted her would be a more passionate embrace.

Keeping his hands on her face but leaning back, he was aware he was pressing his erection against her body. That wasn't the point he was trying to make, but her grin turned salacious. Archer needed to be in charge of this relationship but was finding he was happy for her to equal or take the lead. He'd never been with a woman who was so open about attraction. Having a confident woman in his arms was the sexiest thing he'd ever experienced.

"I need to ask you something?" Archer said.

"Yes," she answered, pressing her hips against him.

Christ, this woman would be the end of him. Yet, he

wanted nothing more than to pull the kaftan over her head and gaze at her nakedness.

"Can we focus?" he asked with a chuckle.

"You have my undivided attention, Archer. Since the moment you entered my back garden with your adorable dog."

Archer looked around her body to find Teddy in the exact spot Erica had been sitting, sleeping. He thought Teddy was faking sleep so no one would move him. Archer didn't blame him.

"Are you still on board with the reckless plan?"

"Yes," she said, frowning. "Are you having second thoughts?"

"No, not at all. In fact, I think I might be in danger of really liking you for a fake wife."

Archer didn't intend to be so forthright. The words tumbled out. Erica smiled, searching his eyes for sincerity. He hoped she found it.

"Would that be such a bad thing?"

"It depends. If you're capable of breaking my heart, I might be in real trouble."

Her face became unreadable. Archer felt her body press tighter to his, but her expression told him she knew what heartbreak felt like.

"We'll be fine, Archer. You worry too much."

"I think we could do with ironing out some details and getting to know each other if we're to fool my aunt. What are you doing tomorrow?"

"Exactly what I'm doing today, but I could do with a break. What do you have in mind?"

"I thought we could go across to one of the uninhabited islands for a picnic. The tide works well to walk across at midday. We'll have a few hours before we need to come back across the causeway."

"Sounds like fun."

"Wear something to swim in, in case you want to take a dip," Archer said.

"Okay."

"Okay," he said, staring down at her mouth.

"Kiss me, Archer," Erica whispered.

Banding his arms around her back, he captured her mouth with his and gave her a hard kiss, holding firm for a few seconds. When he broke the connection, he opened his mouth, and so did Erica, crashing together again. The consuming kiss felt so good. When Archer slid his tongue against hers, his erection grew harder. Erica's chest was pressed against his torso, and he knew she was braless as soon as her erect nipples became obvious. He lifted her as he walked to the chair and sat down. Erica straddled his thighs and placed her hands on each side of his neck, kissing the life out of him. Heavy breathing, strong lips, and the sexiest flicker of her tongue had him dizzy with arousal. He grabbed at the material covering her hips, keeping it decent, but he wanted to drag her dress up far enough to see if she was wearing underwear.

Erica sat back, hand on her chest, taking deep breaths as her chest heaved. The drunk heavy-lidded gaze she was shooting his way made him lose his mind with lust. She wanted him as much as he wanted her, but he couldn't have sex with her. That was a line he couldn't cross if he were to keep his heart intact.

"I could get addicted to this mouth," Erica whispered, swiping her finger along his bottom lip.

Archer licked the pad of her finger and then took it into

his mouth, sucking hard just like he wanted her to do to his dick.

"I should go before things get too heated."

"Archer, I think you already gave me an orgasm from that kiss. I'm on fire," she said, leaving her finger in his mouth while he toyed with her.

His hands held her hips in place, so she didn't feel how hard he was for her. Erica fell forward as she removed her finger and kissed him again. Slow, languid, sensual. She hugged him around his neck, and he barely moved while she explored and teased.

When her hands stroked down his abdomen and to the waistband of his shorts, he stood up, placing her back on her feet. Archer still held her tight to his body but ensured she couldn't get her hands between them.

"Not now, not here," he whispered, kissing her forehead.

He was determined not to fuck Erica, but if he ever failed in that mission, having sex in front of his dog on the patio furniture was not how he wanted it to happen.

"Why?"

"Too many eyes, honey."

Archer stroked the back of his hand across her cheekbone and then threaded his fingers through her hair at her nape.

"Okay," she said. "What time shall I be ready tomorrow?"

"I'll pick you up at eleven. Just bring yourself. I'll arrange everything else."

"Okay, Archer Turner, I'll be ready. Now let me go before I drag you inside."

Archer groaned at her suggestion, dropped a soft kiss on her lips, and stepped away. He whistled to Teddy to get down from the sofa. Teddy trotted to Erica, who let him lick her hand, and then he came to Archer's side.

"Bye," he said quietly and walked away.

It was the hardest thing he'd ever had to do. Archer wanted nothing more than to take her inside and into bed.

TWENTY-ONE

Erica

The following day, Erica watched Archer stride across the lawn. His eyes fixed on her legs. She was sitting on a wicker chair with her feet kicked up on the low wall at the back of the cottage. She slowly, purposely moved her legs as she swivelled in the chair. Archer's gaze remained fixed on her bare legs.

It was a sunny day, so she thought it would be better to wear shorts if they were going to a remote island. Bare legs were easier to dry than wet clothing, she reasoned. Also, to see Archer's attraction was a bonus. Archer may have openly admired her legs, but she couldn't get enough of his thighs. They bunched and flexed as he walked in a solid stride towards her. Erica knew from sitting on his lap how firm they were.

"Are you a leg man, Archer Turner?" Erica said as he neared the wall separating them.

Archer balanced the picnic basket on the bricks but kept his hand on the top while he leaned in to kiss her. A soft press of his lips made Erica let out a sigh. He smelt like fresh washing from the line.

"I've not given it much thought. In those shorts, your legs are sensational, so I am definitely an Erica's legs kind of man."

"Thank you."

"Let's go. Time and tide wait for no man," Archer said, smiling at Erica and holding his hand out.

She took it, laced her fingers, and fell into step with his long stride. He led her down the narrow path at the end of the lawns down to the white sand. Erica shaded her eyes with her hand to look across at the small island across the water. From her viewpoint, it looked to be water everywhere.

"How will we get across?" Erica asked.

"We've got about five minutes to wait, and then all will be revealed," Archer said, setting the basket in the sand. "Whatever could we do in the meantime?"

Erica didn't get a chance to answer as Archer's mouth covered hers. His hands held onto her waist while he devoured her. The kiss became heated fast. Erica was swept away by the passion igniting her body as soon as Archer touched her. In all her years of acting, she never felt a spark let alone the electricity coursing through her body when kissing a man. Her thoughts darted to the kiss she saw Gregg give Monica on her Hollywood star and instantly understood the passion she never had with Gregg.

Archer lit every one of her nerves on fire.

They swayed back and forth as each of them tried to take control. Erica wrapped her fingers around his neck to anchor her body as close as possible. He kissed her slowly, softly, but in the sexiest of ways when he slipped his tongue in and out of her mouth. The temptation to jump up and wrap her legs around his waist was strong. She mentally willed him to carry her over to the rocks as they battled to keep things PG. In the end, neither of them won. Erica needed to take a breather, or else she would've dragged him onto the sand and pulled his clothes off.

Archer pulled away so fast that she swooned for a few seconds, regaining her balance. Then, blinking her eyes in the midday sun, she looked to Archer. He stood with his hands on his hips, and his chin dipped as his chest rose and fell with exertion. Anyone else would've thought he'd been for a run.

"Archer," she whispered.

Archer shook his head and picked up the picnic basket. He looked across to the island. "We can cross now."

Accepting Archer didn't want to talk about the orgasm-inducing kiss, Erica followed his gaze and still saw water everywhere.

"Are we going to walk on water?" she asked.

"Kind of, come on," he said and held out his hand.

Erica followed him, their fingers barely touching as he strode ahead, just the tips hooked together. She could see the sand bank when they reached the water's edge. As the minutes ticked by, the path to the island materialised like magic.

"This is fantastic, like a hidden route to a secret realm."

Archer laughed at her words. "My aunt would say it was a biblical warning not to get up to anything God would disapprove of. Which pretty much covers everything. My dad would warn of the riptides."

"Is it safe?"

Archer looked over his shoulder at her, giving her a wink. "It's safe when you can see the sandbank and the tide is going out. But you don't want to be on this causeway when the tide is coming in. It's faster than you can imagine. You can easily get into trouble if the timing isn't right. If you're with someone and they get into trouble, there is a length of rope and a floatation ring over there on the tree."

Erica turned to look in the direction he nodded. A tree with no branches or leaves at the bottom of the cliff had an orange buoyancy aid hooked onto a dead branch stump. The rope was coiled around the stump underneath.

"If you don't know what you're doing, stay out of the water and get help," Archer warned.

"I'll stick with you. I can swim, but I'm not experienced enough to fight a tide."

"Good plan. I've set the alarm, so we don't forget about the time. There is nothing on the island to act as a shelter if we get stuck."

Strolling, the journey lasted five minutes. Erica guessed she could run the distance in three minutes. When they reached the white sands on Stuart Island, a silence fell about them. No squawking birds like on the main island. The waves lapping at the shore lulled her, relaxing her muscles.

Archer laid out the blanket in the shade of a rock while talking.

"This was where me and my brothers and sister would run away to when we wanted some peace from the house. When our mother left without a word, we were all lost. I remember it was like any other day. She kissed my cheek, hugged me, and wished me a great day at school. Daisy was six months old and in her cot upstairs in the nursery. Jason was tearing around the grand foyer, and Luke crawled around after him. Just like any other day setting off for school. I keep thinking back to see if she hugged me longer or harder."

His confession floored her. So many questions rattled through her head, and none were appropriate to ask. She did, and she didn't want to pry.

"What did you do when you came over here?" she asked as she lifted items from the basket to put on the blanket.

Erica made a runway of food between them, leaving space for Archer to lie down when he was ready. Watching him stand still with his back to her, she glanced at his thighs. Then, chastising herself for lusting after a man talking about his hiding place when he was hurting, she looked away.

With a large rock behind them and Copper Island in front of them, there wasn't much else to see apart from clear water and white sand. The imposing house, Turner Hall, loomed large at the top of the cliff covered in greenery. Edward Hall peeked out above tall trees, its turrets steel grey. Erica toyed around with plates of sandwiches and bite-sized nibbles to be in the order she would like to try them. When Archer turned to face her, she gave him her best comforting smile, hoping he would come and join her.

"I got lost there in a memory, sorry," he said, dropping to his knees and then to his side. "Maggie prepared the food, so we have to guess what's here. She usually makes what she wants to eat, whatever she fancies on the day."

"It looks fantastic. I'm going to try the sandwiches first."

"I didn't think to check. Are you vegetarian or have any food preferences?"

"I'll eat most things once," Erica answered, then took a bite out of a triangle sandwich. "Ham and mustard," she said, lifting the remainder.

"Mine is beef and horseradish. I detest horseradish," Archer said, grimacing.

Erica laughed at his disgruntled face, hiding her smile behind her hand. "You want to swap?"

"I would. Ham and mustard is my favourite."

Erica handed over her sandwich and took his. Archer took her by surprise and leaned in for a quick kiss.

"We should talk about the deal we made the other night," Archer said.

"Do you have a plan?"

"Nope, I hoped you would have made one?"

"Well, we could date for a few weeks. Then you could propose, then we get married."

"Simple, I like it," Archer said, nodding.

They fell silent as they picked their way through the food, exchanging bites of pieces they liked until they were full. Archer packed away the remaining food and dishes and put the basket to the side. When the space was vacant, he scooted closer to Erica, tugging at her waist to lie down next to him. He turned to kiss her forehead when he had her tucked into his side with his arm around her shoulder. A shiver ran slowly down her spine, spreading heat as it reached the base of her back. It was a tender caress a loving husband would give his wife.

"There is a lot more we need to talk about, honey, but I don't want to ruin the mood."

Erica thought the same as she cuddled closer, looking over his bare feet to the water's edge. The contentedness she felt was a strange feeling. When she took time away to learn her lines and research her role, it was in short bursts. After a few days, Erica would grow bored and gravitate to her home in London. Lying on the sand under the blazing sun, she couldn't imagine spending time in a busy city.

"What's on your mind?" she asked.

"We can't have sex," Archer blurted, keeping his hand cupping her shoulder.

"Okay, disappointing, but okay," she said hesitantly. "Can you tell me why?"

"Because this is a transaction. You don't rate marriage anymore. I need to fulfil my aunt's condition to get the business. If I take you to bed, it will make it something else entirely."

"Is that so bad?"

"I can't fall in love with you, Erica. I need to get my family settled. They're relying on me."

"People not in love have sex."

"I'm going to fall for you. I know it. Experiencing how you feel in the most intimate way, I know it will break me when you walk away."

"How do you know I'll walk away?"

"Because that's the deal we struck. You're here for two months, then you'll go back to your job, do whatever it is with the script your reading, and I'll be left here with a broken heart."

"I need to extend my stay with your aunt if we are to date, plan, and marry. We're setting a date for three months, aren't we?"

"Can you afford to stay for three months? I don't mean financially, but with your job."

"I'll need to leave for a week at the end of the two months, but then I can come back."

She needed to get fittings for the movie scheduled straight after leaving the island. But now, with the deal she made with the handsome man, she'd need Yanny to work her schedule without messing about the film production. Now there was a dress to consider and shoes.

"I can check with my aunt about the bookings for the cottages. She'll prefer you stay there far away from my bed until we're married."

Erica giggled at the old-fashioned rules. "When will I get to meet her?"

"We'll let her see us together from afar. Maybe when you have your swim."

"I need to do more than swim. I have to practice holding my breath under water. Increase my lung capacity and strengthen every muscle in my body."

"Is this for your job?"

"Yeah."

"You take it really seriously."

"I have to if I want to be authentic."

Archer went silent again, pulling her closer to his body. Erica liked being tucked against him. She liked feeling his warmth and his protection. Taking a chance on his declaration of no sex, she placed her palm on his stomach. He was hard to the touch. Sliding her fingers under the edge of his t-shirt, she stroked her fingers on his bare skin. When he didn't move or push her away, she splayed her fingers further up his torso. Erica was desperate for the connection. She didn't want a cold relationship, even if theirs was fake.

"I could help you," Archer said, drawing circles on her bare shoulder with the pad of his thumb.

"Help me with what?"

"The swimming, endurance, and holding your breath. I did gig racing here on the island as a kid and teenager. Everyone must know how to be a strong swimmer living on an island. As an oil rig worker, that plan is never to fall in the water. If you did in the North Sea, you wouldn't last very long in the cold water, but I still kept up training."

Erica pushed up and rested her weight on her bent elbow. Looking down at Archer's face, she saw his sincerity shining in his eyes.

"Do you have time? I've been given a plan to do each

day and watched a dozen videos online. It would be great to have someone help me keep track and support me."

"I can spare a couple of hours each morning. We can get to know each other at the same time."

"Thank you so much," she said, leaning down to kiss him.

It was an automatic reaction to kiss him. Archer's soft lips turned hungry as his palm cupped the back of her head. Erica went along with his kiss, sliding her tongue next to his as he rolled them. He nestled between her parted legs, balancing most of his weight on his elbows as he explored her mouth, throat, and collar bone with his lips. She could feel he wanted her, flushed at the knowledge one kiss turned him on. When Erica lifted her hips to shift her position, Archer pulled away and rolled to his back, panting.

"You're going to kill me," he said.

Erica giggled at his over-exaggeration as she sat up. Then, pulling her loose blouse over her head, she flung it to land on his face.

"No looking now then," she said, pushing up to stand.

She shimmied her shorts over her hips and kicked off her shoes. Standing barefoot in the sand with a string bikini, Erica looked over her shoulder at Archer. He had stuffed part of her top in his mouth to muffle his groan.

"You're wearing a wet suit for our practice sessions, right?" he said, throwing the blouse into the space she'd vacated.

"I thought I could try naked, but I don't think your aunt would approve."

"She most certainly would not."

Archer stood to join her, toeing off his shoes as he pulled off his t-shirt.

"The water here is too shallow to swim, but we could

paddle around or sit at the water's edge," Archer said, holding out his hand.

Erica took it and joined him at the water as it lapped over their feet. He explained the tides were too strong over this side of the island to go any deeper, especially for a novice swimmer like her. She accepted what he was saying, and they stood hand in hand, with the water up to their knees, looking at the cliff face.

"Archer?" Erica asked.

"Yeah?"

"How are we going to pull this off without anyone getting hurt? We have to make sure everyone believes us, and then when this ends, I'll feel horrible for fooling everyone. How will your siblings react?"

"It'll be fine. We're not going to meet many people up at the house. Just the staff. Jason, Luke, and Daisy know the deal, and Aunt Cynthia won't care."

"And the wedding, what about the guests?"

"We'll keep it low-key."

"Okay," Erica said, not convinced in the slightest.

He turned her to face him while the water ebbed and flowed around them. "It's not going to be hard to fake falling in love with you," he said.

Erica could've melted on the spot as he cupped her cheeks and pressed his lips to hers. It didn't take long before he wrapped her in his arms, peppering her mouth with soft butterfly kisses. His hand went down her back and into the back of her bikini bottoms. She canted her hips to push against his, encouraging him to pull her tighter against his hard-muscled body. They stayed like that for eternity, with her arms wrapped around his neck and his hands holding her in place. Erica made no plans to stop kissing him. It was her new favourite pastime.

He lifted her under her arms, and she wrapped her legs around him. Archer carried her back to the blanket and laid her down, him covering her body with his. They continued their make-out session until she heard a consistent beeping noise.

Archer pulled back half an inch from her mouth. She could feel his smile.

"We need to pack up and head back. Tide is on the way in."

Archer's breath feathered over her mouth. She was dazed by his passion and the sun, in no mood to move out of his arms.

"If we have to," she said.

"Getting stranded over here would not please my aunt. Bailey would bring the motorboat across, but I prefer not to alert her to any inappropriateness."

Erica pecked his lips just before Archer moved away. She watched as he pulled on his t-shirt, marvelling at his side, back, and torso muscles. He looked strong and powerful. Erica knew without a doubt he would protect her while she was in his care. A sudden wave of melancholy overcame her as she thought about the time she would walk away in three months and return to her Hollywood life. Erica considered giving it all up for this man for the first time in her career. A man she barely knew. These thoughts never crossed her mind when she married Gregg, her ex-husband.

Getting up and dressed, she folded the blanket for Archer to stuff into the basket. Archer helped her up from the sand and brushed her down, taking extra time to ensure the sand was off every inch of her legs. The roughness of his hands sent tingles throughout her body. The tips of her nipples began to harden. Erica was insanely attracted to the man ensuring she was sand-free. How would she cope with being married to him that wasn't real?

"I think you got all the grains," she said, laughing as she pushed him away.

He gave her a sheepish grin, telling her he enjoyed it as much as she was.

It was less than five minutes since the alarm had sounded, and they were on the move across the sand pathway back to their fake lives to begin. The water was lapping at her feet when they had reached the sand on the other side of the causeway. It astounded her how quickly the tide came in.

"No wonder you set the alarm. Another five minutes, and we'd be wading the last hundred yards."

"Yep," Archer said. "No messing about with the water around here. But, until you're experienced, I'd say the swimming pool is a better option for you."

"Agreed. I don't have much confidence in my strength at the moment."

"If you work hard, it won't take long. Then if you're feeling like an adventure, I could take you to see the seals. We can swim with them."

Erica stopped at the junction between the sand and the dirt path winding back up to the back of her garden. "There are seals here, and you can swim with them?" she asked, looking back out to the island they'd spent the last couple of hours on.

"Yeah," he answered and chuckled, tugging her up the steep path. "Don't slow your pace now, or you'll never get up this path. It's fine coming down but a killer to walk back up."

"That's definitely an incentive to become a strong

swimmer. I can't wait to swim with seals," she said, puffing as she trudged up the path.

"And I thought the incentive to become a strong swimmer was to spend time with me," he answered, giving her a wink when he looked over his shoulder.

"Well, there is that. And my job depends on becoming a better swimmer."

"You wound me," Archer said, clutching his heart.

They both laughed as they carried on up the path, passing comments back and forth. When they reached the flat grass lawn, Archer placed the picnic basket on the ground and pulled Erica into his arms.

"Can I kiss you?"

"You never have to ask permission, Archer. I thought I'd told you how much I like you."

"I know, but that was before our bargain. Before we confirmed that we're going to act like a couple who have fallen hard and quickly in love from tomorrow."

"Just kiss me, Archer," Erica said, sliding her arm around his waist and tilting her chin up.

He covered her mouth with his, seeking entry with the very tip of his tongue and then long, languid swipes. Archer pulled out of her embrace just as quickly and kissed her forehead.

"I'll see you tomorrow, honey," Archer said, touching her cheek with his thumb.

"You will. I'll be the one in the pool."

TWENTY-TWO

Archer

When he was a child and a teenager, the west wing of Turner Hall was off-limits. As each elder passed away, the next in line would take up the branch of rooms. If and when he inherited Copper Island, he didn't know if he wanted to keep the tradition.

It was the same for the whole family when his grandfather was alive. The ground floor and lower sections of the building were find to wander, but no one was allowed in the private space.

The rule became iron clad when his grandfather died, outliving his father and making his aunt beneficiary. Archer's dad intended to reverse all the old-fashioned rules surrounding Turner Hall.

There were many arguments between his dad and his sister, Aunt Cynthia. She wanted Turner Hall to be completely private and closed off. In contrast, Archer's dad wanted to open the doors and let everyone in.

He believed the house should be lived in and occupied.

Wandering along the corridor on the first floor, Archer absorbed in the décor, all immaculately kept in the era of the 1930s. There were a few modern additions, fire alarms, water spouts from the ceiling, and other safety measures. If the place did catch fire, it would be dowsed with water quickly. His aunt didn't want to share, but she ensured what she did have was taken care of. Sometimes, Archer thought his aunt cared more about what future generations thought of her than the current family members.

"There you are. Have you settled into your rooms?"

Archer turned towards the voice, knowing it was his aunt.

"Mostly. I think I've thrown away more stuff than I've kept."

"Nothing valuable, I hope?"

"Not at all, just memories of happier times," he said, berating himself for the bitterness in his voice.

There wasn't a day when he didn't miss his dad, and that morning, he'd spent hours sifting through photos of him, his parents, and his siblings. They were all taken on Copper Island. As a child, his parents saw no point in leaving the island as there was everything they needed. Part of that experience, Archer thought, drove his need to explore the world. The other part of exploring the world and not returning to the island during their time off, was the painful reminders of their mother abandoning them and his father never filling the study with his deep laughter again.

"We can't change the past, Archer," she replied.

Archer saw a brief wave of sadness in her eyes before the shutter came down and indifference settled back on her features. She raised her chin and pulled her colourful shawl tighter around her shoulders. The purple and deep red patterns swirled, making a drab-sounding woman look radiant.

"We can't. Hopefully, I can influence the future of Turner Hall."

"Have you found a wife yet?"

"It's only been a couple of weeks, Aunt Cynthia," he replied.

"Well, don't forget to bring her to dinner. I want to meet her before you put an engagement ring on her finger. Do you have a ring?"

"I thought I'd let my future wife choose her engagement ring."

"Don't be absurd. She'll wear a Turner ring. Come to my room in two hours. I'll have a selection ready for you. I will hear no argument, Archer."

"Yes, Aunt Cynthia."

Archer wasn't going to argue. He'd seen his mother's ring. A gorgeous ruby set with diamonds. His grandmother's ring was similar with an emerald. His aunt's rings were stunning. The ring she wore while she glared at him in warning was a sapphire, square cut, loose on her slim finger. He'd remembered she'd always worn it. However, these days it didn't sit as it should. He tilted his head in question, seeing if she seemed slimmer than he'd remembered. Her watch was loose too.

Dismissing the idea she was ill, he put it down to growing older.

Having a ring from the family jewels would take a task out of going into the town. Erica had been emphatic about staying away from people, and this was the solution.

"Two hours, don't forget or keep me waiting."

"Always be on time," they both said simultaneously.

"I am always on time," he replied with a grin.

His aunt harrumphed and turned away, then walked down the stairs. Even now, she shifted quickly at her age, with grace out of his sight. Archer took the back route out of Turner Hall and headed to Edward Hall. He unlocked the main door and walked through the empty foyer like he'd done a dozen times that week. He had helped Erica with her swimming practice in the mornings, and in the afternoons, he had scoured the smaller mansion.

He couldn't shake the coldness of the place. Everything looked clean, grand, perfect for an upmarket wedding, but it felt like a ghost house where that last wedding was decades before, long before he left the island.

Archer had witnessed plenty of weddings taking place in the grand foyer, but the place now felt lost and forgotten. He made a mental note to ask his aunt when the last marriage had occurred and when the next one was booked when he chose Erica's ring.

Taking the wide staircase two stairs at a time, he strode down the red carpet with gold metal trim at the skirting. In the corridor to the left and right were the hotel guest rooms.

Whether he got the hotel, wedding business, or cottages, Archer didn't want to sleep under either of the Hall's roofs.

If he didn't pull off the deal, Archer had already decided he wouldn't stay on the island, preferring to work overseas and away from the ghosts of the past. Archer had no idea what job he would take on the island if he stayed. Pride wouldn't let him stay at Turner Hall at his aunt's grace. He picked up the box of items, and with a stiff nod and a long glance at the floor-to-ceiling stain glass window overlooking the grounds where he'd studied for all his exams, he left the room, closing the door quietly.

TWENTY-THREE

Archer

When he stepped outside and locked the main door behind him, he turned left and headed to see if Erica was at her cottage. It hadn't been long since he'd last seen her, but when he rounded the corner and saw her curled up on the armchair in the shade, he felt his entire body relax. Archer approached quietly, seeing she was asleep, her hands tucked under her chin. The sun was almost shining on her toes as it had moved during the afternoon. He didn't want her to burn in the sun. Crouching in front of her, he stroked the back of his hand over her forehead. Her skin was smooth and warm to the touch. She stirred but didn't wake, burrowing deeper into the cushions. He couldn't stop the grin split his face if he tried. He took a moment to gaze at her cuteness when she was asleep. Her beauty astounded him.

There was no doubting he was wildly attracted to Erica, and the need to sweep her up and take her inside had his hands twitching at his sides. He swelled at the thought of removing her clothes and kissing every inch of Erica to wake her. Instead, he kissed her cheek, deliberately touching the edge of her mouth with his.

"Wake up, honey," he whispered as he hovered over her mouth.

She let out a long sigh and lifted her chin. "Make me," she said, closing the gap.

Her lips parted as he sealed their mouths for a kiss. He dropped to his knees to lean closer as she tangled her tongue with his. He was making her wake up, but every part of his body was on high alert. The arm of the chair hid his apparent erection as he cupped the back of her head. Sighs and deep breathing filled the air as he pressed harder, searching deeper for a connection. This was a deal, but he was drawn to her. He tucked his arms under her legs and back without opening his eyes, lifting her off the chair. There was no hiding he wanted her, so he owned it by sitting back down with her on his lap. She draped her crossed legs over the arm of the chair. Threading his fingers through her loose hair, his eyes remained closed as he kissed her slowly. The lazy kiss changed from soft touches to stretching his mouth over hers to taste her. His other hand dropped to her hip, holding her in place as he lifted his hips. Archer knew he was in trouble making this move to get some friction. The ache was untenable.

At this stage, he was okay with coming in his pants than taking their make-out session to the next step.

"You're so hard," she whispered over his lips.

"I am. I can't help it."

"Let's go inside," she said, kissing the side of his neck and then nibbling on his earlobe. "There's a really comfortable bed."

Archer moved his head back, breaking contact from her

talented tongue and mouth but kept his hard-on and hands where they were.

"I can't," he said, then groaned.

"Right," she said, resting her head on his shoulder. "No sex rule."

"Actually, I have to meet my aunt in an hour, and I cannot be late. If we went inside, I wouldn't be leaving until sun up with neither of us getting any sleep."

If Archer wasn't mistaken, she heard the gorgeous woman squirming on his lap whimper. He felt exactly the same. So why couldn't he just have a fling with Erica, fake marry her, and then walk away? Why couldn't they have a little bit of fun?

That's right, he thought, because he wasn't a fling type of guy. One night or all in, that's the kind of man he was. And there was no way he would be able to have one night and no more with Erica.

"You could come back after your meeting?" she said.

Archer dropped his stare to her hand. Her fingers had found his erect nipple and her thumb gently stroked back and forth over his t-shirt.

"That would be a terrible idea, Erica," he said, not entirely convinced of what he was saying.

"Why did you come over?" she asked amiably, nodding to the box.

He was thankful she knew when to stop pushing him. He lifted her as he stood and placed her back on her armchair. Archer stepped away to go to the box and brought it over. He took out a photo album, flicked to the page he wanted, and turned it to face her.

He smiled as she stroked the picture of him and his siblings on Stuart Island.

"What's your favourite colour?" he asked.

"Are we talking shoes or a sweater?"

"Jewels," Archer replied, observing her reaction.

Her fingers stilled on the picture of four teenagers, arms thrown around shoulders laughing at the camera. He couldn't remember who had taken the photo for the life of him. He knew it wasn't his dad, and his mother was long gone since the picture was taken. Someone had taken it and developed the film, putting it into a photo album. Somehow the album that didn't belong to him found its way into his bedroom.

"Pearls are my favourite, but if I had to choose a coloured gem, I'd pick rubies."

"Okay," Archer answered, hoping like hell there was a pearl ring in the selection his aunt offered.

"Just okay, no clues to tell me why you want to know?"

"It's a surprise," he answered because he had no idea when, where or how he would actually propose to Erica. They'd struck a deal, but he still wanted to propose, so they had a story to tell without lying.

"Are you going to propose Mr Turner? Have you asked my father for permission?"

Archer laughed at her southern drawl, sounding like she was straight from Mississippi. It was a flawless accent, and he wished he could reply like he sounded like the actor Matthew McConaughey. Then he felt his face fall as he thought about her family and friends.

"Should I meet your family? In all this mess, I hadn't considered your family."

"No," she said, waving away his question. "If you want to walk away after three months, there's no point in them knowing we were ever married. People get married in secret all the time. This island will give us the perfect cover."

There was no getting away from her tone that they

wouldn't last. Erica said he would be the one to walk away, but he thought the opposite would happen. She'd already worked it all out. It dowsed his desire to take her to bed. Even a short fling didn't work for him. All or nothing and Erica was already planning his exit.

"Archer?" Erica asked, bringing him back to look at her. When he did, she gave him a soft smile. "Did you hear me because you look like I've stolen your favourite teddy?"

"Nah," he said, stretching down to his box. "He's here."

Archer lifted the old scrappy stuffed toy. He straightened the teddy's bow tie and turned him to face Erica. "He's called Peter. Please don't ask me why. I have no idea. I've had him since I was born, so I think someone else named him, and I went with it."

"He's cute," she said, reaching for it.

Archer handed it over, picked up the box, and placed the photo album inside.

"I went everywhere with it as a kid, and when I became too cool for cuddly toys, he sat on my shelf in my old bedroom."

Erica stood and stepped to Archer, the box the only thing separating them. "Did you hear what I said before?"

"About keeping us a secret? Yeah, I heard you. I get it. I'm sure you don't want your friends and family knowing about the man you married with oil under his fingernails."

She shook her head and then dropped her chin for a few beats before she speared him with a stern stare.

"My darling Archer, how little you know about my family or me. I'd be proud to marry someone who worked for a living, who came home dirty from a long day's work. Please don't make any judgments about me. You'll hurt my feelings. My desire to keep things quiet and secret is to protect you and not me."

Archer's watch beeped before he could ask his question. When he saw the alarm alert him to forty-five minutes until he needed to meet his aunt, his question about her needs left his head.

"I have to go, Erica. My aunt doesn't like tardiness."

"She'll hate me. I seem to be late for everything. I'll keep Peter hostage until you return to retrieve him. If you feel you can't come back this evening. I'll see you at the pool tomorrow."

Erica leaned across the box as much as she could to kiss his cheek and then turned to walk back into her cottage, leaving him alone with a single box of his most precious possessions.

After a shower and a change of clothes, Archer hurried below stairs to the kitchen to swipe up whatever Maggie had baked. Now that he was back in the house, she'd taken to baking in the afternoon. Archer thought she'd have to up her game if his siblings returned, as they all had a sweet tooth. Today was cookies, and by the time he'd run up the stone steps and into the foyer, he'd eaten two. He brushed the crumbs off his shirt and checked his reflection in the front door's glass before striding across the stone floor to the morning room.

Bailey was waiting at the door, checking his pocket watch. Archer had arrived bang on time. With a nod from Bailey, he opened the door for Archer. Archer entered the room and saw his aunt on the far side. The morning room was vast, with a dozen sofa set facing each other down the long galley-style room. On one wall was a fireplace so big you could roast a hog over the flames. On the other side of the room were lead-lined windows. Usually, as the name suggested, the family only spent the morning in the room and then moved around the house chasing the sun. There were two places Archer could find his aunt if she weren't resting in her room. The greenhouse where she cultivated exotic flowers or the morning room.

At four in the afternoon, the sun was high in the sky but shining on the other side of the house. He felt the chill in the room from the old bricks and regretted not wearing a pullover.

"Good afternoon, Aunt Cynthia," he said in greeting.

She sat in a wicker chair facing out the window. The lawns from her vantage point were vast and plain until they reached the tree line obscuring the ocean beyond.

"Please sit down. Bailey is fetching earl grey tea for us."

He wasn't an earl grey tea drinker, and she knew it. But she was, so that was all that mattered to her. Archer accepted this was her house and her rules. So tea for two it would be. He hoped there was a third cookie coming his way.

"Open the box, will you, Archer?" she asked, pointing to the large mahogany box on the tall table a few feet away.

Archer stood and walked to where she indicated and lifted the lid. Inside were rows of rings nestled in purple velvet. The delicate bands with small, medium, and large jewels balanced on top. These looked old, much older than he expected the family jewels were. Most of them were for women, but with their age, they could've been for men in the 1700s and early 1800s. He couldn't imagine how much money he was looking at in the velvet-lined box. And one day they would belong to him. Running his finger along the raised benches, he searched through the dozens of rings, counting as he went. When he got to thirty, he stopped and picked up the gold ring.

"Ah, I see you've spotted it," she said from her seat, not getting up. "That's the family's signet ring. Your father never wanted to wear it. Your grandfather was the last to wear it. If you find a wife and take over the wedding business, I expect you to wear it."

"Is that a condition of the contract we struck?" Archer said, half turning to look at his aunt.

"It's not a deal-breaker, but I want to know you'll take the Turner business seriously. Hundreds of years of history exist in this building and on this island. My brother didn't care for any of it, but he was in line to inherit it. It broke my heart to see him shun all the old ways."

"Why didn't you inherit as the eldest?"

"My father had decided."

Archer waited for more, but his aunt remained tight-lipped.

He didn't wear jewellery and never had, but if it made his aunt happy, he would. He was getting married, and he wanted to wear a wedding band. What was one more ring?

"Which hand do I wear it on?"

"Your grandfather wore it on his left hand on his pinkie finger. His father, your great-grandfather, wore it on his right hand on his forefinger. Your father didn't want to wear it at all. He told our father that it would never be worn as it would get in the way of his work on the oil rigs. But he told me privately he wanted nothing to do with old ways. He hated the way his father paraded the family wealth."

"It's a bit ironic, isn't it, seeing as no one can have any of that wealth until the older generation has gone? It's not like its shared wealth."

"You have a roof over your head and a full stomach, don't you?" his aunt snapped.

"Only if I live here. When we all chose to buy a house in Scotland to be near the rig, we had no help from the family."

"Because your duty is to be here, on Turner Island. You're a Turner, and so was your father, by extension, your mother. You need to find a wife, Archer, or else the Turner legacy will die with me."

His gaze landed on her face. Aunt Cynthia was straight backed, contrite in her outpouring of information and dictation. He didn't like her tone. "It will come to me, won't it? The Island, I mean."

"Only if I will it that way."

Archer stared at her in disbelief, not daring to question if what she was saying was true. He wouldn't put it passed her to be vindictive enough to leave the whole island to charity.

He turned back to the jewellery box and looked at the rings. A delicate pearl set in a silver band was on the top row in the middle. It was simple and beautiful. He hoped Erica would like it. Archer picked up the ring and slid it onto his pinkie finger. He didn't get it passed the second knuckle. He grimaced at the thought he might need to re-sized the ring. His ancestors were lean, slim-fingered. Erica was trim, but as evolution happened in each generation, humans increased in size.

"Who was the last person to wear this one?" Archer asked as he presented the ring to Aunt Cynthia.

She took it from him and turned it in the sunlight. "My mother, I think. She had a choker and earrings to match. I bet there is a bracelet too. Is that your choice? Not going for a big diamond?"

"No, I think my future wife will prefer this kind of ring."

Archer was rewarded with an approving glance. He didn't think he was meant to see it as it was gone as soon as it appeared. Bailey entered the room at that point, informing Aunt Cynthia that her dinner was served. Thankfully he would get out of swallowing earl grey tea and any more lectures from his aunt.

Getting up, his aunt straightened her twinset and patted the bottom of her bun. She turned and nodded to Bailey who left the room, then she turned to Archer, pinning him to the spot.

"Don't forget, as soon as you're ready to put the ring on her finger. I want to meet her first."

"Yes, Aunt Cynthia," he replied.

Archer had no such intention. He would not risk his aunt meeting Erica before he had the ring on her finger. He figured if she said yes to the fake proposal and put the ring on, she would be less likely to walk away after meeting his aunt.

That was his thinking. Whether it worked was another thing. No one voiced liking Cynthia Turner, but anyone who dared say it out loud would risk her wrath.

TWENTY-FOUR

Erica

Archer had gone to extreme lengths to help Erica train for synchronised swimming. He'd told her she needed to spend five hours a day training. It was the end of another week, and Erica was exhausted. On Monday, when she questioned him on his knowledge of the Olympic sport, he confessed he'd spent an entire day watching videos on the internet. He was an expert on the British Olympian team. When she'd strolled around the corner of the grand mansion to the swimming pool, she saw Archer walking towards her with a giant tree trunk above his head. It wasn't the tree that caught her attention but his shirtless torso dripping with sweat. Erica stopped dead in her tracks as he reached the end of the row of logs and dropped it to the floor. It bounced once and stayed still with a resounding thud.

Archer still hadn't noticed her as he clapped his hands together to get rid of the detritus on his hands. When he wiped them on his shorts, the material pulled tight across his thighs, showing the muscles bunching just above his knees.

Her mouth watered.

"Eyes up here, honey," he said.

She hadn't noticed how long she was staring at his legs, but clearly, it was too long by the smirk she saw on his face.

"That's a lot of logs, Archer. What are they for?" Erica tried for nonchalance, avoiding any conversation that she was hot for him, and he didn't feel the same.

"They're for today's fitness session. Hurdling."

"What now? Every day we do something different. Are you sure you're not secretly an army PT instructor?"

Archer was right in front of her now. She could smell his shower gel or whatever he sprayed on himself in the morning. The clean smell of soap had never smelled so enticing. The heat he'd generated lugging the logs to the grounds must have intensified the aroma because she could happily lick him.

"No, nothing like that. If I'm going to do a job, then do it right, right?"

"Yeah, I guess. I'm really grateful you're giving up your mornings for me," she said, looking around his body to the half dozen logs.

"It's only a couple of hours. The rest of the time, you're treading water or doing somersaults. So you don't need me to help you do that part anymore."

Erica thought that was a crying shame. He'd held her waist while she was upside down in the water, toes pointed out of the water as she practised her scissor kicks. Solid hands on her body, making her feel safe as she went through the list of movements she needed to practice to perfection. She would be on set in two months, spending hours on end in the pool they designed for the movie. Her agent had wanted an instructor to come out to Copper Island to give her daily direction, but she thought it was overkill. A half-hour video call in the morning was sufficient for Erica to get her instructions. It wasn't like she had to be Olympic standard, but she wanted to pay Esther Williams her dues in the biopic.

"So, what is the plan today?"

"Warm-up," Archer said, wrapping his arm around her waist.

She liked his style of warm-up. Erica didn't resist when he pulled her closer and dropped his head to kiss her lips. Like each morning, their kiss turned from chaste to passionate so quickly. Archer held her head with one hand on her nape, then tightened his arm around her back. He wouldn't let her move an inch when he kissed her. When his warm wet tongue touched hers, she wanted to climb him —every damn time.

Erica broke the kiss by dropping her head back and laughing. "I'm not sure this is the type of warm-up my muscles need."

"It's nice, though, right?" he whispered against her exposed throat.

"Yeah," she said and sighed. "Really nice."

Erica moved out of his hold and gave him a shy smile. She could see lines were beginning to blur. Erica stepped to the poolside and did her stretches while Archer dropped to the floor and started his push-ups routine. She'd prefer to watch him do the push-up that launched him off the concrete for a second. He did a combination of push-ups, squats, and leaping up. While Erica was more sedate, she could feel her body warming up in the early morning cool air. Partly from her routine and partly from watching Archer. The moment he finished, Erica had her feet wide apart, bent at the waist with her hands flat on the concrete. It was her favourite yoga position. Turning her head to the side to look at Archer, she was treated to him wiping down his chest with a towel. Her eyes looked him over, taking her time on his hips as his shorts hung low. What she wasn't watching until it was too late was him whipping his towel around to a tight strip, ready to flick at her bottom.

"Don't you dare," she warned, not trying to hide her smile.

She liked it when he was being playful.

"It's tempting," he answered, wiping his face with his towel.

His heated gaze had Erica frozen in place, unable to move. For a moment, she thought she'd be stuck in the position forever as her muscles locked. Archer circled her and settled at her rear. Erica could feel his warmth and then his hips against her bottom. It was a risky move, but she pushed back an inch. Archer pushed his hips forward, and it took all her strength not to grind against him. Archer leaned over her bent position and moved his hands along her sides and then down her arms so his hands were flat on either side of hers. Erica puffed out a breath at their nearness, hoping his aunt wasn't watching what they were doing. The erotic dance of seemingly innocent moves was anything but.

"I'm going for a run," Archer whispered into her ear. "Have dinner with me tonight, at your place. I'll bring the food."

Erica swayed her hips from side to side, brushing against him, hoping her tease told him her answer.

"What time?" she asked.

"Seven. I think we should eat inside tonight. More private for what I have in mind."

"Okay."

It was all Erica could manage.

Archer kissed her cheek and then set off running towards Edward Hall. Standing up tall to stretch, she looked up at the windows of Turner Hall. Dozens of reflections echoed back, but with the sun in its position, Erica couldn't tell if anyone was watching.

After a rotation of treading water, swimming laps, and practising turning in a tight circle underneath the water, Erica was exhausted. Training five hours a day took it out of her. She was no slouch when it came to exercising, but the difference between endurance training mastered by Archer Turner and running on a treadmill was starkly different.

She swiped up her towel and staggered back to her cottage, her thighs burning from jumping logs. Weeks had passed since her arrival on the island, and she still couldn't get used to not locking her back door. Erica fully expected to return and find the place either ransacked or a journalist sitting on her sofa waiting for her to return.

True anonymity had been elusive in the previous decade. Erica travelled everywhere with her head down, wearing dark sunglasses. Here, in the glorious beauty of the island, she wore sunglasses by choice. There was no one commenting on what she wore or the state of the highlights in her hair. Erica had never felt so free.

Sadly she was about to ruin her mood.

After a shower and far too long choosing what to wear for her dinner date, Erica padded barefoot downstairs and settled in the living room. She'd set up a video call with Yanny every four days to keep up to date with her future and to see where the world's media had got with her ex-husband and new pregnant girlfriend. Switching into work, reality had become depressing very quickly. With a deep sigh, she hit connect.

"Oh, thank the gods you're here," Yanny said, bursting onto the screen.

"I've never missed a meeting with you, Yanny. Why the panic?"

"I'm sorry. I had these nightmares last night. You cut yourself off completely, even from me. I cannot handle your life alone."

"I don't think I can handle my life alone either. Has it been awful?"

"Because they can't get at you, they're trying me, your agent, and your school friends. The press thinks you're in hiding licking your wounds."

"Do you think we should correct them?"

"Maybe," Yanny said. He'd moved from panicked to manager mode. Yanny sat up straighter now that they were on safe ground.

"Do you have a plan?" she asked.

"How's the wedding planning going? I'm not changing the subject. There is a point to my question."

"It's still on if that's what you mean, but further than that, I don't have a date yet."

"And you're still on track for costume fitting?"

"Yes. About that? It's only five days, right?"

"It should be, unless you want me to schedule other meetings."

"No. I'd rather go straight to LA, get the fittings done, and come straight back."

"I can arrange that. No one needs to know apart from the production team when you're in LA. We won't be able to keep it top secret, but we can make it low-key."

"Okay."

"Do you want me to see if they'll do your fitting in London?"

"If you can swing it, yes, but I don't want to be labelled a diva before shooting starts. I can go to LA on the private jet from Penzance."

"I'll arrange it. Next is your ex-husband."

Erica waited for the bombshell, keeping a staring contest with her manager and lifelong friend.

"Come on, Yanny, tell me the bad news."

"Allegedly," he says, holding up his hands, dropping his chin, and avoiding eye contact. "He's going to file for divorce."

"Oh, for heaven's sake," Erica said, falling back against the sofa cushions. "He's got to know he'll look bad when the truth comes out."

"Well, we could let the truth out, Erica. It would put this whole thing to bed."

"I'm the wronged woman, yet I have to be the arsehole and call him out to be a liar."

"Or you can keep hiding away while he has the sole voice with the press. Up to you."

"Aren't the press bored yet?"

"You have just won an Oscar the same night you find out your husband is cheating on you. The press is rabid. Every magazine from the gutter press to Vogue wants an interview."

"No, they don't. They've earmarked a slot for whoever won best actress. Too bad they didn't make a deal before the event. It gives me more reason not to go into the small town on this island. Word would travel too fast, and then I wouldn't have the freedom to practice in the pool and walk about the grounds."

"You're a harsh lady, but I love you."

"Honestly, spending a couple of weeks here, I have strong feelings of walking away from the Hollywood lifestyle."

"What?" Yanny gave her a mock frightened look. "I'd look awful in rags. What the hell would I do if you retired?"

"It's not all about you, Yanny," she scolded.

"Darling, it *is* all about me," he replied.

Erica laughed at her friend's outrage. She knew he was joking, but it always made her giggle when he made out he was materialistic. Despite how much Erica paid him, he'd never spent more than a fiver on a t-shirt. He had a clause in his contract that if she did give it all up, he had a severance pay of twelve months. Yanny would have dozens of offers to snatch him up if rumour got out she was retiring. She knew for a fact he was constantly offered extortionate deals to walk away from her. Erica knew because he waved it in front of her face each time she fell into diva mode.

"I don't know where I would be if you hadn't bullied your way into being my manager. I'm thankful every day you're in my life."

"All right, all right, stop buttering me up. I can't handle it," he said, mouthing the word *more* at the screen.

"What else is there?"

"Nothing worth knowing. You're busy as all hell once your three months are up. I've pushed everything you had in the third month out, so you have a clear run until you become Mrs, Mrs what?"

"Turner."

"Erica Turner. Nice. From one iconic female actress surname to another."

Erica chatted to Yanny for another hour, going through her schedule for the next six months. She acted casually, but she took her schedule seriously, even though she was late wherever she went. The afternoon raced by after she hung up from Yanny. She read through her lines and researched more about the actress she would be playing. It made her sad working through Esther's life in the 1950s Hollywood and how they were treated. She didn't think the industry had moved on enough, but at least she had more rights than Esther had.

A breeze coming from somewhere in the house caused her to bring the shawl from the back of the sofa over her shoulders as she hunched over, looking at the laptop on the coffee table.

"Hey."

Erica jumped out of her skin at the voice. Knowing it was Archer but getting her body to catch up took a few seconds as she flapped her arms and slammed the laptop's lid down. She was on her feet, walking towards Archer, who stood on the threshold of the living room and the small corridor to the kitchen.

"I'm sorry, am I running late?" she asked as she stood before him.

"It's just after seven," he answered and leaned in to kiss her.

The kiss lingered for a few moments, and she relished his soft lips on hers. To anyone else, it was a loving kiss. To her, she felt it down to her toes.

"I promise I'll be five minutes. Change of clothes, and I'll be back down," Erica said.

"You look perfect as you are," he replied, grasping her hand to stop her from moving.

"I've been in these clothes all afternoon working. I want to change, discard the day to enjoy this evening."

The clothes she wore were supposed to be her dinner date attire but one look at Archer in his deliciousness made her want to change. He wore a shirt open at the neck with dark blue jeans.

"I get that. I'll dish up dinner in the dining room."

"Okay, I won't be long. There's white wine and beer in the fridge. I'll have a beer."

TWENTY-FIVE

Archer

When he arrived at Erica's cottage, it was in darkness. His heart thundered, thinking she'd changed her mind. For someone who didn't want to go into town, the only other place he could think she'd gone was to bed early. He tried the back door, and it was open. Undecided about walking in unannounced, he dithered on the doorstep. The food wafting up gave him purpose to enter her temporary home. Walking through the kitchen, he placed the food on the countertop and followed the noise of nails on a keyboard. He found Erica staring at her laptop screen in the semi-darkness, huddled under a blanket. Just the sight of her made his heart pound. Could he really go through with proposing to this woman when she was only doing it as a favour?

He flipped on the light in the kitchen, thinking he'd do anything to kiss her every day. She promised she'd only be five minutes, so he set about getting plates and cutlery for their dinner. Maggie had made them beef wellington with mashed potatoes and vegetables. The gravy was in a flask.

Unwrapping everything, Archer ferried the food to the dining room, found matches to light the candle, and dimmed the lights.

"The food smells fantastic," Erica said as she entered the dining room.

She wore another loose-fitting dress to the ground, this one off the shoulder in navy blue. Her hair was loose around her shoulders and down her back. The whole looked screamed 1970s, right down to the lack of bra. Trying his best not to look at her other underwear to see if she was wearing any, he pulled out the chair in front of him.

"Dinner is served," he announced with a deep bow.

She walked around the table, holding her skirts as she approached him. Before taking her seat, she stood on tiptoe and kissed his cheek. "Thank you for dinner."

"You haven't tasted it yet. However, I have never eaten anything awful Maggie has made. So I can't take credit."

"It doesn't matter. You saved me the trouble of making dinner."

Archer hurried to the other side seat, which was adjacent to hers. Archer sat at the head of the table, and she sat to his left. The dining table could seat ten people, but he'd positioned them at one end together. Their knees touched when they sat down, and he had no intention of moving. When Erica didn't shift either, he relaxed.

They talked amicably through dinner, discussing his adventures worldwide with his siblings. After some back and forth, they found a city they'd both visited, but between them, they'd covered most of the globe. When the wine was finished, and the dishes were empty, a silence fell between them.

Archer cleared his throat, but he couldn't catch a breath. He'd decided that afternoon he would propose after dinner, but now they had reached the stage of nothing left on the table to eat or drink. Nerves shattered his resolve.

"Archer, are you okay?" Erica asked, placing a hand on his knee under the table.

He shot off his chair at her touch, coughing and banging his chest with the flat of his hand. "I'll be right back," he said.

He raced into the kitchen, took a glass off the shelf, and filled it with water. Then, he gulped down the whole lot and filled the glass again, drinking half of it.

"What's the matter with me?" he muttered, putting the rest of the water down on the side.

"Are you all right, Archer?" Erica called out behind him.

It's now or never, he thought.

Turning around, he dropped to one knee and brought the ring box out of his pocket. Erica looked shocked and held her fingers to her lips, eyes watering but not spilling over.

"Archer," she said, almost breathless.

"I know this is a deal we made, but I wanted to propose, anyway. It could be the only time I ever get a woman to be my wife, so why not make some memories," he said.

She stepped towards him, cupping his cheek. "Ask the question, Archer."

He wanted to scream inside at the ridiculous scene playing out. He was only doing this to get his aunt to give him some of his inheritance early. So why was he so nervous she might say no? He had no idea.

"Erica Taylor, will you agree to be my wife?"

She nodded at him. First, her lip wobbled then a tear

slid down her face. It was as if they'd been in love for years, and he'd sprung the proposal on her. If it were real, this would be the best moment of his life. He opened the ring box and showed her the antique pearl ring.

"Archer, it's gorgeous," she said, lifting it out. She looked at it from every angle, marvelling at the piece of jewellery.

"Let me have it so I can slip it onto your finger," he said, taking it from her hand.

Archer stood to do this part, taking her left hand and looking into her eyes. He kept her gaze as he pushed the ring onto her engagement finger. It fitted. Perfectly. Like it was meant to be hers. If that didn't send him into a tailspin, her following words did.

"I love this ring. I never want to take it off."

"Erica, you don't have to say that. I know where I stand with this arrangement."

"It was a beautiful proposal. I shall treasure the memory even if you don't mean it."

Archer stalled, wanting to tell her that even though right now he didn't think he was ready for marriage, he was very much falling under her spell.

"Do you think we should kiss?" he asked to distract her.

"We should definitely seal our fates. Kiss me until I'm breathless," she said.

Archer tugged her closer by her hand and leaned in. Pressing his mouth to hers, he slipped his tongue inside her mouth, searching for the igniting passion he knew was there. The moment she slid against him, he pressed their bodies together. Hungry kisses were deep and soul-searing as his hands dropped to her waist and then lower. He grabbed her arse, and she moaned into his mouth, flicking the tip of her tongue along the roof of his mouth. His spine tingled, his balls drew up, and if he weren't careful, he wouldn't make it to her bed.

Clutching at her waist, he lifted her, placing her down hard on the countertop, wedging himself between her knees, then yanking her to the edge. Not giving her much time to take a breath, his mouth covered her again, relishing the warmth of her open mouth, the tightness of her calves pressing against his arse. They couldn't be closer if they tried while clothed. He ripped his mouth from hers and stepped out of her hold walking to the other side of the kitchen island. Archer was in a state of arousal so bad that he wanted to rip her clothes off and sink his cock inside her.

Holding back the primal roar lodged in his throat, he drew his gaze back to Erica. She looked at him over her shoulder, not fazed by his indecision. One shoulder and then the other, she pulled down her dress. His eyes were glued to her bare back, her shoulder blades moving as she shoved the dress to her waist. While rearranging her clothing, Archer caught a glimpse of the side of her breast. The curve was enticing, as was her smooth, flawless skin.

"Erica, you are not playing fair," he whispered so harshly she paused for a few moments before lying back on the counter. Her arms draped over her head, so her wrists dangled over the edge nearest him.

"Fuck," he said, pushing his fingers through his hair.

He wanted her, craved her.

"Oh, to hell with doing the right thing," he muttered and stalked around the kitchen island. He positioned himself between her legs again, cupped her breasts, and stared into her eyes.

"Are you absolutely sure you want me to take you to bed?"

"I want nothing more," she said, arching her back to

push her breasts further into his hands.

Archer's thumbs stroked over her nipples, making them harden.

"Bed, couch, hallway stairs, or the nearest wall?" he asked.

"You choose," she answered.

He saw her eyes roll as her lids closed, moaning as he pinched her nipples. He played with her breasts for a few more minutes until she writhed against his hips. Erica was responsive to his every touch, and he loved it. Sweeping an arm under her back, he brought her to a sitting position and clamped his mouth on hers to taste her again. While he kissed her, Archer lifted her off the countertop, bringing her legs around his waist. Knowing the house's layout made his journey to her bedroom easier and quicker. Once he'd ascended the stairs and her mouth had moved to his throat and neck, he again thought they wouldn't make it to a bed. He let her down to stand in the corridor outside her bedroom. The top of her dress still around her waist made her look like a wanton sexual beast, and he loved that too. Never had he experienced this level of connection with a woman. Erica was giving as good as she got, participating in their passionate encounter. He pressed her gently to the wall with his hand flat against her sternum. Archer could feel the sides of her breasts grazing each side of his fingers, teasing him to cup them. Archer wanted to, but he needed to calm down to make their night together longer.

"Take your underwear off, honey," he said, leaning down to take a nipple into his mouth. Swirling and teasing, he sucked hard and bit lightly, getting louder moans from Erica as she shimmied out of her knickers. She let them drop as soon as they passed her hips and then grabbed at the belt on his jeans. Archer let her open his belt, unbutton his jeans, and shove them down but stopped her progress when she tried to dip her hand into his boxers.

Pressing more firmly to her chest, she still her movements. His mouth moved up to her throat and then grazed over her lips.

"I want to touch you first. Please."

Erica immediately dropped her hands and relaxed her head against the wall breaking their kiss.

"You're in charge," she said.

Her words sent Archer into a tailspin. Taking charge of her body was a dream, but he knew it wouldn't last long. It wasn't in Erica's nature to hand over complete control, and he liked her that way. Keeping her in place, his other hand found its way between her legs. Erica shifted her feet to widen her stance and floored him by canting her hips towards him. It took less time than he thought.

He was not in charge, just along for the ride.

When Archer slipped his fingers inside her body, he thought his knees would buckle. But, whether it was the length of time since he'd last taken a woman to bed or the fact this woman agreed to be his wife in all but name, he was falling hard that she was ready for him.

"Let's go," he said, taking her hand and leading her into her bedroom. He shed his clothes as he crossed the room, leaving a trail behind him. When they reached the bed, he turned to Erica. She'd lost her dress along the way too.

"You look wonderful in the moonlight," he whispered as he cupped his hand on her hip. "Come closer, honey."

Archer's eyes were fixed on her breasts. The teardrop shape looked perfect on her slim frame, nipples pointing straight at him. He tugged her the rest of the way, pressing his chest against hers as he interlinked their hands. Falling back on the bed, he made sure she fell on him before he rolled them. Settling between her parted thighs, he paused, then kissed her stomach.

"I don't suppose you have any condoms?" he said, resting his chin on her hip bone as he toyed with one of her nipples.

"Yes," she answered.

"Thank fuck, where are they?"

Erica chuckled and scrambled to sit up, "I'll get them, lie down, get comfy, I'll be right back."

Archer watched as she sashayed into her en-suite bathroom, flicked on the light, and then disappeared out of view for a few minutes. The light went off as soon as she appeared, but it wasn't out before he saw her nakedness. Waving a strip and smiling broadly, Erica joined him on the bed, straddling his thighs.

"I don't know if I should be flattered or disappointed you didn't come prepared, Mr Turner."

Archer groaned at the sound of his name on her lips. The formality was getting him harder for her.

"I didn't want to tempt fate, honey. We were only supposed to kiss if you remember."

"We don't have to go any further, Archer, if you're not comfortable. I understand."

"Oh hell no, we're doing this, even if my heart will be broken later down the line."

"I won't break your heart, Archer."

He watched the small smile on her lips drop as she circled him at the base. Then, with long, slow strokes, she caressed his cock with a hum of approval.

"Your skin is so silky, and here," she said, brushing her thumb over the crown, "is so hard and wet."

"You would make a killing as a phone sex worker," he muttered, unable to handle any more. He blindly reached for the strip, tore off a condom, and sheathed himself. Then he reached up, and grabbed Erica's waist, turning them, so he covered her with his body.

With one hand entwined with hers, his elbow resting on the bed, he positioned himself with his other hand and stroked in an inch. Erica hissed and arched her back, raising her knee and then curling her leg over his thigh. He took his next move slow, pushing his hips, watching her expression, careful not to hurt her. Archer didn't know if the hiss was pain or pleasure, and he'd lost the ability to speak as soon as he felt her heat. Then, taking his weight on both forearms next to her shoulders, he took her in a passionate kiss. She was ready for him. Tongue lashed against his as she opened up for him. At the same time, she pushed her hips up to take more of his cock. That was when all slowness ceased, and they went at it like it was the first and last time they'd have sex. He pushed in to the hilt, his hips pressing against hers, knees and thighs doing most of the work as he pushed harder and faster. Erica's moans became louder, gasps and panting mixed in with slapping of their bodies. Archer knew he would get to his climax before Erica because he was seconds away.

"I should've given you an orgasm first, honey. I'm sorry."

Erica didn't answer him with words. Instead, she slipped a hand between their bodies and hurried her climax along. He could feel her fingers move in circles as they brushed the base of his cock. It wasn't helping him hold back. With a short, sharp expletive, he climaxed. Archer kept moving, slower but still kept pace, hoping she was giving Erica enough friction to get her there. When she hadn't come a minute later, he pulled out. Her fingers still played with her clit, and her pants were still short, but she hadn't come.

"I'm sorry, Archer, it takes me so long to come. It's embarrassing."

"Let me help?"

"Come to my side, slide your fingers inside me and kiss me."

He didn't hesitate to move. After taking care of the condom, he hooked his leg over her thigh and parted her legs. Finding her entrance, he pushed a finger in.

"More," she said.

A second finger joined the first, and he slowly thrust inside her body, finding the perfect spot and crooking his fingers. Erica let out a cry, and he felt the ripple over his fingers.

"That's my girl. Keep going," he said before covering his mouth with hers. He slid his tongue along hers at the same pace as his fingers. In seconds she came. Swallowing her cries and holding her tight, he kept going until she relaxed back into the pillows.

What had he done? It was the most intimate act he had ever experienced with a woman. To his shame, he hadn't remembered ever checking if his partner had orgasmed if he hadn't made her come with his tongue. It was supposed to be a kiss. How reckless had he been to take her to bed?

Archer put his doubts aside and pulled the covers over them, thinking if there was anything downstairs they needed to put away. Erica snuggled into his side, throwing her arm over his stomach as he lay on his back. Sex usually made him sleepy, but now Archer was wide awake, his mind turning over the sensational sex they'd just had. Unable to get to sleep long after Erica was breathing evenly and became heavier next to him, Archer slipped from the bed and headed downstairs. He put away all the evidence they'd had dinner and quietly slipped out the back door.

TWENTY-SIX

Erica

Waking the following morning early, she wasn't surprised Archer hadn't stayed with her. He'd made it crystal clear he didn't want to have sex with her. The other side of the bed was empty, cool to the touch, and the pillows on the other side of the bed were still on the floor from their passionate night. Flashes of admitting she couldn't come quickly and then giving him directions on how to get her off flooded her brain. Trusting Archer with her desires scared the hell out of her. What if he went to the gutter press to tell them how she liked it in bed?

He wouldn't. Erica knew it. The thought made her feel guilty that she momentarily thought so little of him. She wasn't convinced Archer knew who she really was.

Now that she was awake, she got up and took a shower. Flinging on yoga pants and an oversized t-shirt, Erica stomped down the stairs like a sullen teenager. Coffee, toast, and then back to reading her lines. She would have a break from her pool exercises, not that she needed it after the previous night's workout.

The clock on the oven said it was just after eight o'clock, but by the kitchen's heat level, it felt more like midday. Erica threw the windows open while the bread was in the toaster and the French press percolated. They were tall and opened like doors from the window ledge. When the toast popped up, and Erica went to the cutlery drawer for a knife, she realised all the evening's dinner dishes were cleared away. There was no evidence she'd shared dinner with Archer.

The balmy morning heat was getting her hot and bothered, or it could have been remembering how she'd been kissed breathless by Archer on the kitchen counter. Sitting on the windowsill with her back facing the gardens, Erica chewed through two slices of hot buttered toast, thinking about what she'd agreed to with Archer. He'd been adamant that they were not going to have sex, but she ached in all the right places as a reminder they'd had sensational sex. No matter what, she would need to leave him after three months to start filming her next movie. The question remained, would it be forever?

With no exercise routine, and the lack of work due to insisting she went off-grid, Erica was at a loss as to what to do with her day. Reading over her lines didn't appeal, unable to concentrate on anything but the way Archer kissed her.

Deciding she would go for a walk, Erica trudged up the stairs, stripping as she went. Tossing her clothes into the laundry basket, she idly thought she needed to do laundry soon. After a quick shower, Erica was striding across the lawn with her oversized hat and Jackie O sunglasses. She couldn't afford to get any tan lines so near filming, so she dressed in pantaloon cotton trousers and a shirt several sizes too big. She'd got the hedges at the bottom of the lawns when she heard her name being called. With one hand on her head holding her hat, she looked around to see who was calling. Archer Turner was jogging towards her in all his athletic glory, dressed in shorts and a fitted t-shirt. Her mouth watered as she took him in. The muscles just above his knees reminded her of his firm hip thrusts, staying so deep inside her before he pulled out and did it again.

By the time he reached her, she was more out of breath than he was.

"Hey," he said carefully, in his warm voice that melted her insides.

"Hey, you left early this morning," she replied, getting it out before any awkwardness between them could happen.

"I'm sorry about that."

Erica waited for a reason, but he didn't give one, keeping his heated gaze on her eyes. She held his stare until his eyes dropped to her mouth. Thankfully she still wore her sunglasses, hiding her hurt.

"Listen, my aunt wants to meet you. I had a breakfast meeting with her early this morning," he said and held up his hands. "I know. She's family. You don't have meetings with family. It's strange, but that's how it works with my aunt. No other generation does that, my parents never did, and neither do my siblings."

"Okay," Erica replied. He'd justified why he had a breakfast meeting but not why he snuck out after they'd had sex, he vowed they'd never have.

"Are you free tonight?" Archer asked.

"Tonight?"

"Yeah, well, early evening actually. Aunt Cynthia eats at six. So it will all be over by eight."

"Okay," she said and felt the opposite.

Dinner with his aunt scared her to death, not just because she was entering an arranged marriage with a smoking hot man.

"Are you all right under all that disguise?"

"What do you mean?"

Archer took off her hat and held onto the rim at his side, then he lifted off her sunglasses, resting them on her head.

"That's better. I can see you freaking out now rather than assuming. Aunt Cynthia will be fine, and I'll be with you the whole time. She likes control, which is how she exerts her will over me."

"It's a little intimidating, Archer. Are you sure you want to marry me? You could hire an actress," she said, immediately regretting her words. Why she mentioned actress was beyond her, she put it down to the stress of knowing how he feels, skin to skin.

"Lord, no, if I hired an actress, I'd never know how she really felt. At least with you, I have honest reactions when I touch you."

Archer stepped forward, pulled her tight against his body, and dipped his head to kiss her. Conflicted and confused, she hesitated for a few seconds while he pressed his lips to her cheek and then her mouth. Then, she opened to him on the third touch, tasting and dancing as he wrapped both arms around her back and deepened the kiss. Erica felt him, all of him pressed against her. Even with her oversized clothes, she could still get tan lines, so she'd gone without underwear. Her hardened nipples told Archer exactly how she felt about him kissing her. She didn't think she could fake her attraction to him with all her skills and talent.

Erica needed air and space from this potent man. Stepping out of his embrace, she took her hat from his hand and slipped her glasses over her eyes.

"Where should I be at six?" Erica said with a shaky breath, trying to control her blood pressure.

"I'll pick you up at half five, and we can take a leisurely stroll to the main house."

"Okay," she answered, feeling her smile spread. He'd be there with her the whole time. The scary aunt could do what she wanted if Archer stood by her side.

"You're full of words today, honey," he whispered, leaning in once more to plant a kiss on her lips. "If you're going down to the beach, the tide is coming in. Don't be tempted to go across the causeway."

"I'll take a stroll along the shoreline and then come back. What are you up to?"

"Bailey has a long list of equipment to fix. I've spent the morning in the kitchen repairing the toaster and the taps in the mud room."

"I bet this place would keep a team in full-time employment fixing things."

"Yeah, it seems to be that way. Bailey and Maggie tell me they usually get someone up from the town if it's a vital piece of equipment. Apparently, a toaster doesn't rank up high on the list, but I remember Bailey used to love his toast in the morning when the house was quiet. Maggie won't let him anywhere near her ovens."

"I'd better let you go. I think Teddy is waiting for you," she said, spotting the dog over by the gap in the hedge.

She could hear him whine from where they stood, waiting patiently for his master. Erica wanted to call him over but didn't want to interfere with Archer's training of the puppy.

"I'm amazed he's stayed where he is. It's the most behaved he's been since I found him."

"He's cute," she said. "The dog," she added as she sauntered away.

"What about the owner?" he called out.

She chuckled at his question. Then, turning as she walked, she shouted, "in the dog house for running out on me."

Erica jogged away to the sloping pathway down to the beach. She felt lighter now that they'd talked, even though she didn't know why he'd run out.

TWENTY-SEVEN

Erica

Nothing had made her more nervous than meeting Archer's aunt. Auditioning with huge Hollywood stars, interviewing with top directors, stepping up to receive her Oscar. Nothing compared to meeting the formidable woman sitting at the other end of the dining room. The dining table could seat twenty comfortably. Archer had told her it extended for fifty people to dine in the great hall. The cold and draughty room was vast. Chandeliers were high up, dwarfed by the space half the size of a football pitch. If his aunt were attempting intimidation, she'd got it spot on. Erica was seated opposite Archer a third of the way down the table. His aunt was at the head of the table, dressed for dinner in an evening gown and jewels that sparkled under the lights. Archer introduced her to Bailey in the grand foyer, who now stood stoic in the corner awaiting instructions from his mistress.

The clinking of her cutlery seemed to echo throughout the room. Each time she glanced at Archer, he smirked. It was fine for him as he knew all the etiquette required for a five-course dinner with the island's matriarch. Erica was dining with old money, who had exacting standards, and she felt she didn't meet them. As she speared a green bean, Erica idly wondered if Cynthia would talk at any stage during the meal. Since their introduction, which almost had Erica curtseying, nothing further had been said.

They were three courses into their evening, and Archer's aunt hadn't uttered a word. None of them had. A palate cleanser followed a salmon starter, and the main course was finished. Bailey cleared the plates away, and Erica made wide eyes at Archer in a feeble attempt to ask him why there was no conversation. Her family was middle of the road, easy-going but still chatted throughout meal time. Archer clearly couldn't understand what she was attempting to say.

"Have you set a date yet, Archer?" Cynthia asked as Bailey took her plate away.

"We thought we'd have a short engagement, no need to wait when you know you have the one."

Cynthia dropped her chin and stared at Archer, but Erica was staring at Cynthia, gauging her. The older woman reminded her of old Hollywood, saying far more than the words meant. Suspicion laced her words when she spoke again.

"Fools rush in, Archer," she said.

"People only have a long engagement to save for a wedding. We don't have the issue of waiting. We'll speak to the vicar and set a date as soon as possible."

"I imagine there will be some expense, won't there? What about a dress, Erica? You'll want to find the perfect gown to marry Archer Turner, won't you?"

"I will begin at once to search for the dress, Miss

Turner. I can have fittings on the mainland and then bring it back before the wedding."

"Hmm," Cynthia replied. "Flowers, Archer. I'd imagine you'll get those from Narcissi Flower Farm. What about guests? How many are you going to troop through the grounds?"

Erica was watching Archer's reaction to Cynthia's questions. It was veiled in irritation that him getting married was an imposition, but Erica knew differently. Questions flooded Erica's mind. Did Cynthia think she didn't know about the deal? Did Cynthia think Erica was truly in love with Archer and the marriage was genuine?

"There are a lot of questions to answer, Aunt Cynthia," Archer said but looked at Erica. "We can discuss who will and won't be coming to the wedding. Erica and I will go through all the details, and then I can let you know the plan next week. When speaking to the vicar, are there any wedding dates we need to avoid?"

"I'm sure Bailey can tell you what's happening in the wedding hall. I don't get involved with that side of things."

"Okay, I'll talk to Bailey in the morning."

Erica looked directly at Bailey in shock. They were talking about him like he wasn't there. Bailey shook his head infinitesimally at Erica, and she turned her head to look at Archer. A staff member came in, placed a chocolate pudding in front of each of them, and left the room. She was so silent on her feet that Erica hadn't noticed her arrival until the plate came into view.

Erica remained silent for the duration of the dessert course and then coffee with tiny chocolates. Archer's aunt didn't touch her chocolates, but Archer ate one after the other. Four square, delicately decorated chocolates were on a plate in front of her. She took one and ate it whole. The bitterness mixed with raspberry melted on her tongue. For a few seconds, she closed her eyes, savouring the delicious flavours. When she heard Archer chuckle, her eyes snapped open. She glared at him and then looked at Cynthia, wondering what she'd done.

"I think it's time I retired for the evening," Cynthia said.

Bailey was pulling away her chair like a shot as the older woman stood.

"Bailey, can you send hot cocoa to my room in an hour?"

"Of course, Miss Turner," he said and moved out of the way.

"Erica, would you mind walking me out?" Cynthia asked.

Shocked at the request, Erica looked to Archer for confirmation. He dropped his napkin and stood.

"No, Archer, just Erica. She can come back for you when we've reached our destination," Cynthia replied.

Erica placed her napkin on the table, regretting not following Archer's lead and wolfing all four chocolates. Giving the treats a baleful look, she dragged herself away and headed to the end of the table where Cynthia was waiting. Erica was surprised when she hooked her arm through hers. With surprising strength, Erica was propelled forward towards the door. It opened as soon as they were near, and Erica spotted Bailey on the other side.

Cynthia cleared her throat when they were free of the dining room and walking across the grand foyer.

"I am fully aware of who you are, even if my nephew is not. I imagine with your wealth, you are not after his money."

"How do you know who I am?"

"We make it our business to know who stays on the property."

"We?"

"Oh, don't worry, Archer is blind and clueless to a two-bit actress like you. Let me be very clear. You have committed to being his wife. That ring on your finger has been in the family for hundreds of years. You will see this marriage through and never seek a divorce. I will have it added into my will that if you divorce Archer Turner, he and his siblings will lose their entire inheritance."

"I don't understand?"

"The Turners marry for life immaterial if it's a love match or not."

"I'm a divorcee," Erica said.

"That information was clear on your report. I understand he had an affair and is having a child with another woman. If Archer strays, you will turn a blind eye."

"The hell I will."

"Think about Archer, his inheritance, and what he wants to do for his siblings. The apple doesn't fall far from the tree Miss Taylor or is it Mrs Potter?"

"Taylor is my maiden name. Potter was my married name."

"And Turner will be your next and final name."

"This is the 21st century."

"Then give the ring back to me now. I'll break the news to Archer, and you can scurry off the island in the morning."

"I'm not going anywhere."

"Glad to hear it, dear," she said, patting Erica's hand and walking up the staircase to the upper floor.

Erica felt tiny in the grand foyer, wondering what she'd got herself into. When she agreed to marry Archer, she thought it would be just them. But, to have the head of the Turner family dictating what she would put up in a marriage made it very real that she was making a lifelong commitment. Archer had told her she could walk away as soon as they were married. Did he know she was locked in for life if he was to secure his sibling's future?

"Everything okay?" Archer asked, approaching her from across the hall.

He'd worn a navy suit with a white shirt and matching blue tie. In his hand was a napkin. When he stood in front of Erica at the bottom of the staircase, he opened the corners of the bundle of fabric to show her half a dozen chocolates.

"You moaned like you did last night when you ate your chocolate. I want a private audience as you eat these," he said.

"Archer," she said, holding back her tears.

She couldn't handle his thoughtfulness, kindness, and observation of her enjoyment of the chocolates. The coldness coming from his aunt had been a bucket of ice water over her entire body.

He brought her into a tight hold, crushing her to him, carefully keeping the chocolates out of the way. "Whatever she said to you, ignore her. Please tell me you're not having second thoughts."

"She's from another world. I feel like I'm in a tailspin."

Archer brought her to arm's length to look at her. Erica saw his concern etched all over his face and her throat burned from his aunt's words. Her diva persona wanted to yell up the stairs that she had an academy award but stayed mute as the older woman dictated to her.

"What the fuck did she say?"

"Nothing, nothing Archer, it's all good. I haven't changed my mind. I'll be at the altar in a white dress and be your wife. Nothing to worry about here."

"That's three nothings in one speech. It sounds like to me you're going to bolt as soon as I turn my back."

"I have no reason to lie to you, Archer," she said, patting the flat of her hand on his chest.

The heat from his shirt made her keep her hand on his pectoral. She swished her hand to the left and then groaned. He was too delicious for words. Archer put his hand on top of hers, curling his fingers around her hand, and stepped closer.

"Are you feeling me up, honey?" he said in a low voice that set her insides on fire.

"You're insanely handsome. My hands have a mind of their own. I should get back to my cottage."

"Am I invited? A nightcap perhaps," he asked, inching nearer, dropping his head to touch his lips to hers.

Archer brushed his mouth slowly, softly, kissing her with tenderness. She melted against him as his kiss became firmer, his breathing heavier. She was getting carried away, floating with his dizzying kiss.

Breaking their connection, her chest heaving as she took a deep breath. "Archer," she said.

"Erica," he said softly, offering her the napkin of chocolates.

"You can come back only if you don't run out on me again," she said.

"Let's make a pact. I won't run out on you if you don't run out on me."

There wasn't any way Erica would renege on her side of the bargain, not when his siblings depended on this match.

"It's a deal. But can we drop the nightcap stuff? I feel like I'm living in another era. This whole place feels like it is stuck in time."

"Why do you think we all moved away, honey?"

That comment made her sad. The buildings were magnificent, and the art and decorative features were spectacular. She could imagine Turner Hall being a setting for a period drama or a movie set. The thought of the family moving away to get a hold of 21st-century life was too much for her to handle.

"I'm sorry, Archer. I didn't mean to make light of where you grew up."

Archer smiled warmly and took her hand. She linked their fingers and squeezed, relishing the warmth of his hand.

"Let's go back to your place. I feel at home there."

Erica's heart swelled at his words. Never did she think a marriage pact would have been this way. She felt more for this man than she had for her first husband. Could she handle marrying his aunt, too, because she thought there would be more than just her in the marriage of convenience?

TWENTY-EIGHT

Archer

Erica woke him up the following morning while she was asleep, mumbling about raspberries and chocolate. He'd slipped out of bed, hoping she wouldn't wake before returning with the napkin he'd put in her fridge when they'd arrived back the previous night. Archer wasn't feeling like drinking anymore after the wine they'd had with their meal. So they skipped the nightcap.

Locking the back door once they were inside, he took her hand and led Erica to her bed. She didn't resist his move, and he was fucking delighted after he'd high-tailed it out of her bed the last time they'd had sex.

"You're hot," Archer said, lying prone on Erica's bed between her legs, lining up the sweets on her stomach.

"Why, thank you, Archer."

"Your skin is hot, and the chocolates are melting. Hang on. I need to lick it away."

Hearing Erica giggle when his tongue swept over a crumb of chocolate on her ribs under her breast was the best sound in the world. He'd kept his promise and stayed with her tucked against his side all night. Unlike last time, Archer didn't feel the need to run away from the intensity of their connection. He was still thoroughly mixed up about how he should feel. This was an arrangement, yet he could see a future for them. It was evident by the look of fright on Erica's face the previous night that his aunt had scared her or threatened her. Family or not, Archer would shield her from the old ways. His aunt could have her conditions, but they did not include scaring off his temporary wife.

He kissed her stomach and ate one of the chocolates in one go. Then kissed another part of her skin until he reached her breasts and swirled his chocolate-coated tongue over her nipple. After lapping at the hardened bud until it was clean, he took the last chocolate. He brought it up to her lips, brushing it across her bottom lip, smearing the melted gooeyness. Archer swiped, drawing a moan from Erica's throat. She arched her back when he plunged inside her mouth, their tongues swirling. He hooked a hand under her thigh to bring it up high so he could settle his hips between hers.

"This is what lazy Sundays are for, fucking and eating unhealthy food," he said.

"I've never had time for a lazy any day, let alone a Sunday."

"You sound like a workaholic," he muttered as he pushed his hips to simulate what he really wanted to do.

The condoms were just out of reach. Archer didn't want to move from the cradle Erica had created with her arms and legs wrapped around him. They fit together perfectly. He kissed her neck while she hummed her approval, tilting her hips in response to his caress.

"Make me forget I have a job," she said.

Reaching for the wrapper, Archer sheathed and pushed inside Erica.

Fucking heaven.

She released a soft gasp as he pushed as far as their bodies could. The first stroke nearly sent him over the edge. Mindful that Erica took longer to come than he did, Archer took his thrusts slow. Agonising as it was to hold back, he wanted to get her there from his cock. It was a prideful, ridiculous primal need to ensure his woman was taken care of.

"Archer." She whispered his name as a prayer on her lips.

"Yeah, honey?"

"I'm not far," she said.

Her forehead hit his shoulder as she lifted her hips faster to meet him halfway. She was working her friction, and her moans became louder. Archer thought he'd have to wear earplugs the next time because the sounds Erica made when she was nearing her orgasm were too erotic for his control.

"Shall I help?" he whispered, licking the shell of her ear.

"Wow, that feels fantastic," she said.

Archer did it again and slipped a hand between them to find her bundle of nerves. As he stroked his finger, he felt the first pulse on his cock. Keeping to the same motion, Archer kept going for two more thrusts, and then he came so hard. Erica was tight around him, slowing her hips as he kept going. When she tipped over, he thought he was done for. The sensations he felt were crazy hard, getting him half stiff or still stiff. He wasn't sure. Meeting her tempo, he slowed until she sagged back against the pillows. Bringing her face into focus, he kissed her lips and then her forehead.

Archer rolled to the side breathing heavily, taking her

hand in his as he stared at the ceiling. He waited for the urge to get up and leave, but it never came. He was content to lie there in silence with Erica's hand in his. A call to his siblings was waiting for him as they'd been blowing up his phone all day yesterday asking how the meeting had gone, forgetting the time difference between the UK and wherever they were.

"I'm not running out on you, but I have to make a call. I won't be long," Archer said, lifting her hand and kissing her palm.

"Sounds intriguing," she said, turning to her side, giving him a full view of her breasts.

"My brothers and sister. We check in on Sundays now that we're all apart."

"I love that you're close to them. It must be lovely."

Archer cupped her chin, hearing the loneliness in her words. "They drive me insane, but I love them. I'll be right back."

He gave her a quick kiss and then went to her bathroom to take a quick shower. When he returned, Erica was fast asleep with the covers tucked under her chin. He paused for a few moments to let the picture sink into his memory bank. She looked vulnerable, curled into a ball, but beautiful.

He hurried to retrieve his phone and went downstairs to the outside patio. His message alerts filled his screen as he scrolled on the lock screen. They were all from his brothers. His sister, Daisy, hadn't sent a single one. Which meant she was already waiting on the group call.

"Hey guys," Archer said cheerily, giving them his fake grin.

"Well?" Daisy asked.

"More specific," Archer replied.

"When's the wedding? What did Aunt Cynthia say?

When can we meet her?" Daisy asked, holding up a finger for each question.

"Okay," Archer said, holding up his hand. "We haven't set a date, but we will as soon as we've seen the vicar. Aunt Cynthia said very little at the get-to-know-you dinner."

Jason snorted, falling back on the bed he was sitting on, holding the phone up so he could still see everyone. "She never says much."

"When can we meet her?" Daisy asked again.

Archer looked at Erica's bedroom for a few seconds and then looked back at the screen. "At the rehearsal dinner."

"She's there, with you?" Luke asked. "Get her in on the call."

"Erica's sleeping. It was a long night," he said.

"I bet," Luke said.

"Eww," Daisy replied.

"You can meet her at the rehearsal dinner in a couple of months."

"That long?" Daisy whined her words in frustration.

"We have to meet the vicar and set the date, which will be at least a month. There is so much paperwork involved. Then there is Erica's dress and all the arrangements here. I know the wedding manager here will have it all to hand, but I'm sure Erica will want things the way she wants. I'm not fussed, so she can have whatever she wants."

"Have you met the wedding manager yet?" Jason asked.

"No, not yet. To be honest, I've only met the gardener who I didn't know. Bailey and Maggie are keeping information on a need-to-know basis."

"Isn't that a bit odd?" Luke asked.

"He probably lives in town and only comes up here when there's a wedding."

"When's the next one?" Daisy asked.

"I asked Aunt Cynthia last night, and she said to check with Bailey. I'll do that tomorrow. Anyway, how are you all?"

They all nodded and gave their updates. Archer's mind was firmly with the wedding manager and where he had his office. So many things to sort out he didn't know where to start. When he ended the call with his siblings, he tossed the phone on the couch and went back to bed with Erica.

Everything could wait until the following day.

TWENTY-NINE

Erica

After another gruelling week of cardiovascular workouts and breathing exercises, Erica saw improvement. Archer came each morning and mostly kept his hands to himself. She raced over the logs and climbed the tree Archer had picked out for endurance. Bit by bit, he'd built an organic obstacle course. In the afternoons, she practised yoga. Her physique for the movie was lean and not bulky. When Saturday morning arrived, she woke early to prepare for their trip to the flower fields on the other side of the small island. Erica had read the island used to have dozens of flower farms but now only had a handful. They were heading to the Narcissi Flower Farm. Lounging on the couches outside, she picked up the novel Yanny had sent her, along with the rest of the mail he thought she should see. While she was thinking about Yanny, her phone rang. There was no number, but then very few people knew her private number. Specifically, the number they were dialling was Erica Taylor, the Oscar-winning actress.

"Hello," she said, putting it on speakerphone while she continued reading.

"Is this Erica?"

She stayed quiet, not confirming or denying, allowing for an uncomfortable silence until the caller made a decision. They either hung up or introduced themselves.

"My name is Jason Turner. I believe you are going to marry my brother."

Erica snatched up the phone and switched off the speakerphone.

"This is Erica," she replied.

"The same Erica who is going to marry Archer?"

"Yes."

"Can we switch to video call?"

"No, why would you want to do that? It's early."

"I don't give a shit about the time difference, sweetheart. I want to see the face of the woman who bizarrely has agreed to get hitched to the Turner family."

"Just Archer," Erica replied.

"If you think you're just marrying Archer, then he hasn't introduced you to our aunt like he said he had."

A chill down Erica's spine made her shudder. He'd confirmed her suspicions, and she didn't feel good about it.

"I've met your aunt. She's lovely," Erica said.

She wanted to play the fool for a little while. Years of journalists attempting to trick her into saying stuff she didn't mean had her attention set to wary.

Jason let out a howling laugh in response to her comment. She smiled back even though he couldn't see it. She was tempted to switch her video camera on, but her wariness remained on high alert.

"So he has introduced you. It looks like I might like my

new sister-in-law. Tell me, Erica, are you Erica Taylor or Erica Potter?"

Now grateful she hadn't opted for a video call, she brought the phone away from her ear and pressed the speaker button. Placing the device carefully on the tabletop like it was a bomb ready to go off, she remained mute.

"My lovely aunt called me late last night and left me a voicemail, telling me my brother was marrying a two-bit actress. Perhaps I should ensure your intentions are long term."

Jason had emphasised *lovely* when he spoke about his aunt, revealing his dislike for the woman in his tone. She couldn't stay quiet for much longer else, the answer would be obvious.

"I think your aunt may have me confused with someone else."

"Like an Oscar-winning actress?"

"Jason, I have to go. Archer is walking across the lawn towards me."

He was nowhere in sight, but she wanted off the call with Archer's brother without seeming rude.

"I'll take it you are the one and only Erica Taylor who won an Oscar. A character in the film about a woman who enters into an arranged marriage and gets the shock of her life."

"You saw the film?"

"Of course, I saw the film. Half the world saw the film. You're fucking famous without your scumbag husband cheating on you."

"He's not my husband," she replied.

"That's not what the press are saying."

"Don't believe everything you read, Jason. The divorce came through a couple of months ago. It appears he didn't tell his new girlfriend, who confronted me ten minutes before I went up and collected my award, seven months pregnant with his child."

"Wow, she's got some front to do that."

"I split up from my ex-husband a while ago," Erica said a little quieter.

"I'm sorry, that's rough. He's a fool."

"It's in the past."

"I guess you don't value marriage in the same way anymore, which is why you so readily agreed to marry Archer."

"Something like that."

"He's a good guy, Erica."

"Yeah, I'm beginning to see that. Will I have Luke and Daisy calling me too?"

"I doubt it, my aunt doesn't like them, and I'm not going to tell them."

"Thanks, Jason."

"I'm keeping quiet for now. When they find out I knew, I'll be roasted for years, so this plan had better work."

"I understand what's a stake. No marriage, no business, no jobs for you, no place to settle as a family. I get it."

"What do you get out of this?"

Erica remained quiet. She didn't know anymore. When she didn't really know Archer, the marriage could save her pride in the public eye if they knew not only was she already divorced, she had remarried. But now? She didn't know why she continued with the façade if his aunt insisted on a minimum of one year of marriage.

"I don't need the money. I'm going to be a nice person. It's better I do this than some money-grabbing woman who wouldn't be nice to Archer. Not everyone has to have an agenda."

"Oh, Erica, you like him."

Erica rolled his eyes at his tone, all gushing. What wasn't to like? Archer was handsome, kind, and determined to take care of his siblings, even entering into a fake marriage for their sake.

"He's a great person. Of course, I like him. Do you think I'd fake marry a horrible person?"

It was Jason's turn to be silent.

"Are you still there?"

"Yeah, just thinking. Listen, I need to go, but we'll talk again soon. Do not let my aunt intimidate you."

He didn't let her reply before he hung up the phone. A few minutes later, she was still staring at the blank screen of her phone when Archer called out from across the lawn. She watched him approach in long navy shorts and a buttoned pale blue shirt. Teddy was at his side, half running, half walking to keep up with Archer.

Erica stood, brushed down her linen trousers, and went to meet him at the opening in the wall. He kissed her soundly, holding her tight. He nuzzled her neck and then stepped back.

"Everything okay? We can go another day," he said.

She thought she was better at hiding her agitation, but with Archer, he sensed the discomfort of her call with his brother. Jason was going to keep her secret, not that she knew why it should be a secret. Erica searched her mind to understand why she hadn't mentioned she was an actress. It was easy enough to say. She had nothing to share about the humiliating press coverage of her ex-husband parading around with a woman pregnant with their child when they were clearly still married. The press covered every aspect of her life and documented proof that she and her husband were still together when you calculated the child's conception.

"Just work stuff earlier, my manager rang to say there was a delay somewhere along the chain, and I may have to leave at a different time."

"Oh, not sooner, I hope?"

"Probably later. It could coincide with getting my wedding dress."

Archer squeezed her hand and smiled wide, seemingly mollified that all was okay. "Okay, let's go and look at some flowers."

THIRTY

Archer

Archer entered the back door of the kitchens to find Maggie at the stove frying bacon. He felt like the bisto kid inhaling a lung full of the amazing smells.

"Are you hungry?" she called over her shoulder without looking at him.

"Always Maggie," he replied.

"You'll have to eat toast tomorrow along with Bailey. This is the last of the bacon until I can get down into the high street."

"What?" he barked in mock outrage. "No bacon sandwich?"

With the frying pan in hand, Maggie turned in a circle and walked over to the side bench, chuckling.

"Yes, Archer, you'll cope."

"I don't think I will. Is there a national shortage?"

"No. But I'm too busy to leave Turner Hall. You've eaten through my bacon stocks. Miss Turner doesn't eat it. It's only you and Bailey."

"I'll go for you. Is there anything else you need from the butcher?"

"No, Archer. I wouldn't make you go and see the butcher."

"He's still my grandfather even if his daughter ran off and left us."

"Oh, Archer. I'm sure she had her reasons."

"A mother abandoning her four kids, never to be heard from again but apparently is still alive? Yeah, sure, there's bound to be a really great reason for never getting in contact with her children. Not even when her husband died. They never divorced, so she was still his wife."

Archer couldn't keep the bitterness out of his voice. Maggie put the pan down and came over to the bench seat at the kitchen table. Her plump body twisted at the waist, and she wrapped her arms around his body from the side. The harder she squeezed him, the more Archer wanted to lash out. Being hugged by his childhood cook and surrogate mother felt safe and comforting.

"I'm sorry, Archer. I'll get the bacon."

"I'll get the bacon," Archer replied. He looped his arm around to bring her head in close, and he kissed into her hair. "Give me the list, and I'll get everything you need."

"Why don't I phone it through, and you just need to pop in and pick it up. If you don't want to stay and talk then, it will minimise the awkwardness."

"Okay," he said, patting her arm to encourage her to move out of her motherly hold before he started sobbing. "Sounds like a plan."

While Maggie busied herself making his bacon sandwich, his mind drifted back to a couple of days ago when he walked through the rows of narcissi at the farm. Erica had never visited a flower farm before and was in awe of the thousands of flowering plants as far as the eye could see. All the flower farms were part of their upbringing. As the eldest, he could remember going with his parents and grandparents numerous times. His sister Daisy hadn't had the opportunity to run through pathways with their mother. She'd left when Daisy was six months old. His brother Jason had some knowledge of going out as a family, but not many he admits to remembering. Luke was a toddler at two and a half years and remembered little at all. Jason was angry, he was bitter, Luke was indifferent, and Daisy was nostalgic for a mother she'd never met.

He managed to pry out Bailey and Maggie other items they needed in town and took the golf buggy down the hill to collect provisions. Ordinarily, they would have to wait a week or fetch it themselves. With only Erica as a guest, who Maggie told him wanted very little in food requirements over the stock items they'd provided, they only needed to feed themselves and his aunt.

Parking up in a side street, he walked straight to the butchers to get it over with first. When he arrived at the window-fronted establishment, he found there was a queue out the door. The green metal strands acting as a curtain to keep the flies out swished as each person left and the next ventured inside. As soon as he stepped over the threshold, his name was called out.

Archer looked to the man, his grandfather, his mother's father. Pete Boyle. The white-haired man with a ruddy complexion and the bluest eyes was happy to see him. Archer noted he was much slimmer than when he last saw him but looked in good health.

"Maggie said you were coming to collect her order. It's good to see you, Archer," Pete said, coming around the glass counter and bringing Archer in for a bear hug. "It's been too long, and Betty will be thrilled that you're back."

Mrs Boyle was never as joyful when speaking with Archer but was polite.

"You're looking well, Pete," Archer replied when he was let out of the second hug of the morning.

"Thanks," he said and returned to his side of the counter and disappeared out the back, coming straight back with a tray of meat.

"Here's Maggie's order. Lucy has your vegetables next door."

"Okay, thanks," I pop in there next.

"Is Jason, Luke, and Daisy here too?"

"No, not yet."

"How long are you here on the island?"

"It could be forever. It depends on my aunt's mood."

Pete Boyle nodded sagely, his smile slipping from his face. "Well, I hope it goes in your favour. It would be great to see you all back."

Archer nodded, not commenting, and lifted the tray of food to wave farewell.

"Come into The Anchor for a pint. I'm there most evenings," Pete called out to his back.

"Will do," Archer replied, leaving the butcher's shop so others could come in.

He took the fully laden buggy back to the kitchens after a quick trip to the greengrocers and two other shops. He unloaded everything while Bailey and Maggie ferried the food to their rightful places.

"When are we going to meet the future Mrs Turner?" Maggie asked when all the produce was put away.

"Who?"

"We know everything, Archer. The woman you've proposed to, Erica, I think her name is."

"Yeah," Archer said, rubbing the back of his neck with one hand. "I am getting married—Erica Taylor, who is staying in the cottage."

"That's fast work," she answered.

"When you know, you know, ya know," he replied.

"Bring her with one morning for breakfast. She must be running out of food by now."

"I will. Is the mistress of the house in the morning room?"

"Yes, Bailey has just taken her a pot of tea."

"Okay, I'll see you later. If you need me to make another trip, let me know."

He left Maggie in the kitchen, raced up the stairs to the grand foyer, and strode across the marble floor. When his aunt was holed away in her greenhouse, he'd skid along the floor in his socks as it was the only big space where he could mess about as a kid and not knock over a family heirloom when it was raining. Grinning at the memories of happier times when he and Jason introduced their dad to skidding around, he entered the morning room. When the door was open, it permitted anyone to enter unannounced. He hated he had to knock on a closed door before he was allowed to enter, especially when it was the living room.

"Hello, aunt," he said as he entered the room.

Aunt Cynthia was in a pair of tartan slacks and a twin set. One strand of pearls around her neck.

"I hear you went into town today to see that man," she said without looking at him.

Something had her attention out of the window. Archer betted it was a blade of grass.

"I went into town to pick up Maggie's meat order."

"And to speak with Imelda's father," she said.

Imelda was his mother, the butcher's daughter, and not the woman his father was supposed to marry. His aunt had spent every day after Imelda had walked out of the family saying *I told you so* in a million different ways.

"We spoke yes, he is my grandfather."

"Your grandfather is dead, Archer."

"I have two. You can't change that fact. You can't rub my mother's family off the family tree."

Cynthia turned to him, a saucer balanced on her palm and the cup midway to her lips. "You want to make a bet about that?"

"My mother has nothing to do with you. My father's marriage has nothing to do with you. So why do you hate Mr Boyle, anyway?"

"It doesn't matter. The fact is, you're following in your father's footsteps, marrying the first woman to turn your head and not look for good stock to continue the Turner line."

"You've forced my hand with your ridiculous conditions."

"I gave you three months. There's plenty of time to find a better wife."

"You don't know anything about Erica."

"I know all I need to."

"If Erica is not good enough and I'm not allowed to whore my way around town, how the hell am I supposed to find a wife to meet your criteria?"

"We can arrange a match from the lower-level aristocracy."

"No. We made a deal. I find a wife, and you give me the business. That's it."

"You're no better than your father."

"I'll take that as a compliment because, despite your best efforts, he was a fantastic dad."

He didn't let her reply and carried on. "Where can I get in touch with the wedding manager?"

"Ask Bailey."

"He doesn't know who he is. So back to you, where can I get in touch with the wedding manager for Edward Hall. Does he live in town?"

"He lives on the mainland."

"Then I need his number to help Erica, and I organise the celebrations."

"What celebrations? You go to church, get married, and then we come back here for afternoon tea."

"Times have moved on. Erica and I will want to celebrate with our friends."

In truth, he had no idea what Erica wanted, but he was on a roll, pushing his luck.

"I'll locate the paperwork and leave it out for you."

"Thank you."

Archer left the morning room and passed Bailey on the threshold, they nodded, and Archer marched out of Turner Hall to find Erica.

THIRTY-ONE

Erica

Archer pulled his body out of the pool in that sexy way only men could do with powerful upper body strength. The water dripped off him like he was under a shower. Erica ogled him for a few minutes as he twisted to sit on the pool's edge. She marvelled at her soon-to-be fake husband, wondering if she could keep it strictly business. Licking her lips and then ducking under the water, Erica swam to where he was sitting and emerged between his splayed legs. Resting her hands on his thighs, she looked up at his face, and his chin dropped to gaze back.

"Are you ready to meet the vicar?" he asked, hooking his hands under her armpits and lifting her clear out of the water to plant a kiss on her lips. He lifted her higher, and Erica straddled him, balancing precariously on his thighs. Archer held her tight until she settled.

"I feel nervous. My last wedding was done in the local council offices," Erica said.

She stiffened when she ran through what information was required. If Archer noticed, he didn't say anything.

"The vicar will put you at ease. Of course, it helps that you and I like each other, not that the vicar will care if this is a love match or not. He's been the vicar on the island since he was eighteen, so he is probably too old to be too curious."

"Is he friends with your aunt?"

"Most definitely," Archer replied.

She sank down on his legs, relief flooding her. If the vicar were friends with his aunt, then the meeting would go in their favour. Erica had the feeling Archer's aunt would ensure there would be no hiccups. Archer grabbed her arse and pulled her closer, getting her to sit directly on his hardness.

"Visiting the vicar turns you on?" Erica asked, shifting from side to side.

"You in a bikini turns me on. It won't long before our training sessions will be over, so I'm making the most of the view."

"Time seems to be flying so fast."

"When we see the vicar today, he should be able to marry us within one month, then that will leave you free to go."

His words hurt her heart. She was so at home in his arms that leaving seemed a lonely prospect. Archer was matter of fact even if his erection and hands said otherwise. At every turn, he was reminding her the arrangement was temporary. She could leave in a couple of months, except his aunt had thrown in the never get divorced clause. Had Cynthia done the same to Archer? Erica dared not ask. Otherwise, Archer might ask more questions about what his aunt had said to her.

"How long will the meeting be?"

"Twenty minutes tops. I have an outing planned for us first," Archer said.

"Sounds mysterious."

"You'll have to wait and see. But first, we need breakfast, and Maggie wants to meet you."

"The famous cook of Turner Hall."

"The very same. Maker of the best bacon sandwiches. You don't have to eat them. She can make you anything you want."

"I'm not a fan of bread. Well, my stomach is not a fan of bread. I can watch you devour your breakfast like a caveman."

"Caveman, eh?"

Archer shifted his hips, inching near the edge of the pool. He had a wicked gleam in his eye.

"I think you'll find I'm a gentleman," he said. "But for that comment," he added, dropping Erica into the water.

He was standing on the edge of the concrete path when she came back up, pushing her hair off her face.

"I was comfy there," Erica said through a laugh.

Archer gave her a cheeky grin, hands on his hips highlighting the muscles at the edge of his shorts.

"Can't get too used to comfiness, Erica. I'm taking my caveman ass off to get changed. I'll meet you back here in half an hour."

"All right. I'm sorry about the caveman remark. I didn't mean it," Erica called out to his back, walking away. Archer lifted his arms and flexed his muscles in a Popeye move.

Erica sank into the water, treading as she worked her legs and arms, watching him move until he turned the corner around the side of Turner Hall. Then, with a long sigh, Erica swam to the other side of the pool and used the metal steps to get out of the pool. Grabbing her towel, she wrapped her body up and walked back to her cottage. When she met with the vicar, she would have to state her profession for the paperwork which would end up on the marriage certificate. It was on the tip of her tongue to confess when he had her arms around her, but she backed out. Maybe the vicar won't ask, and she can fill in a form.

THIRTY-TWO

Erica

Erica showered, dressed, and was back at the pool in forty-five minutes. Archer was already there, which was no surprise to her as he was on time for everything.

"Being late is diva behaviour," he said as he greeted her with a kiss.

"I have been known for my outrageous behaviour. It's been fully documented."

It wasn't a lie. Erica had very little concept of time. She was ready when she was ready. Everyone put up with it, so she made no amends to change her ways. Archer got her to focus on arriving where you said you'd be when you agreed. Fifteen minutes late was a record for her.

"Good job Maggie doesn't start cooking until we get there. Let's go," he said, holding out his hand.

Erica took it. It only took a few minutes to get to the kitchen door. Archer ducked under to walk through the door opening, and Erica followed, clutching his hand. Each time she met a new person, the expected reaction was familiarity. When Archer didn't know who Erica was, it was refreshing and wonderful to be normal. But as soon as Erica locked eyes with Maggie, she knew she was busted.

"Oh my, Erica," Maggie said, rushing over to take her in a hug. "It's so wonderful to meet you. Erica Taylor in my kitchen, whoever would have thought it."

"All right, Maggie, bit over the top, isn't it?"

"You brought Erica Taylor to meet me," Maggie said.

"Because you asked to meet her. You also promised you'd feed us. We're starving from the morning workout. What's on offer?" Archer said, rounding the kitchen table and dropping onto the bench seat. He patted the space next to him for Erica to join him, but she stayed rooted to the spot. She was pleading internally that Maggie didn't mention anything further. Erica waited for Maggie to turn her back and begin preparations for breakfast. When she thought the coast was clear, she shuffled along the bench to sit next to Archer.

"Ignore Maggie. She is beside herself there is more than Bailey and Jennifer in the house, along with my aunt. We've swollen the numbers."

"Who is Jennifer?"

"My aunt's maid, dresser, I don't know what the modern word for it would be. She gets my aunt up in the mornings and dressed these days and then gets her ready for bed. Years ago she would accompany her everywhere she went. Overseas or to the mainland. A lady's maid would be what she would've been called back in the early 1900s. My aunt still lives in those times, so she treats Jennifer as a personal maid even though my aunt never leaves the house."

"Will I meet her?"

195

"Maybe. She is the same age as my aunt and stays upstairs most of the time."

Maggie turned to face them, looked to Archer, and then pointed to the teapot. "Pour the tea, Archer. Erica, what can I make you for breakfast?"

"I love some scrambled eggs and bacon," she replied, having given it a lot of thought when she was showering. Her lateness gave her the diva tag out in the movie world, but for everything else, she tried to make sure she wasn't too fussy, keeping things simple.

"Cheese in your scrambled eggs?"

"Ohh, why not? I've never had that before," Erica said.

"All right, sit tight, and I'll get the food on the go. Archer, I assume you'll have your usual?"

"Absolutely. I've earned it. And I'll probably earn it later too. We're going to Little Lagoon after we've eaten."

"Oh, you'll have a fabulous time," Maggie said, aiming her comment at Erica. "Archer, Jason, Luke, and Daisy spent a lot of time down there when they were younger."

"No more information, Maggie. It's a surprise," Archer said.

He'd dropped his hand to Erica's leg, his palm resting on her thigh. Archer poured the tea one-handed and pushed a cup and saucer her way. The pretty blue and white flowers on the dainty cup were a contrast to the sturdy mugs in the cottage.

"I know. They're tiny, right? Three sips, and the tea is gone. I have eight cups when I have breakfast here, but Maggie won't hear of having a mug in her kitchen. I guess we've all got our old school traits."

"What's yours?" Erica asked.

"I'd have to think about that. What do I still do now that

I've always done?" Archer was talking out loud, looking to the ceiling and tapping his finger to his chin.

"Family, no matter what, I suppose. I could never walk away from being a Turner, even though I happily stayed away from my childhood home. I'd do anything for Jason, Luke, and Daisy."

"Admirable, Archer," Bailey said as he entered the kitchen. "You have another name to add to the list now."

Archer turned to Erica and kissed her cheek. "I do," he said.

Should she tell him now, Erica thought? Now she wished Maggie had outed her. It would be a lot easier than at the vicarage.

"Here is your food," Maggie said, placing two plates in front of them. "Enjoy."

Erica looked at her cheesy scrambled egg on a bed of spinach. Cherry tomatoes cut in half were in with the eggs giving the whole plate a look of decadence and healthiness at the same time.

"This looks fantastic. It certainly beats my usual toast and marmalade," Erica said.

"Exactly," Archer replied, pointing his fork at Maggie. "Who wants toast when you have this?"

Two slices of bread popped out of the toaster, and Bailey dropped them onto a plate. He smeared butter and then jam.

"As toast offends you so much, I shall take this to my office," he said in a haughty tone.

Archer and Maggie giggled as Bailey walked away.

"Is he okay?" Erica asked, feeling guilty about her comment.

"Yeah. Bailey has a routine and likes to stick to it."

"That's his old school trait," Erica muttered before

taking a forkful of eggs. She resisted moaning after her spectacle eating a petit four at the formal dinner with Archer's aunt. Instead, she squeezed her thighs together at the buttery, cheesy eggs and closed her eyes.

"You eat like you have never tasted food before," Archer commented.

"I'm not a great cook, fairly plain and basic, so if someone so much as puts pepper in a meal, I swoon."

"I'll remember that when I need to apologise."

"Is that likely?"

"I'm a man, so I'll likely do something that will need some kind of sorry."

The three of them laughed at his comment. When breakfast was over, he put the dishes in the hot soapy water to wash up. Maggie told him to leave the dishes to her and get going to the surprise date. Erica loved their relationship. It was easy going with a healthy dose of ribbing, even from Bailey, who came back in with his plate of crumbs and then grabbed the bacon warming in the oven Maggie had put to one side.

Archer told her they would walk to where they were going. It would give them time to digest their food before they got there. Curious about what he had planned, she had convinced herself he was taking her to a fete where there were fairground rides.

She couldn't have been more wrong.

They arrived at a pale blue painted wooden shack with wetsuits hanging outside. The door was wedged open. Archer went inside and returned with a man with shaggy hair still wet. His wet suit was peeled down to his waist, showing off his tanned chest. His wiry frame looked strong.

Archer beckoned her over to where they were standing on uneven ground, a mix of pebbles and dirt.

"You need to wear a wetsuit for what we're doing. The water can be cold out of the sun. Do you want a wet suit to the knee or the ankle?"

She instantly thought about tan lines and hated herself for that being her initial reason for her decision.

"A full wetsuit if you have one in my size," she said.

"Okay," the shaggy-haired guy said and disappeared back into the shed. He popped his head back out and said, "what size feet are you?"

"Five."

If he recognised Erica, he didn't give any indication. Coming to the island was a genius idea of Yanny's, and maybe she could risk going into the town if hardly anyone knew who she was.

"That's Keith, my brother Jason's best friend growing up. They fell out a while back, and I don't think they've spoken for years. He runs the sports tours. Keith is an amazing surfer, but his day job is working the tourist boats."

"Is that what we're doing?" Erica asked.

"We'll go out in the boat, and then when it's safe, we'll go in the sea. It's a small lagoon around here. Keith will take us out, and we'll snorkel back."

"Oh cool, sounds great."

"With the seals," he added.

Erica's mouth dropped open and then grinned hard at Archer. "Oh wow, that's amazing."

"I haven't done it for a long time. Back when we were kids, we didn't have any safety measures. There was no ringed area, to make sure we didn't get swept out to sea or encounter a curious shark."

"Sharks?"

Archer laughed. She put her hands to her cheeks in fright.

"Don't worry. We'll be in the lagoon the whole time. No sharks can get in there unless they can jump the rocks."

Keith came out of the shack carrying a wetsuit on a hanger. The navy blue with a white stripe suit down the side had arms and legs.

"This should fit you fine. You can change in the shack. Just move the pebble to close the door. There's a latch."

Erica thanked Keith and went to change in the dark shack with no windows. She folded her dress and draped it over the back of the chair rammed up against a wooden table. The only things on the desk were an open laptop and half a mug of tea. She noticed there was no password protection screen, just an open tab for a social media site. The whole island seemed to be trusting.

Wedging the door back open, Erica headed back to where Archer and Keith looked to be in a heated discussion.

"I haven't spoken to him for years, and I don't plan to change that." Erica heard Keith tell Archer.

"Okay, none of my business. You both seemed close when we were teenagers."

"A lot of time has passed. We all grow up."

Archer turned his attention to Erica, ending the friction and uneasy atmosphere.

"Let's get you out on the water," Keith said, heading back to the shack. He went inside and came straight out, kicking the pebble and closing the door. There was a padlock at the top, and he clipped it shut. Not so trusting, after all, Erica thought.

Archer and Erica followed Keith to the small boat with a motor at the back. In the time Erica had changed, so had Archer. His suit was short sleeves and ended at the knee, showcasing his muscular calves. They walked over the large pebbles and then onto the sand. The small blue boat was hooked up to a small jetty. Archer got in after Keith and held out his hand for Erica to throw her leg over.

She fell into the boat unceremoniously in fits of giggles.

"Graceful," Archer commented with a smirk, helping her up.

Erica sat on a bench seat opposite Archer and looked out into the lagoon. She hadn't noticed on the sand, but the breeze picked up, making her hair fly about. She took the ends and held them while the boat bounced on the water. Archer sidled across, grabbed her hair at her nape, and then tucked the wayward strands into the back of her wet suit. She gave him a shy smile at his consideration. It wasn't long before Keith slowed the boat and turned off the motor. The silence fell around them as they floated in the middle of the lagoon. Then from nowhere came the sound of seals. She spotted one on top of the rocks, and then more appeared.

"Let's get in the water. I'll fix your snorkel and mask first. Then I'll put mine on."

Erica let him do what he said. This was the first time she'd snorkelled, and she couldn't wait to dip her head under the water. They sat on opposite sides of the boat and dropped into the water at the same time. Archer swam around to her side and took her hand as they swam using their free arm. It was something he'd made her practice in the pool for upper arm strength. For hours over the weeks, they swam up and down the pool switching sides every ten laps. Now she knew why he'd done it. The seals joined them once Keith had powered away, leaving them isolated.

Erica snorkelled around in circles, following one seal in particular. A while later, Archer indicated they swim to the shore. As soon as Erica could stand on the sea bottom, she stood up, and pulled off her mask, smiling wide.

"That was amazing, Archer. Thank you so much for arranging it."

"Seeing the wonder on your face when the seals joined us was worth it."

"It was magical."

The water was up to her chest. Erica swayed back and forth with the movement of the water. Archer brought her close and kissed her. She was grateful she wore a wetsuit because Archer turned the kiss indecent as he devoured her mouth, tasting every inch of her. She let the water give her buoyancy and wrapped her legs around his waist, feeling his erection as she pressed her pelvis to his hips. Still, with their tongues entwined, Archer walked them out of the water and onto the sandy beach. It was a secluded cove surrounded by rocks. He dropped to his knees and covered her body while still kissing her. She was frantic, trying to get closer in thick wet suits. Finally, he broke the kiss and stared down at her.

"Turn over," he said, his chest lifting up and down with his panting.

She did as he asked. Archer pulled the flap across and then pulled down the zip of the wet suit exposing her back. When he realised she wasn't wearing anything on top, he pushed her onto her back again.

"You're not wearing a bra," he said.

"Was I supposed to?"

"I don't know. I've never been this close to a woman wearing a wet suit."

Archer curled his fingers under the collar and peeled it down. It trapped her arms at the side. He looked left and right and then tugged the wet suit to expose one of her breasts.

"Archer," she said as he sucked on her nipple, pulling it hard into his mouth.

"I know, but I can't help myself. You're naked under here."

He left her breast alone, covered her modesty, and left her arms where they were. She sank further into the soft sand under his weight, looking up at his handsome face. He was playful. Her earnest, focused, and resolute man was being daring and playful.

Except he wasn't her man, not really.

"We were the last people to go out and see the seals today, but I'm not going to risk stripping you and having my way with your body," he said.

Archer let out a pretend sob and tugged her wet suit up to her neck. "Goodbye, boobies," he said.

Erica laughed and wrapped her arms around his neck when she was free to move. She cuddled him close, loving the feel of his body on hers, wishing they'd met under different circumstances at a different time. Archer rolled them, so he was on his back. He pulled her to his side, arm wrapped around her shoulder, and they stayed like that in silence for an endless time. Erica could hear the seals in the distance calling out to each other. The water lapped at the sand a couple of feet from their position. But all she could feel was her thundering heart. Sneaking a hand over Archer's muscles, she put her palm over his heart.

It was hammering too.

THIRTY-THREE

Archer

At some stage, he'd nodded off in the afternoon sun with Erica tucked into his side. The vicar would not be angry if they were late, but Archer was never late for anything. He'd shaken Erica awake and kissed her slowly until she was fully alert.

"We need to get moving to see the vicar," he said, cupping her chin and kissing her nose.

It was so easy to be intimate with Erica. Her calming nature soothed his soul. Years of working in a loud, boisterous environment on the rigs had him yearning for something or someone quieter. He was about to lie to a man of God, which scared him more than his aunt reneging on their deal.

The cove where they landed after swimming with the seals was nearer to Turner Hall than the cove where they went out on the motor boat. He walked Erica to her door and told her he'd pick her up in an hour. That gave him enough time to hurry back to Maggie, iron his shirt, and change.

He drove the golf buggy to Erica's cottage and then headed down into the town. Erica fidgeted next to him, looking in every direction but him. He couldn't see her eyes as she wore oversized dark sunglasses.

"Are you okay?" he asked when they stopped at the top of the driveway to the vicarage. Like most of the older homes on the island, the vicarage was large, with land all around. All Saints Church stood majestically off to the right of the vicarage, looming tall above them.

"We're going to lie to a man of God," she whispered.

"Just think of all the couples who get married, thinking they're in love and thinking they will spend the rest of their lives together only to get divorced six months later."

"That's depressing," she commented.

Erica had removed her sunglasses and dropped them into her black handbag. Her trouser suit was perfect for an office worker. He'd never seen her so formally dressed, making him think of a chameleon. He never knew how she would appear each time he saw her.

"What can I do to ease your worry?" he asked.

"Tell me he isn't going to grill us, and I don't have to lie any more than necessary."

"It's going to be fine, don't worry," Archer said.

He was fully confident his aunt had fixed everything for them. Undoubtedly, a donation to the church had arrived in the last few days to ease the interview. They walked to the front door, and Archer rapped the brass knocker. When no one answered, he looked around to see if he could see Father Sheldon Chivers. The only thing he could hear was the birds chirping.

"I'll go around the back. He might be in the garden," Archer said, dropping her hand.

He rounded the corner of the house and walked across the grass to the back of the house. It was quiet there too. Archer was sure he'd made the appointment for today with the administrator for the church. Turning back to meet with Erica again, he stopped when he saw Erica talking to a woman wearing a dog collar. Ordinarily, a female vicar wouldn't have alarmed him, except they were expecting an old family friend. Instead, Erica looked disturbed and uneasy as she made small talk with the other woman. As he neared, Erica stepped towards him.

"This is Reverend Wendy Sprite, the new vicar on Copper Island. Father Chivers retired a while ago."

Stunned by the news and furious with his aunt for not telling him, Archer gritted his teeth, painted on a smile, and stuck his hand out to shake the vicar's offered hand in greeting.

"It's great to meet you. Have you been on the island long?" Archer asked.

"About a month. I came for my predecessor's retirement party. Your aunt sure knows how to say thank you in style. The grounds at Turner Hall are gorgeous."

Archer wanted to laugh and then howl at the turn of events. Murderous thoughts entered his head about his aunt and her manipulating ways.

"Thank you. It's an amazing house to grow up in, with plenty of space to run around and climb trees."

Making small talk was painful. Erica squeezed his hand with a look of sheer terror on her face.

"I'm sorry I was running late. Shall we go into the house, and I can make us some tea?" the vicar said.

"That would be lovely," Erica replied, saving Archer from rescheduling after speaking to his aunt.

They entered the house and followed Reverend Sprite to the kitchen at the back. She flipped on the kettle while Archer felt lost in a place he'd spent many hours in as a choir boy along with his brothers.

"Did you know Father Chivers?" Reverend Sprite asked while she grabbed three mugs from the open shelving above the kettle.

"All my life," Archer replied.

"It was a shame you couldn't come to his retirement party," she said.

Erica gave Archer a side glance, and he understood why. There was an undercurrent to her tone.

"What reason did my aunt give for us not attending?"

"She said none of you likes the island. I can't see why that would be. It's lovely here. Everyone is so friendly, and the views are to die for."

"I'm an electrician. My three younger siblings, Jason, Luke, and Daisy, are a chef, medic, and crane operator. Until recently, we all worked on the same oil rig. We wouldn't be granted permission to leave during our three-week stint for a retirement party."

"Ah, understood. Your aunt didn't explain about your jobs."

Archer had a whole ream of points he wanted to make about her assumption of why he hadn't come to say goodbye to a man who had helped him through his mother leaving. His faith had wavered, and Father Sheldon Chivers was there for him.

Reverend Sprite brought the tray of tea mugs across to the table with a plate of plain biscuits. Fully aware of Erica's agitation at the change of events, he rested his hand on her bouncing knee. To his relief, she stilled immediately.

"Tell me how you two met?" the reverend asked.

"We met on the island," Erica replied before lifting the mug to her lips.

"Was that a few years ago? Your aunt said you haven't been back for some time, Archer."

"This year," Archer replied.

"But you've only been back a few weeks if you couldn't come to the retirement party."

Archer felt like MI5 was interrogating him. He turned to face Erica and waited for her to look at him. When she did, he was rewarded with a megawatt smile lighting up her whole face. It was the first time she hadn't looked terrified in the last half an hour.

"It's been recent. But when you know, you know," Archer said, looking directly at Erica.

He lifted her hand and kissed where the pearl ring rested at the bottom of her finger. His lips were pressed against her hand, but he still managed to swipe the tip of his tongue between her fingers. Watching Erica's cheeks pinken made him grin. He was further delighted when her eyes widened.

"Don't you young people want to live together first? Divorce rates are on the increase."

Erica coughed on her mouthful of tea at the remark.

"My aunt wouldn't entertain the idea of me living in sin under her roof."

"That's not the only reason you're getting married, is it? To appease your aunt?"

"Have you ever been in love, Reverend Sprite?" Archer asked.

"No."

"My father died in front of my youngest brother. He just dropped dead, and there was nothing anyone could do for him. No one is promised tomorrow, so what reason is there to wait if you know you've found the woman you want to marry?"

Archer heard Erica's sharp intake of breath but didn't look at her, holding her hand tighter.

"Ah yes, I was told about Luke. He's the medic, isn't he?"

"That's right."

"I'm sure that was a difficult time for him."

"For all of us. We were all there on the platform that day."

"I'm sorry for your loss Archer," Reverend Sprite said, sincerity lacing her words.

"Thanks. Shall we get back to why we're here?"

"Of course, I'm going to grab my notebook to ask you a few questions."

As soon as she left, Erica sagged on her chair. "I nearly had a heart attack when the reverend approached me while you were around the back of the house. I swear my life flashed before my eyes. This is a car crash," she said.

"We'll be fine, honey."

"I'm sorry to hear Luke had to witness your dad dying."

"It was a bad time, made worse." Archer stayed silent for a few beats. "This isn't so bad with a new vicar. I will be having a conversation with my aunt in the morning. It's almost like she doesn't want me to get married."

"She wants you to get married, trust me."

"Is that what she said to you in the grand foyer."

"Yes."

"Then what game is she playing?" Archer said more to himself than Erica.

Before they could talk more, the reverend returned with a leather-bound notebook and sat back down. Wendy took a long sip of her tea and opened the book to a blank page.

"So, Erica, what's your full legal name?"

"Erica Taylor."

"Spelled like the actress?" the reverend said, keeping her eyes on the paper.

"Yes," Erica said quietly.

"And your profession?"

Erica let out a long exhale and then cleared her throat. "Actress."

Archer turned to look at Erica, startled by what she'd said. He thought she was a writer, had even commented that she was a writer, and Erica hadn't denied it. All along, he thought she was genuine, but she was playing a role.

"I thought I recognised your face. You look so different without all the makeup and glitz. Congratulations on your Oscar."

An award-winning actress, Archer thought. He didn't need to watch movies to know about Academy Awards and how notable they were. Archer hadn't met just any actress. He'd unwittingly enlisted the help of a professional. Boy, did she play her part well.

"Thank you," Erica said in a quiet voice, head bowed.

"But aren't you still married? Your husband is with the other woman?"

"I divorced my husband months ago. I wouldn't believe what you read in the press who only want to sell copies. I keep my private life out of the public eye, and no one knew we'd separated and then divorced. I'd like to keep it that way."

"Of course, I am the keeper of all secrets." The vicar shifted in her seat, moving to look at Archer. "And you,

Archer, you said you're an electrician. Is that what you want me to put on the marriage certificate?"

"Yes. My middle name is Edward, Archer Edward Turner."

"Oh, isn't that marvellous? All your names are six letters. And Erica, you won't have to change your initials."

The reverend was being cute, and he wanted to punch something. The rest of the get-together passed in a blur. Archer knew he answered the questions with his hands wrapped around a cold mug of tea. By the time they left, Erica was silent, and Archer was ticking like a bomb. He drove like his arse was on fire as fast as the golf buggy would go and came to a screeching halt outside Erica's front door. He sat still, not trusting what would come out of his mouth.

"Are you coming in? We have a lot to plan now she's confirmed we can marry in a month."

Archer still couldn't form any words.

"You lied to me," he said eventually.

"I have always told you the truth," she replied, picking up her handbag and sliding off her seat from the buggy. "Goodnight, Archer."

Archer watched dumbfounded as she walked away. He was expecting her to defend herself, but she was right. She had never said what she did for a living, and he had never asked her. It didn't help his heart knowing this. His heart thought he'd been betrayed that his feelings weren't reciprocated. But then, he'd never asked how she felt about him beyond their agreement either.

Pocketing the buggy keys, he jogged to catch up with Erica. She didn't use the front door. Instead, Erica strode around the side of the house to the rear. He was hot on her heels, and he knew, she knew, he was there. Erica tossed her handbag on the couch and opened the back door to the kitchen. This time Archer didn't follow. She needed to invite him in. He wasn't that much of a caveman invading her home if he wasn't welcome.

While she was gone, Archer googled her name and read the first three news articles. They were all about the Oscars and what followed afterwards with her husband and the other woman. He was more confused than ever and wished he'd never looked. She was clearly on the rebound.

He saw the grim expression when she came back out in a sundress and bare feet.

"You're an actress," Archer said.

"Yep," she answered, banging the two beer bottles onto the coffee table.

She tossed the handbag on the floor and stretched out on the sofa. Archer inched forward and then took a seat on the chair opposite her. Erica had closed her eyes, taking deep breaths in and then out.

"You should've told me."

Erica turned her head his way, narrowing her eyes. "Why?"

"Don't you think it was important to tell me?"

"Again, why? What's wrong with me being an actress, too lowly for a rich boy like you?"

Enraged by her accusation, Archer stood but stayed rooted to the spot. "The problem is, I'm in love with you, and you're acting. You were using me to save face from your husband."

Erica swung her legs to put her feet flat on the floor, and then Erica yelled.

"You're using me to get your inheritance." Her breathing was heavy again.

As her chest rose and fell, Archer couldn't take his eyes

off her breasts because her nipples were clearly defined against the cotton fabric of her dress.

"Wait, what? You're in love with me?" Erica asked.

"Forget it," Archer replied and took off across the lawn into the darkness.

He'd collect the golf buggy later once he'd calmed down.

All he could think about was the way she kissed him. Surely she couldn't fake that, could she?

THIRTY-FOUR

Archer

Getting in to see his aunt was a challenge. Bailey had told him she was too unwell for visitors every day for a week. He didn't believe Bailey but didn't blame him. His aunt was Bailey's employer, so he was loyal to whoever paid his salary.

After a week of being sent away, he decided he would go around Bailey and speak with his aunt. Bailey was a creature of habit, and Archer could easily set up an accidental meeting. Getting up early and ignoring the splashes coming from the swimming pool, Archer crept along the outside of Turner Hall to the morning room. He heard Erica calling out his name, but he kept going. Nothing and no one was going to prevent him from seeing Aunt Cynthia.

While he felt shitty ignoring Erica, he needed to speak with his aunt before confronting Erica, and they worked through the situation.

He reached the side window he knew was never locked and fitted his bulky body through the gap. Archer would be waiting for his aunt when she came down for her morning tea. Like Bailey, his aunt was also a creature of habit. If she were genuinely unwell, she would stay in her room. Ten minutes later, the door opened, and Bailey stepped in, closely followed by his aunt in slacks and jumper. She clutched a shawl around her shoulders. He was sitting in the armchair opposite where she sat.

The maid followed with a tray of tea and biscuits.

"Good morning, Aunt Cynthia," Archer said as he stood.

"Archer, how did you get in here?" Aunt Cynthia barked.

"The entry was unlocked."

He wasn't technically lying.

"I see," she said, giving him a disapproving glance.

"Set the tea down, will you? That will be all."

The maid glanced at Archer with concern and then hurried away. Bailey closed the door after her, and they were left alone.

"I don't have long before Miss Shaw gets here. What's on your mind?"

"You didn't tell me Reverend Chivers had retired."

"You never asked. Do you want me to list all the people who have left the island since you were here last?"

"You let me believe getting a booking with the reverend would be straightforward."

"Did you not get a date set? I had a letter to say your marriage at the family chapel would happen in three weeks."

"You could have warned me we might have had more trouble securing a wedding date."

"Why would you have more trouble? You're wildly in

love with Erica Taylor, are you not? Whirlwind weddings are not uncommon."

"If I didn't know better, I'd swear you were making this more difficult. You are the one who put the stipulation in place for me to find a wife."

"For you to gain something you are not entitled to yet."

"You own the entire island. Why the hell are you making me jump through hoops to get to wedding business and cottages?"

"I don't want to argue about this anymore, Archer. You have your wife-to-be. You have your wedding booked. So what exactly is the problem?"

His aunt dropped into her chair and pulled the wrap tighter around her body, seemingly weary. He didn't buy it for a second. His aunt was a master manipulator and a bitter one at that.

"Are there any more surprises you will spring on me?"

A knock sounded at the door, and Bailey entered with a woman behind him.

"How are you today, Miss Turner?" the woman asked as she approached his aunt.

"You can go now, Archer," his aunt said.

"Archer Turner?" the woman asked as she held onto Aunt Cynthia's wrist, her fingers at the pulse point.

"Yes, that's me," he said, not recognising her.

"I'm Heidi Shaw," she replied.

"Keith's sister?"

"The very same."

"I'm sorry I didn't recognise you. How are you?"

"I'm doing great. It's been years since I last saw you, probably when all four of you were together before Jason set off for college."

"It's been a while since Keith and Jason have talked."

"Yeah. We came to your dad's funeral but stayed at the back. We didn't want to upset him on such an awful day."

His aunt wrenched her hand out of Heidi's hand, hiding it under her shawl. "Have you come to reminisce or check up on me?" she asked.

"I'll get going. Congratulations on being the island doctor," he said.

"I'm a nurse. The midwife, actually. I double up on the house calls for routine check-ups to take the weight off the surgery. Most of my time is in the car going to see the pregnant women on the island, so doing your aunt's monthly check-up is no bother."

"And if you stopped talking, you could get along with what you should be doing," his aunt said.

Archer raised his hand to wave farewell and left the morning room. He was in no doubt his aunt was avoiding him all week.

By the time he'd gone outside to meet Ralph, the pool was empty, with no ripples on the surface. He doused down the disappointment of not seeing Erica, of missing her. Three weeks until they were married and three weeks until he got his hands on the business that would employ his siblings. He'd marry a woman who was only pretending.

It was what they initially set out to do. Unfortunately, Archer was the fool who fell for an actress.

Archer strode to the gardener's shed at the foot of the lawns hidden behind the tallest trees to find Ralph. He was sitting in a deck chair, looking at a woman in a trouser suit.

"I'll make sure he does his homework, Freya. I appreciate you coming out to the Hall to give me the assignments."

"It's no problem, Ralph. I caught a lift with Heidi. We carpool while I see students, and she sees the mums to be."

"Who is pregnant here?" Ralph asked.

"Heidi is doing Miss Turner's check-up."

"She's strong as an ox and will outlive us all," Ralph said.

Neither had seen him come in, and he didn't want to eavesdrop anymore.

"You got that right," Archer said and stepped further into the shed.

He pivoted to the side and took a look at who the woman was. He recognised her instantly as Freya Riley, high school teacher, and Luke's childhood best friend. She was the only one Luke let close to him aside from his siblings.

"Oh, Archer, it's great to see you. I got a postcard from Luke this morning. It's from Spain, but who knows if he's still there."

She came over and gave him a big hug.

"To be honest, I don't know where any of them are this week. We'll catch up on Sunday. I'll tell him you got his card."

"No need, there is technology these days, and I can send him a text without having to send him a letter in return."

"There's always been the technology to do that, yet you both always insisted on writing to each other," Archer said.

"I love getting random post. Then reading about his travels over a mug of tea. When I get home from teaching, it's the best thing to do."

"I shouldn't keep you. My aunt will sail through her medical check-up and get Heidi to leave as soon as possible."

"Yes, I need to get back to classes too. Good to see you,

Archer. Hopefully will see you around town. Don't be hiding up here like your aunt."

"I'll try to be sociable."

Ralph laughed along with Freya. She said her goodbyes and left the shed. Archer had agreed to look at the lawn mower Ralph had said wouldn't work. Trying to figure out what was wrong with it would take his mind off Erica, her smooth skin, and all-consuming kisses.

THIRTY-FIVE

Archer

Once the lawn mower was deemed irreparable by his hands, he called Nate at the boatyard to see if he could come up to the Hall to assess if the machine would ever cut grass again. Once Nate was assured Archer's sister wasn't at the house, he agreed to come the following day. There were too many questions floating around Archer's head about the friends they all had as teenagers that now behaved differently. Nate's animosity to Daisy was one he would deal with another time.

Jason would be on a flight on Sunday, so they'd brought the call to Saturday evening for a catch-up. Archer logged in on time to find Luke already there, swigging a beer and looking bored.

"How long have you been on the line?" Archer asked before he'd said hello.

"An hour, go my world clock mixed up. This is my third beer."

"Should make the call lively," Archer replied, laughing.

A loud siren sounded when Daisy came on the line, making them all jump. She put her palm on her chest while she looked over her shoulder.

"Scare the crap out of me," she said.

"What was it?"

"Police van. The Italians clearly don't have volume control."

Luke shook his head in amusement, taking another swig of his beer.

"Where are you, Luke?"

"Don't you recognise your own home?" he asked, moving forward, so most of his head filled the screen.

"Not with your ugly mug in the way. Are you in the house in Scotland?"

"Yeah, got bored travelling. So I thought I'd start sorting out this place if we all end up back at Copper Island."

"I've moved into Turner Hall," Archer said.

"She let you in?" Jason said, joining the call. "Sorry I'm late, guys, been to the movies, and the film lasted longer than I expected."

"What did you go and see?" Daisy asked.

Archer groaned internally. If his brother said Deal with the Devil, he would shrivel up and die.

"Deal with the Devil," Jason said.

Jason's face was impassive, but Archer knew his brother and Jason going to the movies to see the film that starred Archer's maybe wife, who he was avoiding, was not a coincidence.

"Oh, I want to see that film. Is it any good?" Daisy replied.

"Erica Taylor is phenomenal in it. I can see why she

won the Oscar. Just a shame that all the negative press about her overshadows it."

"That's awful, isn't it? I think the other woman is faking that pregnancy. It all seems like a publicity stunt for her to get ahead in acting," Daisy said.

"Who the fuck is Erica Taylor?" Luke asked.

"She's a movie star. Where have you been, living under a rock?" Jason said.

"No, just off-grid. We do it when we have time off from the rigs."

Archer was leaving them to squabble while he and Jason had a staring contest. Archer wanted to know how he knew.

"So, Luke is in Scotland. Daisy is in Italy. Where are you, Jason?" Archer asked.

"London."

"You're all much nearer than I thought," Archer said.

"We're getting ready to come to the island. Have you set the date?" Luke asked.

"Yeah, it's in three weeks. Did you know Reverend Chivers has retired?"

"Blimey, I'm not surprised he must be ninety by now," Luke commented.

"Yeah, I suppose. It seems odd not to have him on the island. He's featured in our lives so much."

"Who is his replacement?"

"Reverend Wendy Sprite. She was mighty suspicious of my whirlwind romance," Archer said.

"They must see many arranged marriages in their line of work. It's their job to ensure you're going into the marriage for real reasons."

"Except I'm not. I felt like I was going straight to hell telling her lies."

"How did Erica feel about it? It's a shame you're not marrying Erica Taylor. She'd win the lady reverend over," Daisy said.

"Yeah, shame," Jason said, sarcasm dripping from those two words.

"We fought. I don't know how she feels. I'm not even sure if we're still getting married."

"What did you fight about?" Daisy asked.

"I thought she was a writer, even mentioned it, and she never corrected me," Archer replied.

"What does she do for a living?" Daisy asked.

"She's an actress," Archer replied.

"What's wrong with that?" Daisy said.

"Fuck off," Luke barked. "You're marrying Erica Taylor, and you had no idea she is hands down the sexiest woman alive?"

Jason was laughing behind his hand. "I thought you didn't know who she was?"

"I just googled her, man. I knew her face, and I just didn't know her name. Damn fine woman," Luke said.

"Erica, your Erica is *the* Erica Taylor," Daisy asked, her voice raising an octave.

"Yep," Archer confirmed.

"And you didn't know?" Luke said. "She's stunning and everywhere, not just in films. Adverts, charity, everything."

"No. It seems she's able to play the part really well." Disdain licked at Archer's words.

"Now, hold on there," Jason said. "You have no basis that she is faking her affection for you. It is possible she likes the straight-laced, never late to anything, type of man."

"Have you two, ya know," Daisy asked.

"You can ask if they've fucked," Luke said.

"I don't want to ask it, eww, but are you two more than just faking a relationship for the dragon?"

"Daisy," Jason chastised.

"Sorry. Have you been more than friends?"

"Yeah. I've taken Erica to Stuart Island across the causeway, we went to the flower fields, and I took her to swim with the seals."

"You're in love with her?" Jason asked.

"Of course he is. We're talking about Erica Taylor. Who wouldn't be?" Luke said.

"But she's an actress, and she hid it from me," Archer said.

"You didn't ask her what she did to earn a living. You didn't ask her how she affords to rent out five fucking cottages on Copper Island," Jason said.

"Well, that's rude, prying." Archer felt twelve years old with his feeble reasoning.

"You're marrying the girl. Wouldn't you ask the basics?" Daisy said gently.

"Clearly not," Luke muttered.

"So what was the fight about? Did Erica say she didn't like you? Was she just filling a role? Did she tell you she's only marrying you for your ability you can fix anything?" Daisy asked.

Archer shook his head to Daisy's questions. "I can't fix the mower," Archer grumbled.

"That mower is older than Aunt Cynthia," Jason commented.

"Listen, go and talk to her. See if she still wants to go ahead after you've been an ass. You're the best judge of character I know. You know she's not faking it because you took her to your favourite places. Deep down, you know you wouldn't have fallen for someone who wasn't more than skin deep. So go and grovel, apologise and make sure the wedding is on before I pack this house up into a million boxes," Luke said.

"What he said," Jason replied.

"Yeah, Archer. Be nice to Erica. She seems lovely," Daisy chipped in.

"All right, guys, I'll see her, get things straightened out."

"Report back in the morning," Jason said.

Archer hung up from the call, fed up with being told what to do even if it was the right thing.

He closed the laptop lid and drummed his fingers, looking down at what he was wearing. He was still in his long shorts and t-shirt from attempting to fix the lawn mower. While he remembered, he sent a text to Daisy to ask her why Nate would only come to Turner Hall if she weren't there.

Tossing the phone on the bed, he jumped into the shower and changed before heading to Erica's cottage. He rapped on the back door, and there was no answer. Risking her wrath, he turned the doorknob, and it opened. Walking into the kitchen, he knew the place was empty. None of her personal belongings had gone as there was a shawl strewn over the back of the chair and a novel she'd been reading with a bookmark sticking out three-quarters of the way in. He stepped closer to see what she was reading and saw a folded piece of paper with his name scribbled on the front.

Gone to London to do movie stuff and pick up my wedding dress. Send me a message if you no longer want to get married and break the deal.

Archer took note of the number she'd scribbled and stored it in his phone. He'd wasted no time telling her the deal was still on but could he talk. Erica replied instantly,

225

saying she wouldn't have any time to speak meaningfully and they could talk when she returned in two weeks.

"Two weeks? Am I planning this whole wedding?" he thundered to nobody.

Then he made a call. "How quickly can you leave Italy?"

THIRTY-SIX

Erica

Travelling at a moment's notice was a luxury Erica took for granted. Having the money to book a private charter helicopter had its benefits when she was nursing a broken heart. Erica was still on the tarmac when Archer's text came through to say he still wanted to get married, and the deal was still on. Flying as the only passenger, she felt guilty. Erica contacted charities on the island to see if they needed anything transported to the mainland. While they were loading up, Erica debated speaking to Archer but couldn't risk being overheard. Whatever he had to say could wait until she returned.

"Okay, that's it, Miss Turner. I'm grateful for your kindness," the man said after sticking his head through the door opening of the helicopter.

"No problem. We'll bring back your deliveries in two weeks."

"Fantastic. You've saved us so much money."

"I'm happy to help," she said, then slid on her sunglasses

when the burly man stepped from the helicopter to stand away.

She prayed he was another man who didn't know who she was.

The flight back to London seemed to take seconds, and they soon landed at London City Airport. She had a car waiting to take her to her house in Kensington. When Erica had left, dozens of journalists were crowding at her house's front gates. Yet, as she stepped from the car, the road was quiet. London smelled different since she'd been gone. The island's fresh air had changed her senses, and she craved it already. The driver came with her to the door, placed her overnight bag next to her, and waited until she opened the door.

Erica thanked him, and she was once again alone. Being alone in the cottage was relaxing and calming but alone in her large house, she felt lonely. Leaving her case at the foot of the stairs, Erica made her way through the open-plan living room and into the kitchen. The vastness struck her. Picking up her post, she took it to her study, which was the smallest room on the ground floor. Heading back to the kitchen to make a snack and a coffee, she smiled at the flowers in a vase, left by Yanny as a welcome home surprise. Unfortunately, the flowers didn't smell as fragrant as those from the flower farm on Copper Island.

Sighing, she waited for the kettle to boil and told herself comparing everything to the equivalent on Copper Island would not ease the ache in her heart.

Erica settled on the sofa, read her post, and then tossed it to one side. She wasn't comfortable, restless in her own space. Deciding to go to bed early, Erica rummaged in her handbag for her book, only to remember she'd put it down when she wrote the note for Archer.

○

The following morning, Erica hoped for a better mood, but it didn't come. It hadn't rocked up when Yanny buzzed on her intercom.

She let him in through the gates and then greeted him on the threshold of her home with a hug.

"Are you okay?" Yanny asked her as he examined her face.

"Yeah, all good," she said, attempting to keep the sigh from escaping.

"You haven't told your face the message. It looks like someone took your favourite teddy away."

Sighing, instantly remembering Archer's dog and the cute teddy she'd held hostage that sat on her bed. She wondered if her heart was breaking. Archer thought she was acting the whole time. How could he believe that?

"My head is all over the place. Please tell me you have me busy for the next two weeks."

Yanny led the way into the kitchen. He went to the coffee machine and helped himself to a cappuccino. Erica passed on caffeine and opted for water instead.

"You have meetings every day for the movie, dress fittings, script changes, you know the drill. Then, a couple of magazines are desperate to interview you, and then there's your ex-husband."

"Gregg? What about him?"

"He wants an audience."

"Did he say why?"

"No, but I suspect it has to do with his relationship with the wench going off the radar?"

"Trouble in paradise?"

"Possibly, but I have no idea what that has to do with you. You're divorced. What can Gregg possibly want?"

"I suppose one meeting won't hurt. Can we make it at a public place but inside?"

"Sure, what are you thinking, lunch?"

"Make it somewhere expensive next week. It will allow me to reacclimatise to London life before I face him. He's going to want something. I just don't know what it is."

"I'll squeeze it in. Tomorrow you have the fitting for your wedding dress," Yanny continued with his list.

Another sigh escaped Erica. She'd talked with the dressmaker every few days, tweaking what she wanted. The dressmaker already had her measurements, and the fitting would ensure they'd translated. The lady making her wedding dress made all her red carpet gowns. Erica paid well enough that the dressmaker only worked for her, so it didn't take long when she needed a dress. Erica chose a simple design to help with timings, but it was detailed enough to make her feel special, even if she felt like shit.

"What's going on, Erica? Are you going to tell me why you came earlier than planned?"

"My profession never came up in conversation. Archer thought I was a writer because he saw me with a manuscript a few times. He never asked, and I never said. It was a fake arrangement, so we didn't need to delve into our whole lives. Just know enough to fool his aunt."

"Except?"

"His aunt knew exactly who I was and thoroughly disapproved of who I was. She called me a two-bit actress. I nearly took the bait but resisted. When we met with the vicar, we had to state our professions as she was new to the island and wasn't sure if I was Erica Taylor, the actress, or not. When we got back to the cottage, Archer was furious.

230

He now thinks I faked liking him, and then he told me he'd fallen in love with me."

"Oh shit. That's a lot to unpack. So he's in love with you?"

"Yeah. The thing is, I think I fell a little bit in love with him too. I loved that he didn't know I was Oscar-winning actress Erica Taylor. I hadn't worn a scrap of make-up the whole time I was on the island. We got really close and spent time together every day. It felt so good, and now he thinks I don't care about him."

"Do you think you should go ahead with the wedding?"

"If it were the original deal, then I'd say yes."

"But?"

"His aunt pulled me aside and said if I don't stay married to him for a full year, she'll write Archer and his siblings out of the will. She told me I couldn't ever get divorced while she was alive. So getting their hands on the business is the only way they can be assured of staying together."

"Four siblings that like each other? I don't believe it."

"His brother Jason tracked down my mobile number. He gave me the speech and said he would keep my secret safe. He didn't need to, and really, I outed myself."

"What are you going to do?"

"Go ahead with the wedding. We joked at the beginning if we hated each other, the house was big enough to live on opposite sides and not see each other."

"That's no life, Erica."

"I know, but I feel responsible for their happiness."

"And what about yours?"

"I spent five years with Gregg, and look how that ended."

"So you're going to give up a year of your life to rescue

four people, three you have never met, because you feel obliged to carry through on a deal you made when you were lust drunk. You'll also be breaking the law."

"Yes."

"Maybe time away will give you perspective. By the time you return, you'll have a better view of what you're going to do. I'll stand by you no matter what, but I wouldn't be a good friend if I didn't tell you I think you're bonkers."

"You'll give me away, right?"

"Aren't you inviting your parents?"

"I think the fewest people possible is best if I'm going to break the law and lie in front of a woman of the cloth."

"A female vicar, interesting, how very progressive of Copper Island."

THIRTY-SEVEN

Archer

Archer strode across the grand foyer and hugged his sister. "Thank the Lord you're here. What took you so long?"

Daisy shuffled out of his hold and straightened her clothes. Archer knew he hugged too hard for too long, but that was how he showed his love.

Daisy looked at her watch and then up to her brother. "It's not even twelve hours since you called in an SOS."

"I'm sorry, I'm freaking out."

"Well, I'm here now, so I can help you straighten your head. Where's Erica?"

"She's gone."

"For good?"

"I hope not."

"Explain while you show me where I'm sleeping."

"Would it be weird to take the guest room in Erica's cottage? That way, you don't have to see Aunt Cynthia if you don't want to."

"Are you kidding me? I'd happily keep the home fires

burning for the superstar actress. If you manage to get her back onside, she will be my sister-in-law. Which means she's really marrying me too."

"I need her onside, Daisy, not scare her off," Archer said, hooking his arm around her neck as they walked across the foyer.

"Is the Dragon home?" Daisy asked.

"Yes, she is," came the booming voice from their left.

"Fuck," Daisy whispered and stilled next to Archer.

"Aunt Cynthia," Archer said. "You're up earlier than usual."

"That's because I got a note to say my only niece was on Copper Island."

"Did someone wake her up?" Daisy asked Archer quietly enough that her aunt didn't hear.

"Bailey would be my bet," Archer muttered.

"What are you two whispering about?"

"Daisy needs breakfast, and we were arguing who would be cooking."

"Unlikely, I'm sure you two will go straight to Maggie."

"Probably," they both said and shrugged.

"Make sure you come and see me later this morning, Daisy Turner. I'd like to understand what your plans are for a career."

"I'll work it out with Bailey when a good time would be," she replied.

Aunt Cynthia turned on her heel and went into the morning room.

"Try not to piss her off until I get the paperwork for the business. It's in your interests too. Make sure you have a speech ready for when she wants you to tell her what you want to do when you grow up."

"I bet she thinks we're all kids and have no idea how to live alone, let alone do a skilled job on an oil rig."

"Let's eat. I need food."

₀

During breakfast, they managed to pry out of Bailey who the wedding manager was and where they could find him. It turned out that the manager didn't live on the mainland at all but had an office in the town and lived a couple of streets away. Archer drove the buggy into town and parked up. Daisy speed-walked behind Archer, asking him to slow down.

"Grow longer legs," he replied.

"Very amusing. That comment got boring when I was six."

"I have a million things to do, so it's jog next to me or have a piggyback."

Archer could hear Daisy thinking through her options. Then, with a long sigh, he slowed his pace to walk side by side with his sister, who had dropped everything to come and help.

"I'm sorry, Daisy, for snapping. I'm worrying over a wedding that might not even take place. I know Aunt Cynthia is lying or withholding information. Did you see Bailey's face when he had no option but to tell us?"

"I don't know why he was so reluctant."

Archer stopped outside the greengrocer and searched for the side door behind a moveable hoarding. Archer pressed the intercom while Daisy squeezed into the space next to Archer.

"How the hell are people supposed to find him with a giant cut out of a tomato in front of the door?" Daisy asked.

"I can't imagine there's much passing trade. His office might operate on an appointment-only basis."

"That's true. I wonder how many couples come over from the mainland to see Edward Hall?" Daisy asked.

Archer kept his finger on the buzzer after there was no answer the previous five times he pressed it.

"Are you looking for Stan?" Lucy said.

"Yes, Stan Myers, do you know where he is?"

"Fishing, probably. He will be at the end of the east causeway."

"Thanks," Archer said and placed his hands on Daisy's shoulders to steer her out of the confined space.

The east causeway was a few minutes' walk away, and to save time, Daisy jumped on Archer's back. A lone man was sitting in a blue and white deck chair with a fishing rod in its holder. The line was out into the harbour. The man was fast asleep with his green bucket hat over his eyes. His fingers interlocked over his rounded stomach.

"He doesn't look like a wedding planner," Daisy whispered as they approached.

"No, he doesn't."

"Are you Stan Myers?" Archer called out, attempting to mimic a police officer.

He'd never seen a man move so quickly out of a deck chair before. Stan stood straight, pushed the hat to the back of his head, and squinted in the bright sunshine.

"Yes, I'm Stan. Who wants to know?"

"I'm Archer Turner, and this is my sister Daisy. We were informed that you run the wedding business up at Edward Hall."

Stan took off his hat and scratched the back of his head. His grimace told Archer something was not right.

"Yes, that's me."

"Is today your day off?"

Archer hoped he'd say yes because if he were fishing on his aunt's payroll, he wouldn't be a wedding planner for long.

"I'm self-employed. I organise many events around the island, including weddings up at the hall. I fish when it's a nice day, and I don't have any appointments."

"How can prospective bookings or future bookings get in touch with you if you're not in the office?" Daisy asked.

"The phones are diverted to my mobile," Stan said, taking his phone out of his pocket. "Anyone wanting to get married at Edward Hall comes from the mainland. It's too expensive for the locals."

Archer wanted to change that immediately. Locals would have a severe discount if they wanted to get married up on the cliff.

"Well, I'm not sure if I'm a local anymore or from the mainland, but I need you to help organise my wedding."

"Congratulations," Stan said, dropping his hat and stretching his hand out. "We haven't met. I moved here when I met my wife. She's the local. I'm still considered an outsider. It's been ten years."

"I'd give it another forty years, and they may consider you a local, but don't hold your breath," Daisy said.

Stan chuckled at Daisy's words, and Archer liked him.

"I was sorry to hear of your father's passing. I really liked him. I'm sorry I don't remember you, Archer. Or you, Daisy, I think you'd all left by the time I was hired."

"Yeah, ten years ago, we were either on the oil rig or studying. So it's not surprising you didn't know us. Dad returned on his downtime, but we never did, preferring to travel the world."

"When are you getting married?"

"Three weeks," Archer said.

"Shit, really?"

Stan started to pack away his fishing gear, stuffing his hat in his jacket pocket. Archer and Daisy watched as he hastily got this stuff together.

"Is that a problem? Aunt Cynthia said there aren't any bookings for the next couple of months. I'd have thought the spring and summer would be busy."

"I guess times are hard, and the rich folk are saving their money," Stan said.

"You seem to be panicked," Daisy remarked, trying to hide her smirk at the man patting down all his pockets for something.

"Three weeks isn't long to organise a wedding. This will be the first one we've had this year. Everything is in storage. How many guests will you be having? Where are my fucking keys?" Stan said, exasperated, forgetting he'd asked a string of questions.

"There, on your tackle box," Archer said. "We don't have to iron out all the details right now, do we?"

"It's best I know exactly what you and your bride want, then I can get to work. I'm sure Ralph will help me haul everything out. I'll need to make sure the furniture is perfect. Oh god, is Cynthia Turner coming?"

"I imagine she would as she's my aunt, and she owns Edward Hall."

"This is going to be a nightmare. The lady scares the shit out of me. Nothing is ever good enough. Do you know what her favourite phrase is?"

"We could give you a list, but I want to know what she uses on you," Daisy said.

"*I suppose I have to lower my expectations.*"

"You have to ignore her baiting. I'm sure you do a great job. Does she keep you on retainer?" Archer asked.

"No, I get paid per wedding. I prefer it that way, so when I'm not working on a wedding, I can help with the events on the island with a clear conscience."

"All right, Stan. Why don't you come up to the house tomorrow? I'll have all the details you need. Do you have a list I can look through?"

"Sure, I'll email it over to you. Here," Stan said. He pulled out an envelope from his tackle box and pulled out the contents, shoving the pieces of paper into his pocket along with his hat.

"Write your email on here," he said, handing over a stubby pencil and the envelope.

Archer printed the email address clearly and his mobile number.

"Thanks, Stan. What time tomorrow?"

"I'll be there from seven. You'll find me in the basement of Edward Hall, where all the wedding stuff is stored. Come and find me when you're ready."

"I've never been married before, so please take this comment as I mean it. Why are you freaking out?"

"Cynthia Turner's nephew is getting married in three weeks. Trust me. She will want perfection."

"And what about my bride and me?"

"Doesn't even factor," Stan said, waving his hand in the air. "But if you can fill the list in and bring it with you tomorrow morning, we can get to work."

"Okay," Archer said, feeling the panic shift from Stan to his bones.

He didn't know what Erica wanted for a wedding, and she wasn't speaking to him. Filling in the form would be a challenge.

"We'll see you in the morning. I'll be here too, Stan. So that's three pairs of hands to pull off a Turner wedding."

Daisy's words seemed to bounce off Stan. He looked to the sky, muttered some words, and then picked up his rod and tackle box.

"See you in the morning," Stan said and stalked off the causeway.

"How many weddings have you attended?" Archer asked Daisy.

"None. What about you?"

"None. We're fucked."

"Daisy burst out laughing. Come on, let's go and get a pint. We can have our very own *Don't tell the bride.*"

THIRTY-EIGHT

Erica

After ten days of living back in London, Erica still missed the island and the handsome man she left behind. He'd peppered her with random questions about the wedding she didn't care about. She'd talked Yanny's ear off every evening about what she should do. As each day passed by, she realised marrying Archer would be a mistake for both of them. Finally, on the penultimate day, Erica went to pick up her wedding dress. She was still intent on talking to Archer when she returned to the island to tell him it was a bad idea.

Settling at a table outside a restaurant on the patio area, Erica took out her paperback and waited for her lunch to arrive. Her dress was hanging up somewhere inside. The hostess took it from her like it was fine china and promised to take good care of it. The patio area had five feet high shrubs giving a subtle note to passers-by that attention was not welcome.

"Is this seat taken?" A man's voice said, interrupting her reading.

Erica looked up at the good-looking man standing on the opposite side of the small square table she was sitting at. His short spikey blond hair reminded her of a surfer with its natural bleach blond tips and his tanned face.

"I'm engaged," Erica replied, holding up her hand with the antique pearl ring on her third finger.

"I know. To my brother. Is this seat available?" he asked again.

"Yes," Erica said, carefully tracking his movements as he gracefully sat, unbuttoning his suit jacket and smoothing his tie down his broad chest.

"I'm guessing you're Jason."

"Why?"

Jason sat back with a smirk. The only evidence she could see he could be unruly was his hair. Dirty blond and sticking up like it wouldn't behave.

"You were the only blond in the childhood photos."

Nodding, Jason made himself comfortable at the table in the corner of the restaurant. "Yes, I'm Jason. Can I have lunch with you? I promise this is a friendly get-together."

"So friendly, you gate crashed. How did you find me?"

Feeling more relaxed now, that he had stated he wasn't there to hand out bad news or behave like a male version of his aunt, Erica dropped her book into her bag.

"The gutter press. They snapped you coming in and uploaded it onto their website."

"And you, by chance, were looking."

Jason grinned, leaning forward with his arms resting on his thighs under the table. "I came back to London a few weeks ago. I wanted to know if you were still here when Archer said you did a Houdini act on him. Google alerts are fantastic. However, you've been holed up in your house.

Beautiful place you have in Kensington, by the way. Very secure."

A server handed Jason a menu and left them alone.

"Your brother ignored me for a week, wouldn't speak to or look at me. He knew I had movie commitments, so it was hardly a disappearing act."

"You told him you'd be gone for five days, then in your note, you said you'd be away for two weeks."

"And he said he wouldn't run out on me."

Jason took a breath in and then exhaled through his nose. Sitting back and giving Erica his undivided attention, after making his choice from the menu, he stared her out.

He lost.

"My brother is methodical, doing things in order rather than multitasking. He couldn't talk to you until he had talked to our aunt. Aunt Cynthia gave him the run-around claiming to be ill when she wasn't. He gate crashed her morning tea and got his answers. Then he called us for advice. Finally, he came to your cottage to discuss everything, yet you'd gone."

Erica chewed on those words, knowing they would be true. It wasn't like she'd ignored Archer over the last ten days, but she had only answered questions he'd asked. There was no deviation, no small talk or sexy talk. Erica hadn't dialled his number because she couldn't bear to hear his voice. All she had in her head was his final words, *forget it*, on repeat.

"The risotto is lovely here, and so is the steak," Erica said.

"You come here a lot?" Jason asked, picking up the menu.

Erica was grateful Jason didn't push his point any further. She understood he was looking out for his big brother. She'd do the same if she had siblings. The conversation had grown too serious, and she was getting stressed.

"It's one of my favourite places to eat," Erica said.

"Mine too."

"Are you a foodie?"

"I'm a chef. When I'm in London, I come here to eat and speak with the kitchen brigade."

"Oh hell, don't tell them that. It'll freak Pedro out."

"You know the head chef here?" Jason asked.

"Yeah, we go way back when he worked in another restaurant, and I was a struggling actress in the theatres. I'd pop into his place and eat late at night after the place closed, and all the staff would eat together. They were simpler times."

"Archer is freaking out," Jason said.

The change in subject jolted her from good memories. She thought talking about food would dissuade Jason from piling on the pressure.

"Why?"

"He's planning a wedding with no idea if the bride is coming back."

"I said I was coming back. I've answered every wedding question he's asked."

"Yeah, but they weren't with much feeling, just simple yeses or nos."

"What more does he want? It's a wedding for show, to get you all the business so you can settle together. It doesn't matter much if the flowers are yellow or white."

"You have added two names to the wedding party, and you're one of them."

"Yanny would kill me if I didn't invite him."

"What about the rest of your family?"

"I don't really see them. We're not close, and I'm an

only child. Plus I'm not dragging anyone else into the lie that doesn't already know. By the time we separate, I hope my parents won't find out, and they can pretend to disapprove of their daughter with one divorce."

"I'm sorry you feel that way. Are you having second thoughts?"

"Completely. I don't think this is a good idea. But I made an agreement, and for the sake of all of you, I'm still returning to the island in a couple of days. I'll talk to Archer then, tell him my fears, and if he still wants to get married, I will walk down the aisle and smile for the cameras. Lord knows I've done that a thousand times on the red carpet."

"Erica," Jason said, stretching his hand out and clasping hers. "You're making me sad. I think Archer cares for you a great deal. He is busting his ass to get everything ready for when you come back."

"That's the problem. Why is Archer doing that when he said I was faking how I felt? I don't sleep with just anyone. I've never felt more like a whore when he told me I was acting. I shared stuff with him I've never confessed to anyone."

The waiter came out with their food, and Jason pulled his hand away to make room for his food. Then, Jason leaned forward and dropped his voice when they were left alone again.

"There's no reason why you two can't get married for real."

Erica mirrored his position, holding her hair back out of the way of the food.

"The ink is still wet on my divorce papers. My ex-husband cheated on me with a much younger woman. My ego and heart are still bruised, Jason. Getting married to a good man like Archer and believing we have a shot? That would be foolish because I don't trust my judgment or feelings."

"Then let me judge. Archer has sent an SOS for us all to return to help. Daisy has been there for a week and a bit. Luke is on a flight home, and I'll be coming back in a couple of days."

"Do you need a lift?"

"I can book my own flight."

"There's space on my flight. I'm taking across a heap of stuff for a charity organisation on the island, but all that is going in the hold. There are spare seats. It would be ridiculous for you to book another flight. Yanny is coming too, but that still leaves two more seats. Are you staying in London?"

"I have a hotel room."

"Let me know where you're staying, my driver will pick you up the day after tomorrow, and he can drive us down. You can spend the time catching me up about your family history and why you think Archer and I make a good match."

"I'm up for the challenge," Jason said.

"Good. Let's eat."

₀

When Erica arrived back at her home, there were a couple of photographers waiting for her. Unfortunately, one got too close, and she held up her hand—the one with her engagement ring on.

"Who was your lunch date, Erica? Is he the man you're engaged to? Is Jason Turner your fiancé?"

Erica was still amazed at how quickly information was sought or bought. Making no comment, she entered her property, leaving them on the pavement, behind locked gates. Yanny was her first call.

"Two things," she said. "One, we have an extra person travelling with us to Copper Island, and second, the paps think I'm marrying Jason Turner."

"Was he the guy you had lunch with? It wasn't on your schedule," Yanny said.

"He's Archer's brother and the person we're giving a lift to Copper Island. How did the press get wind of it?"

"My sources say one of the other patrons took your picture when the, and I quote, *strikingly handsome man joined Miss Taylor for lunch. Has she finally got over Gregg Potter and under Jason Turner?*"

"How did they know his name, the reservation was under my name?"

"I don't know, but I'd guess someone bribed the staff if he paid the bill."

"Yes, he did. Dammit, someone took a note of his name on the credit card."

"You know the drill by now."

"It still shocks me."

"And that's why I love you. You still have the naivety. Hollywood hasn't made you bitter."

"Marriage has, though."

"Are you still going to break it off?"

"Jason reckons we're a good match, me and Archer."

"Well, you do really like him."

"For the right reasons?"

"Who cares if he makes you happy."

THIRTY-NINE

Erica

The helicopter had landed at the small airport on Copper Island, and the four people in the aircraft stared at each other. Jason had corralled Luke into coming with them on the same flight. Sitting next to Yanny, Erica crossed and uncrossed her legs as she stared out the window. Jason pulled his head back from sticking it out the window, chatting to a man below.

"What are we waiting for?" Yanny asked.

"Nathaniel, apparently. He's the only one who can operate the forklift truck. You seemed to have carried an entire shop with you," Jason said.

"I told the charity to get whatever they wanted to transport ready. It's good they took advantage of all the space offered. It will cut their transport costs down drastically."

"True," Jason said and nodded. "They're unloading now. Nate's on his way."

Half an hour later, Ralph was driving towards the helicopter in the larger golf buggy. They scrambled off. Erica looked to the horizon, sighing at the view of the blue waters. She could feel her muscles relax hearing the seagulls squawk.

"Is that it? All the luggage?" Ralph asked.

"Yes, that's it," Erica replied. "Thanks for coming to get us.

He hooked the dress carrier Erica handed him and hung it up at the back of the vehicle. Jason lifted the cases into the trailer at the back, and then they were on the move. The journey from the small airport up to Turner Hall was quiet as a private road linked the two places. She wondered why the first time a boat took her across. Jason explained that only the family got to use the private road. Guests came across by water.

Erica held onto the grab handle as Ralph navigated the small roadway up to the top of the cliff. Then, finally, they arrived at Erica's cottage, and she was surprised to see it looked occupied. Pop music blared from the upstairs window. A few seconds later, a woman popped her head out of the open window and waved madly at them.

"Why's that woman in my cottage?" Erica asked, looking up at the beautiful woman with tousled dark hair.

"That's Daisy, our sister. I'm already exhausted by her enthusiasm," Luke said.

Yanny chuckled and got out of the buggy first, moving to the back to take the bags out of the trailer. Jason joined him, taking the dress bag from the back.

"Is she living with me now?" Erica asked, not entirely upset at the idea of the company.

"When we all lived on the island, our home was Turner Hall. Daisy hated living there and said her aunt picked holes in everything she did. If our aunt is still alive, Daisy will never sleep a night at Turner Hall."

"They don't get on?"

"Not at all. Daisy calls her The Dragon."

"Oh dear, not exactly happy families," Erica said.

"Not for a very long time. Let's go in, and you can meet our pint-sized human bottle of champagne. She irritates the fuck out of me, but I still love her," Luke said.

"You guys are all close. I'm envious," Yanny said.

"We have our fights like any other family, but we would drop everything if one of us were in trouble."

"That doesn't sound good if you're all here. Is Archer in trouble?" Erica asked.

Luke halted her progress up the path by grabbing her wrist. "You tell me, is he?"

"We'll soon see. I hadn't thought there would be this much of an audience when we arrived."

"You'll get space. I'll make sure of it," Luke said.

Erica stepped back into the cottage she was familiar with and looked around to see all her stuff was where she left it. The shawl over the chair in the kitchen was folded and placed on the seat.

"Hi, I'm Daisy," the woman from upstairs came running across the living room to hug Erica. "I'm so happy to meet you. We've organised the best wedding you can imagine."

Erica groaned inside. Was there still going to be a ceremony? The earnest look in Daisy's eyes gave her hope Archer had thawed out since they'd last talked.

"Thank you. Is Archer here?"

"Um, yes, but there is a situation."

"What's going on, Daisy?" Jason said.

Erica, Yanny, Luke, and Jason all faced Daisy. She bit into her bottom lip, looking at each of them in turn.

"They've been yelling at each other for a while. It's why I had the music up."

"Who is arguing, Daisy?" Luke asked.

"Archer and a man. He arrived half an hour ago looking like a shambles. I swear he slept in his clothes on the overnight ferry. They're in the middle of the lawn out the back. No one's thrown a punch yet, but it has that vibe."

As a unit, the four of them moved to the back door, led by Erica. As they stepped out into the covered patio area one by one, Erica sucked in a breath.

"Oh shit," Erica said.

"This is not good," Yanny said.

"Who is that with Archer?" Erica heard Luke ask.

To her surprise, both Jason and Yanny answered at the same time. "Her ex-husband."

Erica strode away towards the two men who were staring each other out. Archer's arm muscles bunched as he fisted and unfisted his hands at his sides. Dressed in black board shorts and a black t-shirt, he looked menacing against Gregg's creased suit and shirt.

Tearing her eyes away from Archer, she looked to Gregg. "What are you doing here?"

"You didn't attend the lunch we arranged, so I was forced to come here instead."

"How did you know I'd even be here?"

"Who is this guy?" Archer asked. "He turned up here an hour ago scaring the shit out of Daisy by banging on the cottage door. She called me to say a strange man was trying to break into the house. Daisy thought it was a crazed fan, and I came over."

"I'm her husband," Gregg said.

"This is Gregg, and he's my ex-husband," she told Archer at the same time.

Archer took a step towards Gregg, but Erica slipped between the two men facing Gregg.

"Take a step back, Gregg. You're no match for Archer," she said.

In every aspect, she thought. Erica could feel the heat coming from Archer at her back, but he wasn't touching her. All she wanted to do was fall back into his arms and find comfort. Instead, Gregg looked over her shoulder and took several steps away, running his hands through his hair.

"Why are you here, Gregg? Yanny told you I couldn't make the lunch meeting."

"But you could have lunch with Jason Turner, your fiancé," he said, spite oozing from his words.

"I'm not marrying Jason Turner. Where the hell are you getting that from? And why do you care? You asked me for the divorce, and you'll have a baby soon with Monica."

"It's not my baby. I've been a fool, lured in by the lying bitch," Gregg said.

"Hey, no name-calling," Erica barked, pointing her finger at him. "Be respectful."

"She tricked me into thinking I was the father of the baby. I'll call her whatever I like," Gregg replied.

"You're no better," Erica screeched. "You were having an affair while we were married before we split up. You're a hypocrite, and you're a lying bastard."

"What happened to respectful?"

"Fuck off," Archer said behind her.

Gregg looked over her shoulder and completely changed his demeanour. "I'm sorry, babe. I don't know what I was thinking. When she told me she was pregnant so soon after I'd slept with her, I thought I had to do my duty and stand by her."

"But you didn't think it was dutiful to stand by your wife and not fuck around?" Erica said, spitting her words out.

Archer had curled his fingers around Erica's bicep. It was a loose grip but one that could tighten in a second should she decide to lurch for her ex-husband.

"You were never home, always on set filming your latest movie or promoting. It was a lonely life."

"You knew what my life was like before we married. Countless times you told me you didn't mind I was away. I trusted you."

"I'm sorry," Gregg said, holding his head in his hands. "Can we talk? Somewhere we don't have an audience?"

Erica looked to her side and saw Yanny, Daisy, Jason, and Luke standing in a row with pensive stares.

"I need to take a shower. Where are you staying? I'll meet you at your guest house."

"I have nowhere to stay. I came in these clothes. I needed to see you."

"Fucking hell," Archer said behind her.

Erica craned her neck to look at him. His eyes dropped to her face. All she felt was comfort, even if he looked at her with frosty eyes.

"If you're not marrying Jason Turner, then all these people can back off and let us talk."

Teddy barked at her feet, his yap aimed at Gregg. Erica bent to scratch the dog's head and let him lick her hand in greeting. She was glad the dog was on her side.

"Are there some spare clothes Gregg could change into?" she asked Archer.

He rolled his eyes and looked at his two brothers. Gregg was nearer Luke's physique than Jason or Archer.

"I'll be back in ten minutes. You, arsehole, do not go into that cottage. I'll come back with some clothes and can take you to get a shower. You stink."

"Thank you," Gregg said. "I want to make amends with my wife."

"Ex-wife," all the Turners and Yanny said simultaneously.

Erica wanted to cry at the support she had from the surrounding people. The last thing she wanted to do was have a conversation with Gregg. What was the point? Archer hadn't stepped in or volunteered he was marrying her, not Jason. Daisy has confirmed the wedding was still on, but that didn't mean Archer was happy about it.

FORTY

Archer

"Where are you going?" Jason asked once he'd caught up with Archer.

"Luke's old room. There's bound to be clothes left in the drawers."

"Luke has stayed with Gregg, so he doesn't move, and Daisy went inside with Erica."

"This is all so fucked up. What the hell is that man here for?"

"I don't know, but Erica looked as pleased as you were to see him. What happened before we arrived?"

"I was having a cuppa with Maggie and Bailey when Daisy called. She was whispering, and I couldn't hear her, so she hung up and sent me a text and a video of Gregg hammering on the front door. I ran like the wind. By the time I got there, Gregg had come around the back, standing on the lawns calling out Erica's name."

"How did he know which cottage was hers?"

"I've no idea. You know how helpful the townspeople

are. They must have known the guest was living in the first cottage, or else he tried the others, and Erica's was the only one that looked lived in. I was grateful Daisy had locked the doors when she went to bed. The banging woke her up."

"What was his reason for coming to the island?"

"I didn't get that far, didn't know who he was until he said after you all arrived. I was yelling at him for scaring Daisy. For coming onto Turner land without permission. Whoever told him where Erica was staying obviously didn't know about the rule of no trespassing without permission."

"We can find out who that was later. Gregg is still in love with her. You can tell in a blink."

"That's what I'm worried about."

"You didn't exactly greet her warmly."

"I was too busy trying not to punch him."

They'd reached Luke's room, and Archer went straight to the chest of drawers in the far corner. He pulled out sweat pants and a t-shirt. Gregg could go commando for all he cared. Archer was not rooting around for underwear for the arsehole.

"What about shoes?" Jason asked, going to the closet and opening the door.

"Fuck's sake, dude."

Jason held up a pair of shiny black brogues. "Look, if they go for a walk to stop you from eavesdropping, he will need shoes. Erica will not take him seriously with dress shoes and shorts."

"How the fuck would you know?" Archer asked, flopping down on the bed. Archer bounced twice, thinking Luke had a better bed than him.

"We had lunch a couple of days ago when I was in London. And we may have talked a while ago."

"How long ago?" Archer narrowed his eyes at his brother.

"Before the call where you told us she was a megastar with a megawatt smile," Jason said, closing the door and coming to stand in front of Archer.

"I distinctly remember not telling you she had a megawatt smile."

"Okay, that was just me, but yeah. I checked Erica out, chatted to her, and we became instant friends."

"Talking twice is not instant friends."

"You jealous?"

"Insanely, let's get going."

Jason chuckled as he slapped his brother on his back and took the clothes from Archer's arms. Looking at his brother, Archer relaxed now that he was there.

"Thanks, brother," Archer said. "Thanks for coming."

"You holler, and we'll be there. Always."

When they arrived back onto the lawns behind Erica's cottage, Luke was standing with his arms folded, with his feet a foot apart. Archer knew the stance meant he didn't like Gregg any more than he did.

"He's still standing, it must mean something, and Erica's nowhere in sight," Jason commented as they came nearer.

"Follow me," Archer said to Gregg's back.

The man turned around, relieved to see Archer. That could only mean Luke had given him advice that was threatening. For a second, Archer felt for the man. Luke's quiet chats were not pleasant. He never laid a finger on anyone, but he sure knew how to threaten. Archer took off in the direction of Turner Hall and the shower by the swimming pool. He waited for Gregg to get washed and changed, then escorted him back.

Erica and Daisy sat on the sofa under the covered patio,

with Luke, Jason, and Yanny opposite. Luke spotted them coming first and stood. The other four stood too and put their coffee mugs on the table.

"Let's go for a walk," Erica said to Gregg when they arrived.

She didn't wait for an answer and whistled for Teddy to go with her. He ran to catch her up and stuck by her side. Archer's heart filled with love for the stray dog and his protectiveness of a woman he barely knew.

It brought to the surface his own feelings for Erica.

"Do not touch her," Archer said as Gregg moved to join Erica.

"I've already had the speech from your brother Luke."

"Doesn't mean it's sunk in, does it?" Archer replied. "I mean it. Do not upset her."

"I know her better than you do, dickhead. She is my wife."

"Was your wife. You gave her up. Now she's engaged to someone else."

"Whoever he is, he won't win. I'll get her back."

"Come on, Archer, join us for a coffee. We haven't seen each other for weeks," Jason said, taking Archer's arm to steer him away. Archer let him, but only because he didn't want to put Erica in a position to have to explain. If she hadn't already told Gregg who she was marrying, it wasn't his place yet.

It riled him he couldn't speak to Erica first, couldn't tell her how he really felt, how much he missed her. So he kept a wail inside as he watched Gregg jog to catch Erica up. Teddy barked and moved to Erica's other side, away from Gregg.

"That's my boy," Archer said aloud and laughed.

He joined his siblings on the sofas. Someone had brought out juices and a platter of pastries.

"Where did they come from?" Archer asked.

"I got a basket together to welcome Erica back. As a peace offering for invading her home," Daisy said.

"Are you best friends now?" Luke asked, jabbing her in the ribs with his elbow.

"I really like her, Archer. Please make sure you marry her," Daisy said.

"I can't make her marry me, Daisy, but I sure hope she isn't considering getting back together with her ex-husband. There is nothing to make her go through with the deal we struck. She is free to walk away. Along with my fucking heart."

"Aww, Archer. It will all work out. I just know it," Daisy said.

Unconvinced, Archer munched through a couple of pastries and listened to his sibling's banter. He'd missed them over the last few months since he'd been back on the island. He'd hoped like hell he could convince Erica of his true feelings because he needed the wedding business to get Jason, Luke, and Daisy back for good.

The coffee was gone, and the sun was at its full height when the stories ran dry of their travel escapades since they split after leaving the rig. The lull was interrupted by Teddy running across the lawn, barking his head off. He came to a skidding halt next to Archer and repeatedly barked. The unrelenting sound didn't stop when he ran off but stopped when Archer didn't get up. He came back and forth a few times.

"I think he wants you to follow him," Daisy said.

When Teddy noticed Archer had stood and began walking, he sped off across the lawn to the top of the path.

Archer looked to the others and shrugged his shoulders. He followed at a walking pace until Teddy ran back to him, still barking. When he ran away, Archer jogged to catch up with him. Archer could hear the others behind him right on his tail. When they got to the fencing and looked down to the beach, they could see what had panicked Teddy.

"Fucking hell. She's stuck in a riptide," Luke said, jumping the fence and running down the pathway. Archer was next, and he just knew Jason and Daisy were following. They were all strong swimmers, but any strong swimmer knew not to put themselves in danger.

"I'll stay with Teddy," Yanny called after them.

When they reached the sand, they kicked off their shoes and went to the shoreline. Erica was moving away from the shore, treading water.

"Where's Gregg?" Luke asked.

Archer didn't give a shit where Gregg was. He'd left Erica to fend for herself. Anger boiled in his veins, staring at the woman he loved, drifting away from him. He couldn't help the metaphorical reference to his love life.

"Look, down there. He's crawling out of the water," Jason said.

Archer looked to where Jason was pointing down the beach. He watched as Gregg face planted the sand.

"Daisy, go and see if he's okay. If he is, tell him I will kill him for leaving Erica out there."

Daisy took off at a run to tend to Gregg and he turned back to see how far Erica had drifted.

"What are you going to do?" Jason said.

"I'm going to fucking get her," he replied, pulling off his t-shirt and dropping his board shorts, so he was just in his boxers. He didn't want to be weighed down with any heavy clothing.

The riptide wouldn't drown Erica, but it would take her further from the shore. It would be her tiredness that would cause her to drown.

"You're not going out there unaided. Let me get the float and rope," Luke said.

Archer willed Luke to hurry as his brother ran on the loose sand to the tree line and unhooked the floatation device and the length of rope. He returned, tied the rope around Archer's waist, knotting it tight, and handed him the float.

"I got this end. You know what you're doing?" Luke said.

"Yep. We've all been trained to do this."

"Is she going to panic?" Jason asked.

"No. She'll be calm."

Archer didn't wait for any more questions and entered the water away from the riptide and swam out to her. As he got nearer, he could see Erica's eyes were half-mast from her exertions. How long had she been there? He swam parallel to the shore and got behind where she was. Archer blinked, and she went under for a few seconds before she popped up again, spluttering. He approached her from behind and put his arm over her shoulder and under the armpit on the opposite side, guiding her to float on her back. She thrashed until he spoke.

"I've got you, honey. Hold on to the float. I'll get us to shore."

With the emotion of almost losing her, he tried to stop the blurring of his eyes with unshed tears. He needed her to be safe, to talk to her, to tell her he loved her.

All Archer had to do was keep hold of Erica. True to his thoughts, she remained calm and heavy in his arms. She was like a stone. Archer looked to shore to see Jason tow them along the beach and out of the rip tide. When they were pulled to the sand, Archer lifted Erica into his arms as soon as he could stand. Luke rushed into the water and untied the rope around Archer's waist. Gregg and Daisy met him when he stepped onto the dry, loose sand.

He stopped and looked at Gregg, his soaking wet clothes sticking to his body. "What the fucking hell were you thinking? You wanted to get your wife back, so you thought leaving her stranded in the sea was a way to go?"

Erica was heavy in his arms and out cold. He needed to get her dry and warm, away from the arsehole he was glaring at.

"Get him off the island," Archer said to his siblings.

"I'm sorry, I thought she knew how to swim out of a riptide. Erica has told me about the sandbank making a causeway out to the island. I wanted to see it, but she said not to go out because the tide was coming in. It came so fast that we argued, and both got swept away. She tried to make me come to shore, but I wouldn't listen."

"Get out of my sight," Archer roared.

Gregg jumped at Archer's voice and tripped when he backed away, landing on his arse. Archer strode by with an exhausted Erica and climbed the pathway. When he got to the top, Teddy and Yanny were waiting.

"Is she okay?" Yanny asked, taking her hand and kissing the back of it.

"She should be fine, just exhausted from treading water for so long. I'm going to get her back to the cottage and into bed. Do you know where you're staying tonight?"

"Don't worry about me. Daisy is sorting me out, just concentrate on Erica."

Letting out a whine, Teddy jumped up Archer's leg.

"She's okay, buddy. You saved her life," Archer told the dog.

Teddy jumped up Archer's leg again, trying to get to Erica. Archer dipped down into a crouch so Teddy could lick her face, and then Archer made his way across the lawn to the cottage. Taking the stairs two at a time, he went to her bedroom and into the bathroom. She was coming round but still groggy.

"Archer?" Erica said.

"Yeah, honey."

"You came running," she said, lifting her arm to cup his cheek.

It was entirely unhelpful as he tried to remove her wet clothes, but he let her caress his cheek, still holding back the tears that he could've lost her.

"I'll always come running. We all will if you're in trouble," Archer replied.

Erica's head hung like she was drunk. He'd sat her on the chair in the corner by the shower unit, but it wasn't proving easy.

"Archer, is everything all right?" Daisy called out.

"Are you alone?" he shouted back.

"Yeah, it's just me. Do you need help?"

"I do, she's like a dead weight, and I don't want her to get a chill."

Daisy entered the room and undressed Erica while Archer held her upright. Between them, they got her washed, dry, and into PJs. Daisy watched Erica while Archer took a shower and put on the clothes Daisy had brought up.

When he was changed, he returned to the bedroom to see his sleeping angel tucked in under the covers.

"Where's Gregg?" Archer asked Daisy, not taking his eyes off Erica.

"Luke took him down to the port side in the buggy. He's going to make sure he's on the next boat off the island. I think he would have chartered a boat himself if there wasn't a ferry due to leave in the next hour."

"I could've lost her, Daisy," Archer said, relieved Gregg had gone.

"But you didn't, focus only on that fact. I'll leave you two alone. Your phone is next to the bed on charge. If you need me, send me a message."

"Thanks, Daisy. I owe you. I owe all of you."

"You don't owe us anything, big brother. You've spent your whole life looking out for us. This is the least we can do."

Archer hung his head and then took a long breath through his nose. He heard the door click closed, and he looked up to find it was just him and Erica.

Walking to the other side of the bed, he stepped out of his shorts, pulled off his t-shirt then climbed into bed. He was an experienced swimmer, but even he was exhausted from the rescue and carrying Erica back.

Archer brought her tight to his side and drifted off to sleep.

FORTY-ONE

Erica

Laughter filtered through from somewhere Erica couldn't pinpoint. Her mouth was dry, and her body ached. She was wrapped in warm arms under a covering and felt like she was suffocating for a moment. Then, jerking awake, Erica sat up and blinked several times to focus on where she was.

"Are you okay?" A sleepy male voice said next to her. She realised it was Archer.

"I think I had a nightmare. I thought I was suffocating."

She sank back down on the bed and turned on her side to look at Archer. It didn't take too many seconds for her mind to remember why her body ached.

"You may have those startling moments for a while," he said carefully, looking back at her with a gaze she hadn't seen before. The last time she was him, he was frosty and distant, and now all she saw was raw emotion.

His hand stroked her arm from shoulder to wrist, his eyes following his movements.

"I thought I was going to die out there. Gregg left me

and swam away. I didn't know what to do. If you hadn't pushed me with all that training, I think I would've gone under sooner."

"How long were you out there for?"

"About twenty minutes, but it felt like longer. I tried to tell Gregg not to go out on the sandbar, I could see the water coming over his feet, but then he lost his footing and got caught."

"So you went out to save him," Archer said, encircling her wrist with his fingers.

His movements were gentle and innocent, but she could tell he was holding back the rage for her situation.

"I thought it was still shallow enough."

Archer's eyes snapped up to hers, and his lips thinned. "Rule number one when saving someone from drowning is never putting yourself in danger."

"You did."

"That's different. I knew what I was doing and how to get you out of the riptide. Plus, I was not going to leave you out there."

Her heart melted at his conviction. Their fingers entwined, knotting together and then falling loose as he played around.

"Where is Gregg?" she asked.

"On the mainland, Luke put him on a ferry."

"He was so angry, Archer," Erica said and then sobbed, bringing her hands to her face.

She was pulled into a bear hug cocoon in his arms as she let out the anguish from earlier in the day. He made soothing noises lulling her back into a calm state. Snuggling closer, she lifted her chin, so her face was pressed against his throat. Erica could feel him swallow hard, and he tightened his arms further.

"Why was he angry, honey?"

"He blamed me for the divorce, even though he filed for it. Then he blamed me for his girlfriend, tricking him into thinking he would be a father. I felt so bad because he really wanted a family, and I wasn't ready. Then he blamed me for her rejecting him because he was willing to raise another man's child. Then he blamed me for making him sign a prenup which made him penniless. Apparently, she walked away when she found out he had no money. She assumed he would get money from the divorce. That's when he confessed he was already divorced, and there would be no money coming."

"And you still risked your life for him?"

"He was in trouble."

"And you came running."

Her breathing evened out, the cold hard truth of the risk she'd taken. "And I got into trouble. How did you find me?"

"Teddy. He came running across the lawns, fixated on us following him."

"I need to treat him in some way. What do dogs love?"

"Attention and loyalty, they give it back in spades."

Erica fell silent. Now was as good a time as any to tell him what she'd decided on the flight over. Surrounded by Archer's family, she realised she couldn't go ahead with the marriage like it was a business deal.

"Archer," she said eventually.

"Please don't say it," he whispered and moved his head to kiss her lips. "Please don't break my heart."

Erica automatically opened for him, welcoming his passion as he kissed her, but she had to stop him. Putting her hand on his chest, she gave him a shove but didn't leave the confines of his arms.

"I can't marry you, Archer," she said, breaking out into a sob.

He held her tighter. "Why not?" The words came out as a wail.

She had to plough on, get it all out, so Archer knew where she stood.

"I thought I didn't care about marriage after Gregg was so disloyal and easily broke the vows meant for life. But watching you with your family, getting to know you, your mind, and your body, I can't let it happen. I know you need the business for your family, but it feels wrong to marry just for money."

He'd turned back on his side, eyes watering at what she was telling him. He clutched both her hands in his. "And you couldn't learn to love me?"

"No."

Archer fell silent and turned onto his back, covering his face with his hands. "Am I so awful that you couldn't love me?"

Smiling for the first time in hours, she tugged on his bicep, but he wouldn't budge, wouldn't look at her.

"I can't learn to love you because I already love you. I don't want to marry you to fulfil the requirements of a bitter old lady. She pulled me aside in the grand foyer that night to tell me if I didn't stay married to you forever, she'd write you out of the will. She insisted I go through with the cere-mony no matter what. She needs me to marry you, but I don't think she cares if love comes into it."

"You love me?" Archer said.

Archer turned back and then covered her body with his, moving her legs apart with his thighs so he could nestle without putting too much weight on Erica. His forearms were at her head, mouth covering hers as he moved his hips.

Erica wanted to answer him, but he wasn't letting her away from the searing kiss he was lying on her. His tongue swept into her mouth so slowly and tentatively that she thought her shiver would never end. Archer knelt back in a swift movement that had her dazed for a moment. Bare chest, broad shoulders on display for her. She hoped forever.

"You love me," he stated. "Love. Me."

Erica nodded as tears formed in her eyes. She could feel her mouth fill with water from nerves. He hadn't said it back.

"So if you married me next week, it would be for real and not save my siblings and me?"

"Yes, but do you want to marry me?"

"I've always wanted to marry you. I meant the proposal, and I would've meant the vows even if you hadn't."

"Archer," she said.

He looked down at her body. Erica felt her nipples pebble at his gaze, but she didn't move an inch. Archer tugged off her pyjama bottoms and panties and then pulled her up to a sitting position to discard her top. When she was naked, he slipped off the bed, turned the lock on the bedroom door, and pushed his boxers off as he approached the bed again.

"Do you want to have kids?" he asked.

"I do."

"How soon?"

Erica was ashamed when she visualised her movie schedule, which would start in two weeks.

"Anytime," she answered, not caring. If he got her pregnant there and then she wouldn't show until after filming.

Archer gave her a salacious grin and crawled up the bed to resume his position covering her body. "No need for condoms then," he said as he entered her.

Erica sighed as he pushed inside. Hearing Archer's groan in her ear, she wrapped her legs and arms around him. It didn't take either of them long to reach their climax. Quietly they exclaimed the peak of their passion, hard throbs over Archer's thick cock as he kept going, sliding inside and out. The realisation she had come just from his cock was making her heart beat wildly. Archer's lazy thrusts turned into hard pushes again. Erica was racing towards her second orgasm as Archer reared up. Soft love-making the first time had turned to hard fucking the second time.

He put his hands flat on the mattress, then balanced on the one hand, grabbing the headboard so he could slam into her harder like he wanted to be buried deep. Erica was aware of the laughter coming from somewhere, so she closed her lips as she moaned through her escalating orgasm until she couldn't stand it any longer and grabbed a pillow to scream into. Archer let out a roar as he came, pushing in hard one last time to seat himself to the hilt. The laughter instantly stopped. Archer pulled the pillow away from her face and gave her a wide grin.

"You should've just let it out, honey. They were going to hear us, anyway."

"I can't ever face them again," she said, embarrassed that they'd been overheard.

"Don't be embarrassed. They'll be glad that we're still together."

"We're going to get married," Erica said in amazement.

"Yeah, for real."

"Let's get showered and dressed and join the others to give them the good news." Archer tugged her off the bed and led her into the bathroom attached to the bedroom. "We also have a dog to lavish all our gratitude."

FORTY-TWO

Archer

"I now pronounce you husband and wife. You may kiss the bride," Reverend Sprite said in the family chapel.

Cheers went up from the small crowd assembled for the wedding. Archer looked to his aunt, who was tight-lipped and sat still where everyone else stood and hugged. He didn't give a shit. He'd married Erica Taylor for love and not because his aunt blackmailed him into it.

"Come here, Mrs Turner," Archer said and snaked an arm around her back to bring her in for a kiss. He dipped her back and kissed her soundly, keeping it decent for the vicar and his aunt.

"Can you come and sign the registry, and then you can join the others to celebrate your marriage?" Reverend Sprite asked.

Archer led Erica by the hand into the tiny room on the chapel's side. Archer took a seat first, signed his name, and then Erica followed. Next, their witnesses, Yanny and

Jason, came and put their signatures on the marriage's official documents.

"Until I saw you two say your vows, I would've put money on the fact you were conducting an arranged marriage for the sake of the Turner legacy," Reverend Sprite said.

"What makes you say that?" Archer asked.

"Something Reverend Chivers had said when I met him. He said to watch out for the Turner children if they marry. He said only one Turner had married for love, and it had gone badly wrong."

"Let's not talk about the past," Jason commented when the rest of the group fell silent.

Archer clutched his bride's hand and squeezed. "We're going to break the mould, honey," he whispered.

"You have another document to sign, Archer," Jason reminded him.

"I'll be back in no time. My aunt said she would sign over the business as soon as the ink was on the marriage certificate," Archer said to Erica.

"Okay, I'll be over with the punch bowl, getting drunk with Yanny," Erica said.

Archer was thrilled she had got on so well with his siblings, and they loved her too.

"Teddy, are you staying or coming with me?" Archer said to the dog, who wore a fetching bow tie for the day.

Teddy moved to Erica and sat at her feet.

Erica laughed that the dog Archer saved was now loyal to her. Archer kissed her cheek. "I saved you both, and now you're both mine forever."

"Damn straight," she whispered back and kissed his cheek.

Archer left the chapel, noting his aunt was nowhere to be seen. Walking towards Turner Hall, Jason, Luke and Daisy fell into step.

"Do you think she'll go back on the deal?" Jason asked.

"No, not a chance. She is many things, but she doesn't break a deal," Archer said.

They rounded the corner of Turner Hall at the rear and saw Bailey standing at the doors into the conservatory. That room linked to the morning room where he knew Aunt Cynthia would be.

"Congratulations, Sir," Bailey said as they reached him.

He held a tray with four tumblers and a single whiskey measure. The four siblings took a glass each, necked the liquid, and placed the glasses back on the tray.

"She's waiting for you," Bailey advised, meaning not to hang around.

Archer led the way into the large room filled with the entire history of the Turners and went to the opposite end to where Aunt Cynthia sat at his grandfather's writing desk with a stack of papers.

"Only you sign, Archer. The business will be yours and yours alone to take on," his aunt warned.

"Understood. I wanted Jason, Luke, and Daisy here to know the cottages, hotel, and wedding business can give us jobs and an income," Archer said.

His aunt grunted and flipped to the back page where she'd already signed her name. Archer scribbled his signature on two copies with an ancient fountain pen he thought had been used in his great-grandfather's time.

Aunt Cynthia collected the documents, sliding one into an envelope and sealing the end. She turned it over to show Archer the address.

It was the family's solicitors.

"This will go off on Monday morning so he can re-do my will," she said.

"Of course," Archer replied. "Are you coming back outside for the party?"

"No, I'll let you all enjoy yourself. All the standing around has left me tired."

"Thank you for standing by the arrangement. I won't be staying in Turner Hall now I'm married and own the cottages. Erica and I will live in the cottage she's been staying in."

A flash of regret washed across his aunt's face for a second or two, and he felt guilty for leaving her on her own in the main house. But then, she'd been on her own in Turner Hall for some time, and it was her own doing. Neither he nor Erica wanted to eat at set times. Or be under any scrutiny. The cottage was perfect for their needs, and they would have good memories of how they came together in the first place. Shaking off the guilt, he picked up the papers and rolled them into a tube.

"Goodnight, Aunt," Archer said.

The four of them walked out of the morning room and then to the conservatory. Bailey wasn't there. He hoped that meant he'd gone to his rooms to change to join the celebrations. It was a small gathering with a simple food menu Jason had designed and enlisted a couple of chefs to prepare to give Maggie the day off.

"What do you think the catch is?" Luke asked as they crossed the lawns from Turner Hall into Edward Hall.

"I don't know, but let's go and chat with Stan Myers. I think he should be able to tell us. I have a hunch I know what's going on."

They reached Stan, and he shook hands with them all, offering his congratulations to Archer.

"It was a grand ceremony," Stan said.

"Yes, and it all came together so easily. You must be well-practiced. You'll be a great asset to the business," Archer said, holding up the rolled legal document.

"What's that?" Stan asked, paling.

"I own the wedding business, Edward Hall, and the cottages. Aunt Cynthia signed them over to me as a wedding present."

Archer wasn't going to tell the man the real deal. He wasn't a Turner.

"I see. Well, that makes you my boss."

"I guess it does. Tell me, Stan, how many weddings have you done for Cynthia Turner at Edward Hall?"

Stan grew silent, eyes wide as he thought about Archer's question. Archer knew weddings had taken place when his grandfather was alive as he'd witnessed them, but he was dead six years.

"How many, roughly over the last six years? I don't need an exact number."

"Um," Stan said, scratching his head, seemingly holding a phantom fishing hat.

"Or to the nearest ten, just give me an idea?" Archer pushed. Jason, Luke, and Daisy looked on, bemused at Stan's discomfort.

"The thing is Archer. Can I still call you Archer?"

"Sure, I don't want to be Mr Turner. What's the thing?"

"Your aunt enlisted me to be the event organiser as I do all the events on Copper Island. She hired me when your grandfather passed away."

"That makes sense. I remember you saying my aunt

paid you per event rather than keeping you on salary. How many fees have you earned in the last six years?"

"Including your wedding?" Stan asked.

Archer was losing patience at Stan's stalling.

"Yes, Stan, how many?"

"One, well, none as you haven't paid me. You bought the business, so you are now responsible for paying my fee," he muttered.

"No weddings?" Jason asked.

"She never called on me to arrange a wedding. Everything was in place, and advertising was happening. There is a website and email, but no weddings took place."

"So there is no wedding business up here?" Daisy asked.

"Not since your grandfather left this earth. When he went, your aunt let everyone go who looked after Edward Hall as soon as the last event took place. She honoured the bookings already in place, but there weren't many as old man Turner was in his nineties when he passed. Miss Turner didn't take any interest in the hotel operations or the events."

"And you're only telling me this now?" Archer said.

"I figured now you own the business, and you'll find out soon enough. I was under oath not to tell anyone what your aunt was doing. She ran the business into the ground. So there is no business," Stan said.

Archer felt for the guy who looked like he wanted to run away.

"It makes sense why the kitchens were empty of anything useful," Jason said.

"And why the chairs and tables needed to be sorted in storage. Thick layers of dust were all over them," Daisy said.

"Thanks, Stan," Archer said, dropping his head back, looking skyward. "Stay for the party, won't you?"

Stan shook his head. "I need to get back into town. My wife needs to get to work, and I'll take over looking after the kids."

"Okay. How many events do you organise for the island?"

"About forty a year, give or take."

"That's a lot for one man," Luke said.

"I have an assistant. She is amazing. We do it together."

"Do you pay her?"

"We take a fee from each event. My wife earns the main salary in the household."

"We are going to resurrect the wedding business, Stan. Would you prefer to be on salary or paid by the event?"

"Can I still organise the events on the island?"

"If you can handle both, then yes."

"I'll take the salary," Stan said without any hesitation.

"Let's talk in a couple of weeks after I've come back from my honeymoon, and we can iron out the details."

"Thanks," Stan said, looking more relieved as the minutes ticked by. "Have a great honeymoon."

Stan Myers hurried away, leaving the siblings alone.

"So there is no business. You went and asked for a Turner business, and she knew it wasn't operational," Luke said.

"I'm sure she would call it a life lesson. I should've pushed for the books for you to look at, Daisy," Archer replied.

"What's done is done. We need to come up with a new plan," Jason said.

"I'll work one out when I'm on honeymoon."

"Sounds romantic," Luke said and snorted. "Where are you going?"

"To London. Erica is filming immediately for her movie.

While she's on set, I'll draw up plans of what the fuck we're going to do. When I have that, I can let you know how we're all going to fit into the plans."

"You said you're moving into the cottage with Erica. What about us?" Daisy asked.

"I thought we could take a cottage each. The fifth one can be for guests when we have friends come and visit. Turn Edward Hall back into a hotel as well as a wedding venue. I also thought we could expand the events to endurance training. The grounds are vast enough and I did a mini endurance test course to prepare Erica for her film role."

"When you didn't know she was a movie star," Jason quipped.

"All right," Archer said good-naturedly. "I'm never going to live that down, am I?"

"No, not a chance," Luke said, throwing an arm around his shoulder. "You come up with the plan, and we'll fall in line."

"I need a drink, and I need to find my wife," Archer said as they walked to the wedding party.

"If The Dragon ran the business into the ground, why did she let the cottages to Archer?" Daisy muttered.

"She probably needed to make it look like there was a business. Erica booked last minute after we were given notice on the rigs," Luke said.

"She's a shrewd old dragon," Daisy said.

Thank you for reading Reckless Kiss, the first book in *The Turners of Copper Island* series. I can't tell you how happy it makes me you spent the time reading it. The next book in the series is Stolen Kiss, and find out about Jason Turner. If this series is your type of story, then check out Jackson's Bay series while you wait. If you want to keep up to date with my future releases, sales, and giveaways, click HERE for my newsletter.

READER MESSAGE

Archer and Erica's story in Reckless Kiss was so fun to write. I fell in love with these two as I do with all my characters. Check out Stolen Kiss if you want to continue with this series.

If you get time, a rating or review would be amazing.

Want to keep up to date with my news? Then click HERE to subscribe to my newsletters. All news goes to email subscribers first.

Take care

Grace

ABOUT THE AUTHOR

I was born and raised in Wales, in a sleepy town just outside Cardiff. Developing a love of stationery at a very early age, I still can't pass a pen shop without nipping in for a quick look around.

Writing and publishing since 2012, I have many books in my back catalogue, all in the Romance genre. They range from Rock Star Romance to Small Town Romance to Family Sagas. Be warned, the stories have a steamy heat level!

In a nutshell?
21st Century Romance—Writing about understated powerful women. Understated love stories with a powerful message, each and every time.

THE THIS LOVE SERIES

A rockstar romance spanning the years. A woman coming to terms with survivor's guilt and a man who will never give up on her.

THIS LOVE ∼ THIS LOVE ALWAYS ∼ THIS LOVE FOREVER ∼ FIVE CHANCES

THE JACKSON'S BAY MINI-SERIES

The Met Gala meets The Cannes Film Festival. Anyone who's anyone is heading to the Ipris Gala event. Six families, strangers at the beginning, become ever entwined by the end.

Sunshine & Lightning ∼ High Heels & Summer Mornings ∼ Wishes & Promises ∼ Strangers & Heroes ∼ Sister & Brothers ∼ Flashbulbs & Champagne

THE RED & BLACK SERIES

A record label series. Each of the record label owners and senior staff have their story told. Intrigue, revenge, rival record labels, and a whole lotta heat.
Charcoal Notes ∼ Crimson Melodies ∼ raven acoustics ∼ cardinal lyrics ∼ Onyx Keys ∼ Vermillion Chords ∼ Inky Rhapsodies ∼ Magenta Symphonies ∼ White Wedding

THE TALBOT GIRLS NOVELLAS

FESTIVE, SMALL-TOWN NOVELLAS TO WARM YOUR HEART.

Stranded at New Year ∼ His Christmas Surprise ∼ Under the Mistletoe ∼ Snowflakes at Dawn

Standalone Novels

The Stranger's Voice ∼ Hollywood Spotlight ∼ The Girl Upstairs

Sign up to my email list HERE

ACKNOWLEDGMENTS

My husband of over two decades is my ever love. Each story I write has a little bit of him in the hero.

Many people have supported me over the years with my novel writing. They should all be mentioned in every book as they shaped the writer I am today. I am thankful that I have a team behind me who keep me straight and make me laugh.

Not everyone helps on every book, but there are still there, cheerleading from the sidelines.

No one will love my characters as much as I do, but when I see a review that accurately says what I feel when I write about them, it is the most satisfying feeling in the world.

I am grateful to my readers. May you keep enjoying my books.

I also want the thank the makers of *Maltesers*. Without them, these books would not be published.